John Augustine Wilstach

The Angel and the King

And other Poems

John Augustine Wilstach

The Angel and the King
And other Poems

ISBN/EAN: 9783743396814

Manufactured in Europe, USA, Canada, Australia, Japa

Cover: Foto ©Andreas Hilbeck / pixelio.de

Manufactured and distributed by brebook publishing software (www.brebook.com)

John Augustine Wilstach

The Angel and the King

MR. WILSTACH'S POETICAL WORKS.

TRANSLATION OF VIRGIL.

The Complete Works of Virgil, translated into English Blank Verse, with variorum and other Readings, and Notes, and ample Index. In two volumes, crown octavo, gilt top, 1222 pp. $5.00. Houghton, Mifflin & Co., publishers, Boston and New York.

*₌*This translation is the first English translation of the Complete Works of Virgil. Dryden's, although usually assumed so to be, is not complete.

TRANSLATION OF DANTE.

The Divine Comedy, translated into English Rhymed Verse, with Notes and Illustrations. Ample Index. In two volumes, crown octavo, gilt top, 1011 pp. $5.00. Same publishers.

*₌*This work gave the first specimens used in typography of the new character (ɐu) invented by Mr. Wilstach to represent the Greek diphthong (ε ἰ) an invention which was brought into further notice by the Cyclopædia of American Biography (Vol. VI., p. 558). The metrical system used in this translation was invented by the translator for the purpose of this work.

THE BATTLE FOREST.

An Epic Poem. Two editions, the last, of 80 pp., 25 cents. The Mail & Express, publishers, New York.

The Battle Forest is also made part of the present work.

THE PRESENT WORK

Is a complete collection of Mr. Wilstach's Original Verses, including Earlier Poems, Satires, Ballads, Sonnets, and Humorous and Miscellaneous Poems.

THE ANGEL AND

THE KING

AND OTHER POEMS

BY

JOHN AUGUSTINE WILSTACH

BUFFALO
CHARLES WELLS MOULTON
1893

CONTENTS.

PAGE.

POEMS.

THE ANGEL AND THE KING.

"ARISE!" an Angel said to Charlemagne,
    The guardian angel of his life and weal,
"Arise, arise!" so God commands, "and steal!"
The King awoke, and said "My senses reel,
Heed pay I none to dreams so wildly vain."

But scarcely had again the power of sleep
    Sent the King's eyelids rest from wearying days,
    When came again the Angel, and his gaze
    Fixed on his ward; and all his heavenly ways
Showed he was charged with God's own warn-
        ings deep.

"Arise! Arise! O King, nor make delay!
    Ye must foul Satan's nest invade with fire!
    Thieves rob ye of your crown, and in the mire
    Would trample dead our time's most honored
        sire!
Arise and steal, I beg, entreat and pray!"

The King arose, in armor full him clad,
    His trustiest sword then buckled to his side,
    And ventured forth to see what might betide;
    But found all sleeping, sentry, servant, guide;
The eyes of all the Angel freighted had.

"To no one else than thee could it be given,
  Thou art the only lord hath conquered me,
  From all the King's keen plans I still am free,
  He who my lands hath taken and liberty,
And to a life of stealth and robbery driven.

"This tells thee Elbegast I am, but now
    Make of my gratitude, Knight, whatever
          proof."
  "If Elbegast thou art, in my behoof,
  Let me thy stealthy methods put to proof
Teach me of thy pursuit, the where and how."

"The King's own self to rob I seek to-night,
  But tell me what *thy* purpose is and course."
  "Yes, freely will I, but no stealth nor force
  Will I against the King employ, remorse
Would haunt me ever if that noble Knight

"At my hands should sustain a single wrong;
  He as to me has been deceived, misled;
  Nor would I in the house burglarious tread
  Of mine put, where with honest food was fed
A family claiming lineage short or long.

"I go to-night that robber of the poor,
  Duke Engerich of Engeramond to spoil;
  If thou take part, 'twill give thee little toil,

Thou must, like me, much like a blind mole
    moil,
I know just where is kept his diamonds' store."

The pair went on, and brought the diamonds
    back,
    And heard, behind a screening portière,
    Duke Engerich say unto his wife, "Desire
    Thou hast to know what high deed may trans-
        pire
Before to-morrow's sun; hast thou the knack

"To keep a secret? Then I'll tell thee, dear,
    To-morrow dies the King; full forty men
    Are sworn to beard him in his guardless den,
    While careless he with prayer-book or with pen
Feels no suspicion, nor e'en trace of fear."

The morrow found the King surrounded firm
    By loyal guards, of whom was Elbegast one;
    Came Engerich with a troop all frolic and fun;
    But ere the night their trifling lives were done,
Was quickly quelled of traitorous deeds the germ.

THE SWORD OF CÆSAR.

OFTEN in the wars of Gaul
  Cæsar fought midst dangers fearful
Round him Roman braves would fall,
Slain by men who heard the call
  Of their country's summons tearful.

Numerous tribes were in revolt,
  Carnutini, Aruveni;
Cæsar's presence gave no halt,
Came assault upon assault,
  Thick as drops in tempests rainy.

Such the havoc and the strife
  Of the Eduan troops elated
Was that Cæsar for his life
Fought 'gainst men whom child and wife
  Sent into those battles fated.

Once a Gallic horseman caught
  Cæsar from his saddle lifted
As a muscular feat, nor thought,
As the Gallic lines he sought,
  What a prize to him had drifted.

The Sword of Cæsar.

Cæsar found the Gaul was gay
   With the feat athletic solely,
And so praised him that to say
To so just a critic nay
   Never could he straightly, coldly.

Cæsar's quick wit made him feign
   Himself of a Spanish legion,
And his dialect theirs, in Spain
Shibboleths such he learned, to gain
   Victories glorious in that region.

He succeeded in the ruse,
   Passed well for a prisoner Spanish,
Each was ready for a truce,
Saw the Gaul of force no use,
   Dread his captive bade he banish.

Crassus' self in Cæsar's hand
   Had a weapon placed of beauty,
Diamonds graced it, rubies grand,
Gems from many a foreign strand,
   Cæsar's sword for show or duty.

"Ah, a rich man have I here,
   Carries with him gold and splendor,
To my heart this sword is dear,"
Said the Gaul, in naught severe,
   But of Cæsar's feelings tender.

"I will give it thee, my friend,
    But alone by way of ransom,
I'll pursue this forest's trend,
And will safe be at its end,
    You will have a present handsome.

"If you do not take it so,
    I will give it to your prefect,
You will lose it, lose the glow
Of its flashing gems, and know
    That in shrewdness you've a defect."

"Give it me," he quickly said,
    " 'T will me bring a fame extended,
I will wear it when I'm wed,
And then place its beauty dread
    Juno's shrine to gladden splendid."

Cæsar handed him the sword,
    While down from the withers gliding,
Left the Gaul the bauble's lord,
Sought the covert, and, adored,
    Was again his army guiding.

Peace and with it, travel came,
    And so Cæsar used his leisure
That one day a town of fame
Drew him and his friends to claim
    From its groves and temples pleasure.

In one temple Cæsar smiled,
  'Mongst its votive offerings glancing,
Joy he felt as of a child,
Seeing there the sword beguiled
  Gaul's gay cavalry's plumage dancing.

"Take it, Cæsar," said his friends,
  When he them the tale related,
But he said: "No! awe attends
Here my sword, and with it blends,
  And the sword is consecrated!"

WALTER OF WIRBACH.

WALTER of Wirbach heavenly aid received,
    Direct, divine, and from the Queen of
      heaven.
A Knight he was, intent on feats of arms,
Intent on winning favor from the eyes
Of one: the maid whose champion true he was.
Much had he prayed the Mother Venerable,
Much had besought the Star of every Sea,
Of human woe or joy, much had bewailed
Before her altars his unworthiness.
But now the day had dawned, the tournament
Must him at Darmstadt victor hail or doom
To overthrow disastrous, and he felt
A terror in his heart insuperable.

But as he moved all stately in his gear
Of steel and gold and crimson, he beheld
A road-side niche wherein an altar stood,
Surmounted by a picture of the Queen
By all the heavenly hosts and thrones adored.
Down from his fierce, impatient steed he came,
And tethering it, so that it might still bear
Its master, when his homage should be given,
He knelt and prayed, prayed long and earnestly,
So earnestly that him an ecstasy
Enfolded, and his soul was lost to earth
And wafted into heaven.   And from the frame
Of that rude picture came the Virgin forth,
And took his arms, sword, helmet, doublet,
      greaves,
Breastplate and orders pendent from its links,
And with all these her radiant self invested,
And the ponderous lance took in her glorious
      grasp,   .
And pulling down the visor, that the crowd
Might deem a Knight and not God's Mother
      there,
Untethered the keen steed, and rode him forth,
Into the lists, and drove as drives the bolt
In storms all foemen from the field, all prizes won,
And came, and tethered there again the steed,
Put gear and weapons in their former place,
And took her station in the homely frame.
The Knight awoke, all happiness, all joy,

Knowing an easy victory would be his,
But knowing not it was already won.
Wild shouts of welcome met him, floral wreaths
Came showered by delicate hands, and every eye
Sought recognition from the champion, and the
    smile
The lady of his love him gave assured
The happy hero that his future life
Was bound in blessedness from heaven, from
    earth;
And then the stoled priest pronounced them one,
And the Church owned in both of them the best
That Beauty and that Chivalry e'er gave
To Christ and to the Mother who him bore.

THE SERPENT OF ZURICH.

L ONGFELLOW'S verse, which lacks no
    grace nor charm,
Gives, with that rhythm clear the poet's lines
Make miracles of beauty and of taste,
A legend of the Bell of Atri; John
He calls the King who therein figured, name
Assumed because the legend named no King.
The Bell of Atri might be rung at will
By any seeker after justice, and at once
The judge appointed for that circuit ear

Should give, and aid to the appellant; now
Zurich a legend has of Charlemagne,
Which has a similar tone, that when encamped
The Emperor was on that calm coast divine
Where Felix bled and Regula for the faith,
The Emperor gave an order forth that all
Who grievances had might ring a certain bell,
And he in person would respond, and come.
From whatsoever business to give ear
To all demands: he did so: justice prompt
Was in that simple court imperial, and content
The people had with admiration mixed
For the good monarch.   But one day 'twas found
That from some cause mysterious rang the bell.
Investigation showed the amazing fact,
A serpent from the lake had grievances.
The monarch summoned came, the serpent met
And questioned.   Bowed three times the beast,
Then sought the sea.   The monarch, following,
        found
A tortoise had usurped the serpent's nook.
The usurper was deposed, destroyed, and came
The serpent once again before the king,
To place within his drinking cup a stone:·
The lapidaries said a diamond 'twas
Of carats unexampled, and of cost
More than the kingly crown, and that a spell
It held which bound the owner (now the king)
In homage and subjection to the will
Of whomsoever might the bauble wear.

Wisely the monarch gave it to his wife,
Wisely she ruled the mightiest King on earth,
Wisely, when death her took, the bauble passed
Unto a holy bishop: all because
To beasts or unto men the King would grant
The claims of justice, and their wrongs redress.

The legend of the Bell of Atri turns
Upon neglect a noble steed sustained; this
Of the Thurian lake, upon a serpent's wrongs;
For, in old times, the serpent sacred was,
As symbolizing wisdom: Holy Writ
This strangely manifests, and poems old:
We read how fiery serpents slew, and one,
Pole-held, aloft, of bronze refulgent, saved,
In Edom's wilderness: and, as one came,
Tinted with checkered stripes, blue-gold and
         lithe,
From loved Anchises' tomb, hushed heroes' hearts,
While some it deemed the genius of the place,
And some that it the attendant was which held
Converse at times with the great Trojan's ghost.

ZEMARAIM.

STOOD Judah's troops and Benjamin's in one
        host,
  And 'gainst them Israel's rose, a mighty horde:
Israel which made idolatry its boast,
  And Judah which still bowed before the Lord.
Jerusalem Judah's sovereign sent with men
  Four hundred thousand for the strife equipped;
Rebellious cities sent forth troops as when
  The waves of ocean rage by tempests whipped:
Eight hundred thousand was their number grand,
  And Jeroboam o'er them kingly sway
Held as the ruler of the recreant land,
  And through false Gods he sought to win the
      day.
Jerusalem's King Abijah was, and ware
  Was he of fight against such desperate odds,
But, high of soul, he drove away all care,
  And said: "The word that closes strife is
      God's;
Armor and weapons are of merit none ,
  Without the approving sign from heaven sent
      down,
"'Tis heavenly force proclaims the victory won,
  And not the tinsel of an earthly crown.

I as God's representative will fight,
　　Secure that he will watch the event, and aid
With unseen weapons him who hath the right,
　　And panic fear send through the ranks dis-
　　　　mayed."

Then stood for battle on Zemaraim's mount
　　The rival hosts, the stronger in two bands,
Each equal its antagonist in count:
　　In ambush one, the two like iron hands.
These iron hands on God's friends were to close,
　　As twixt two millstones is the crumbling grain,
And give unto their sacrilegious foes
　　Ensigns and weapons, and of blood a rain.

Jerusalem's monarch then stood forth for speech,
　　But not unto his own host went his voice,
It went in warnings forth, that they might reach,
　　To Israel's King, and chide rebellion's choice:
"Ye, King and men of Israel, hear me: gave
　　Our Lord to David royalty o'er all
For ever, and with that high King and brave,
　　Whose songs and laws alike rule court and hall,
Made thereupon a covenant of salt.
　　The covenant stood until King Solomon's son
In Israel's righteous march commanded halt,
　　The King a child, young Rehoboam, won
By arts, conspiracies and frauds of men
　　Whom Belial rules, and now God's realm

And ruler ye confront. Him ye should ken
God hears, God aids, and ye God will o'erwhelm.
  Why, have ye not calves worshipped built of
        gold?
And have ye not God's priesthood wholly
        scorned,
  Great Aaron's sons, for all good traits extolled,
And foreign rituals followed, vainly warned?
  Do ye not make priests now of any man
Who brings for sacrifice a bullock young
  And seven rams?   Gold, cattle, is your plan:
A man's possessions wake your fawning tongue.
  But we have not forsaken the divine
And holy God, and Aaron's priests are ours,
  They exercise their duties with design
To follow out their God-appointed powers.
  Morning and evening send they to the skies
The sacrifice, and fragrant incense sweet,
  And prayers and meditations high, arise
For worship apt, for sacred musings meet,
  And on the table pure the shew-bread they
Place as required, and every evening glows
  Light from the golden candlestick's array
Of beauteous lamps in law-adjusted rows.
  The charge of God we keep, whom ye despise,
And God our captain is in this our fight,
  His priests shall sound our trumpets, and your
        eyes
Shall see the bloody traces of His might.

But yet the fight's not on, be wise in time,
Reject not Israel's God, but him embrace:
 Your ill-advised rebellion is a crime,
But He will not withhold from you His grace."

 Response came none, the trumpets broke the
   hush,
And Judah shouted for the onset: came
 The two arms of the ambush them to crush:
But, as a mighty forest swept with flame,
 So was that two-fold host, midst panic fear,
Devoted to the sword of Judah, wild
 The crimson flame God-ruled swept far and
   near: .
Five hundred thousand corpses grim defiled
 Zemaraim's vales; and Bethel fell, and towns
Jeshanah and her neighbors; and the ring
 Of clustering cities, where sedate abounds
Fair Ephraim's beauty, owned God's favored
   King.

PHIDIAS AND POLYCLETUS.

[Memes, in his History of the Fine Arts, attributes the skill of
Phidias to the spontaneous overflowings of inspiration. Cicero, in his
Brutus, pronouuces the works of Polycletus to be absolutely perfect.]

PHIDIAS.

IN his studio, hesitating,
    Phidias stood, his mind debating
O'er an antique legend Grecian,
        And in art its place and use.
'Twas that story of the foretime,
Of the dimly distant war-time,
When the giants grim Phœnician,
        'Neath the lead of Typhoœus,

Stormed the heights Olympian proudly,
Braved the thunders sounding loudly,
Scattered all through heaven their terror,
        And on Gods turned levin loose.
Changed to bird and beast immortals
Left in haste the ethereal portals:
As a goat in ways of error
        Wandered forth the routed Zeus.

To a magpie shrunk Apollo,
He whom Mars and Pallas follow.
"Gods have here," to Polycletus
    Said the artist, " no excuse;
So me grieved my stately Juno,
How I prize her, boy, 'tis you know;
Such defeats might easily meet us
    In the traits of vain Chloreus.

"What defeat the realms infernal
Gave to one, whose love eternal,
Tried by every blast of sorrow,
    Made him to his pledge obtuse,
And engulfed Eurydice's beauty,
And made vain the arduous duty
    Of a minstrel whom no morrow
    Will renew, unique Orpheus!

" Much less strange seems that old story
Not, I mean, of Cycnus' glory,
But that myth wherein Poseidon
    Wrought, through spite, his won-
        drous ruse,
When, against the Lapithæ mighty,
Into many a crimson fight, he
Sent a maid, war's steed to ride on,
    Changed into divine Cæneus.

"Thou has learned from me her features,
Happiest I of artist teachers,
And I grieve that, in the æons,
        She, transformed, was once a goose.
We have each, boy, in his leaning,
Sought from earth and sky their meaning,
I, Orion reaping pæans,
        Thou that wilt be a Tydeus.

        "Love I much my work exalting,
And in it shall make no halting;
And have often deemed division
        Might not justly seem abuse.
Let me now propose our labor
Shall be shared, and each, a neighbor,
Plod his path terrene, elysian,
        Labyrinths both, each a Theseus.

        "Let me cope with forms ideal,
Let thy chisel seek the real,
Let thy faun walk musing, curly,
        Anwering to love's tightening noose,
Leave with me Jove's court and eagle,
Noble thou, while I am regal,
Slighter forms be thine, but burly
        Be my mighty Capaneus."

POLYCLETUS.

"I accept the mission, master,
Plans of thine ne'er knew disaster,
Bronze be mine and marble maidens,
 Our rivalry shall have truce,
Men shall almost hear the thunder
As they scan thy works of wonder,
Eves shall bloom for me in Aidens,
 Thou the shapes seek of Proteus.

"Fame will make her cringing minions
Us attend, and then, on pinions,
Like the fleet-winged sons of Boreas,
 Drive with zeal all us traduce;
Courteous we will have no quarrels,
· Peace consists with work and morals;
Iris need ne'er guard us glorious
 As whilom she did Phineus.

"Known be we, each, as a worker,
Not an idle, aimless lurker,
From Tarentum's Gulf to Smyrna,
 From the Æthiop to the Rus;
Valleys through and glades Arcadian,
Isles Cycladic or Strophadian,
Each of all he gains an earner,
 Happier, e'en, than was Cretheus.

"Need is none that I, in ages
Which illumine poesy's pages,
Full of jubilant dances Pyrrhic,
    Should be driven to the refuse;
Though I may not sip of nectar,
Much of godlike's seen in Hector,
Noble lines are written lyric,
    Epic, too, of Odysseus.

"Ariadnes, Ledas, human
Have in bondage brought the numen
Of thy Gods by charms o'erpowered
    Thrown around them, bright, diffuse;
Heroes have had heavenly powers
Given them in decisive hours;
For Andromache's hand no coward
    Was her spouse renowned Perseus.

"Let us take from boasters warning,
Boasting's oft repaid with scorning.
Throngs that loved fair Atergatis
    Summoned hate from ocean's ooze,
So that, by the Nereids angered,
Dragon scales and talons clangored,
Till the killing visage, that is
    Fell Medusa's, saved Cepheus.

"Wisely men shun methods lawless;
Let our work, like Vulcan's, flawless,
Fair Pandoras bring and culture;
 Let's avoid Mount Caucasus;
Too advanced may be ambition;
It may cause find for contrition;
It may feed another vulture
 With another Prometheus.

"Let us shun the histories fateful
Filled with saddening shudderings hateful;
Rather than rich banquets odious
 Let us seek the anchoret's cruse.
Legends as of Arethusa
Ne'er can make our art the loser;
Art should follow tones melodious,
 Rather Thalia than Tereus.

"Not the bark through Tartarus ringing
At Alcides, but the singing
Of the maids who golden apples,
 For their father Hesperus,
Guarded 'gainst the hero peerless,
Even in face of Ladon fearless,
Symbol of high force that grapples
 Even with Sea-Gods like Nereus.

"Rather ours the festivals Elian,
Or those on the lofty Pelion
Than those led Thebes' sweet princesses
        Into murder's grimy sluice,
When they, taught to treat all mildly,
So enthused were that they wildly
Tore, midst pitiless base excesses,
        Into pieces good Pentheus.

"Let us leave, alike, to dreamers
Subjects fit for vacant schemers
Whom the drowsy God reclining
        Sparges with his poppies' juice.
We will court the past, the present,
Hero, queen, and sage, and peasant,
And the myths, nor e'er designing,
        Either, plans which quell Morpheus.

"So shall shine in art our city,
Skillfuler none, as none more witty,
And, besides, to genius tender,
        Rivaling brilliant Syracuse;
And for genius shall a synonym,
Which each doubter shall find win on him,
Be thy name, enshrined in splendor
        Such as lent to sons Atreus.

THE SEAWARD TOKEN.

The true significance of the statue which, in the year 1820, was discovered in the Grecian Archipelago, beneath a cliff, the summit of which it is thought to have crowned, in the Island of Melos, and now the gem of the Louvre, has been, from the date of its discovery, a theme of controversy among the antiquarians. Some insist that the statue should be called a Venus; others are equally confident in calling it a Diana. After a study of the statue, pursued for a series of days, in the pavilion appropriated to it, in the Louvre, the writer submits that it may be a representation of some mortal maid or matron whose features the artist copied from life.

SHE is speeding a kiss from her lips,
 A love-token fervent and free;
Her eyes bend her form to the ships,
 White wings on the blue of the sea.

Her robe falls with negligent grace,
 While forth leaps the blaze of her charms:
Is it calm fills her exquisite face,
 Or hides its repose her alarms?

Is she daughter, or sister, or wife?
 Is he lord of her home, or her heart?
Is he merchant or warrior? Rules strife,
 Or rules peace? Does he come, or depart?

Right royally poised is her head:
 Does he go with his army to Troy,
A King with his squadrons dread,
 Or a prince with the freaks of a boy?

Far over the Cycladic wave
    Her beauty gleams like a star:
Does she watch, with a sigh, for the brave,
    And point out his pennant afar,

Or seeks she to number the pearls
    That shall garnish her wedding trousseau,
Ere yet the proud ship unfurls
    Her flag in the harbor below?

Ask not! The mysterious past
    Has words which recede and recede,
Has words heaven's rulings lock fast,
    Has words only angels may read.

OCEAN CURRENTS.

[As Longfellow, in his "Seaweed" treats of the Atlantic agitated by the equinoctial storm, so, in the following verses, an endeavor has been made to treat, in a similar metre, of the Pacific warmed by the southern current.]

WHEN salutes the waves Pacific
        The prolific
Hot stream of the southern seas,
    Landward in its warmth it blisses
        Sends with kisses
Shoreward borne upon the breeze,

From the islands equatorial
        T'wards the boreal
Zones it has its jubilant sweep,
All the blooms of Polynesia
        Bathing Asia
Through its forceful current deep.

And from distant myrtled moorlands,
        O'er our ore-lands,
Dimpling soft our tinted lakes,
Breezes come to bathe our mountains,
        While from fountains
Dim, remote, sweet influence breaks.

Ever inward, smiling, smiling,
        Care-beguiling,
Fragrance each far valley yields
Plants here fruits and health abundant,
        And redundant
Wealth distributes o'er our fields.

So, when breezes warm and fragrant
        Strike the vagrant
Dreams the poet wrap, arise
From each zone of passion ancient,
        Howe'er transient,
Glimpses of a paradise.

Gleams come in from Indian oceans,
　　　And emotions
Seize his soul, which peoples gone,
In their seats, firm-fixed or shifting,
　　　Found uplifting,
In the songs of many a swan.

Love and will are his, and glory
　　　Gilds the story
Of the visits of the tides
Bringing boons from where old nations
　　　Visitations
Have received, and wreck abides.

Ever inward, smiling, smiling,
　　　Like the filing
Fays that fill the mimic stage,
Come and bless his lines the glorious
　　　Though laborious
Tributes of each mind and age.

MONTE CASSINO.

THE train sped on, from Rome to Naples
　　　bound,
Through poppied fields and wedded elms and
　　　vines,
Through many a stretch of fair historic ground,
　Past mountain-streamlets, ruins, towns, and
　　　shrines.

And gay the Land of Labor in the sun
  Spread forth its mingled beauties to the eye,
Rich with the spoils which stalwart toil had won
  All palpitating in the summer's sky.

Rome had entranced my thought and all my soul,
  Her hills, called seven, but counting twelve,
    were mine,
With these impressed I saw contented roll
  The journey on through scenes else deemed
    divine.

And was not Naples also in my thought?
  Naples, the queenly city by the sea?
The fame of its heights, bays, and mountains
    wrought
  Chains adamantine for their prisoner me.

The midway station reached, was stopped the
    train.
  And had some heavenly adjutant fixed my
    place
It could not have been happier fixed to gain
  The wondrous vision there before my face.

There, on a lofty height, a castle rose,
  Superb in air, and of a guise so grand
And so magnificent in warlike pose,
  I deemed it a great bastion of the land.

'Quick, quick,' the question flew to all around,
    'Tell me what scene is this me so enchants?
Who is the genius of the place? And found
    Is that great spirit in his usual·haunts?'

And, without waiting for response, I said:
    'Like to the lightning's zigzag is the path
That climbs the mountain to its royal head!
    No mountain, surely, such a diadem hath!'

Men told me here war had no part nor lot,
    Unless that war where heavenly powers con-
            tend,
That always this a consecrated spot
    Had been where earth and heaven had seemed
        to blend.

That here Apollo, in far dates remote,
    Before came Christ to claim it as a home,
His lofty altars owned, and on them smote
    His priests full many a bleeding hecatomb.

The ancient worship ceased, and came the new,
    New symbols, knowledge new and high and
            pure,
But much remained of beautiful and true
    Left by the old that ever shall endure.

Nature remained the same, and ancient seats
  Firm-fixed foundations furnished the new faith;
In some things one religion but repeats
  That which, in other words, the older saith.

Came Benedict with nerve and heavenly gifts
  And changed the worship of the Sun-God's
    shrine
Into that form and faith which manhood lifts
  Serenely into heights and thoughts divine.

Down in the plain, in Roman days, there stood
  An amphitheatre for sports antique;
Perhaps, like to the Flavian famed, with blood
  Of martyrs slain its buried annals reek.

Casinum, in more recent days, a town
  Stood on the slope the plain betwixt and crest,
Then, from the Middle Ages' terrors, down
  It slipped, and, save its name, is lost the rest.

Tell they that once Guiscard the Cunning vowed
  To rob the brethren of their citadel:
His men disguised him carried in a shroud
  Up to the heights as for a funeral.

Arrived, the corpse a lively Knight became,
  Flashed forth the mourning train in sword and
    helm,
And 'twas no arduous task the place to claim,
  And by brute force the weak to overwhelm.

And at one time Italia's lawless sons
   Said: 'Let us all this long tradition break,
Plant on Apollo's heights our storming guns,
   And from the priest his prized possessions take.'

And all the world stood silent, but came forth
   From Britain's statesmen earnest words and
       wise
Of protest 'gainst the wrong, and men of worth,
   Moved by the ages' inarticulate cries,

Albeit in some sense hostile to the saint,
   Denounced the profanation, and thence came
That noble hearts in Britain's parliament
   Averted thus an outrage and a shame.

Sped on the ponderous train upon its course,
   Sped on my journeyings and my voyage thence,
But feel I to the full to-day the force
   That moment had, that wonderment intense.

To-day, although a score of years have passed,
   I seem the splendid vision yet to see;
So palpable 'twill be while life shall last,
   And I with thought and memory blest shall be.

THEOPOIÏA.

DEIFICATION.

THERE'S an homage strange the ancients
    Have in times remote attempted,
And 'twould seem that other ages
    Are not from the vice exempted.

'Tis the flattery that to greatness,
    Wealth, or power, attributes splendor,
Calls a man a God, and worship
    Seeks divine to him to render.

Julius Cæsar so was worshipped,
    Priests burnt incense to him daily,
He who, honoring Jove Olympian,
    On his knees climbed Ara Cœli.

So a boy, gay Bassianus,
    Placed the world's dominion over,
In Jerusalem's Holy of Holies,
    Would claim rivalry with Jehovah.

Women have been so exalted
    That the bright ethereal spaces
Yet Callisto show, and Pleiads
    There record their worth and graces.

But in soberer times Augustus
    Would not suffer such abasement,
Would not let his realm an idol
    Make of him to heaven's defacement.

Albeit when the great Aurelius
    Marcus died, the people, mourning,
Placed for worship, through their reverence,
    Statues his their homes adorning:

Homage finding reasons readier
    Than Racine's, who died supinely
When upon him Louis the Fourteeenth
    Frowned, instead of smiled, divinely.

Once a king, in ages feudal
    Hidden by time his name and nation,
Had a flatterer who him "Godlike"
    Called, as helping his own station;

Him called "God" even on the highways,
    And so full of adulation
Were his words, heard there by strangers,
    That they heard them with sensation.

Some heard with sensation servile,
    Others heard with just abhorrence,
Till one of these last retorted
    With remonstrances in torrents.

"What! A God you call your lordling!
　One alone is God! Be bended
Unto him each knee!" His anger
　Plainly showed him much offended.

But his words quite failed their object,
　And, the folly not receding,
Blows the courtier gave the stranger
　And him left all bruised and bleeding.

Then, in triumph, he the king sought,
　Told his story, but not grateful
Was the king, he deemed his courtier
　Had a wrong done base and hateful.

But, a while the king reflecting,
　Of his rigor all relented,
And, as custom willed, a cake sent
　To his worshipper demented.

This meant: " I again receive you,
　Be my friend, again the fulness
Of my favor claim, and canceled
　Is my hatred of your dulness."

But the courtier, full of dinner,
　And somewhat in mood atoning,
Sent the cake unto the stranger
　From the rude encounter groaning.

Opened showed the cake its contents,
  Gold and gems in plenteous measure,
And was seen no more the stranger
  With his providential treasure.

THE KNIGHT'S ADVENTURE.

A Knight there was of knightly worth the
      flower,
  The Fearless Knight and Faultless men him
      named,
  Thus was he through admiring nations famed,
  And loved he truth, nor e'er was he ashamed
In favor of his foe to own its power.

He owned his King in feats of strength his peer,
  And fealty made him grant his knighthood
      best,
  A point his men-at-arms would oft contest,
  But this on all occasions he confessed,
This noble Knight without or fault or fear.

Disguised, on one occasion, he went forth,
  In knightly faith intent the good to aid
  To chastise those who on the helpless preyed,
  Or sire, or grandsire, widow, wife or maid:
Where laws were dead lived hope in knightly
      worth.

Not far had he passed forth upon his road,
When met he of his henchmen brave a band:
They bade him, as the custom was, to stand,
Not knowing him the master of their land,
And that to him they feudal homage owed.

"For knighthood's honor tell us, noble Knight,"
They said unto the patient horseman, " who
The best knight is of those most valiant two,
The King and him the Fearless Knight, be
true,
And show herein a just discernment bright."

"The King the best knight is e'er saddle pressed,"
Responded then the unknown cavalier;
Response which met with grudging sneer on
sneer:
" We such an answer will not tamely hear,"
They said, and of his arms themselves possessed,

Then dragged him from his saddle quickly down,
And placed him on a meek-eyed palfrey's back,
Their prisoner for the dungeon and the rack,
As punishment for all his treason black
In turning from their master to the crown.

Soon, on the road, another knight was seen,
He too disguised, and this knight was the
King:

"What prisoner, and accused of what, d'ye
    bring?
Meseems is here a strangely curious thing,
A knight a prisoner made by rustics mean."

"Good sir," the spokesman said of those stanch
    clowns,
"The Fearless Knight he basely slandered hath,
  We dragged him from his saddle to the path,
  And leave thou him unto our righteous wrath,
  And add to ours thine own indignant frowns."

"Speak, prisoner, why hast thou such injury
    wrought
  Upon the fame of one who, though my foe,
  I will defend, for he (I chance to know)
  Hath knightly truth, and power to send a blow
Direct as any knight in lists e'er fought."

Responded then the prisoner, deeming not
  He spoke unto the King: "Good sir, the blame
  These men upon me bring is that the name
  Of my good King I honored, for they came
Upon me in the road, and of me sought,

" To know my judgment in the question plain
  'Which knight of all is best,' and my offence
  Is that I said 'The King,' and they have thence
  Me 'traitor' termed upon the slim pretence
That I the Fearless Knight held in disdain.

"The reason, sir, why thus my judgment goes,
    Is simply this: because it is the truth.
    In battle I would meet him without ruth,
    He and myself have battled since our youth,
But truth this tribute to his knighthood owes."

Then to the henchmen said the King: "Return
    Unto your homes, and leave the knight with
        with me,"
    Then face to face him saw from bonds made
        free,
    And kneeled before his prisoner, and said, "Me
Make *thou* a knight, nor my devotion spurn!"

THE LEGEND.

1608, 1865.

WAVES kissed our gunboat; no royal river,
    No Guadalquivir, e'er shone more bright;
The war was over, and men were meeting,
    With friendly greeting, fatigued with fight.

"Ah, there is Jamestown," my friend said,
        smiling;
    Our hours beguiling, he tales would tell
Of days departed, in times colonial,
    To men baronial, what things befell.

I heard him gladly: "Our enemies Southern
  We own as brethren, their legends fair,
By one who knows them, to lines of history
  Imparting mystery, can harm it ne'er."

"No," said he blandly, "the tongue is truthful,
  Albeit, when youthful, romance it sways,
I but repeat them, as came they handed,
  By grandsires landed, from earlier days.

"You see the church there, whose ivied gable
  O'er fact and fable its ruins rears?
Ah what has time done! This river flowing,
  In beauty glowing, seems like the tears

"Its triumph cost us, in tides commingled,
  Where oft have tingled our ears amazed.
War rose aforetime in these same regions,
  And then its legions for deeds were praised

"Which came from changes 'twixt clashing races
  Of differing faces and alien lands,
When from the ambush the well-aimed rifle
  The life could stifle of joyous bands.

"And tells serenely that gable's prattle
  Of ancient battle and strange release,
For on its site once there stood a maiden
  With graces laden and loving peace.

" There Pocahontas, the tale's not idle,
  Had her fair bridal to Rolfe her lord,
And there her father, renowned Powhatan,
  In robes not satin, gave pleased accord.

" But who was saved there?   The captain famous
  Shall any shame us from doubting 'twas?
Yes, those who idols demolish tell us
  That truth is jealous, and here with cause.

"They say the fair scene we all delight in,
  Where stood a Titan prepared for death,
 Was of the Black Bear, the Indian Bankee,
  What time there sank he with stifled breath,

"And that the angel who, 'neath the impending
  Blow came with rending cries to desist,
Was not Pocahontas, 'twas dusk Tetehee,
  Whose strong entreaty no heart could resist.

" And that the chieftain Opechancanough
  'Twas 'neath whose banner rose the event,
And she his daughter, but that enlisted
  Therein, and assisted, the Captain, and went

"With him to capture the Black Bear (criminal
  Without faith or hymnal) Pocahontas's sire.
But stands in triumph that pleasing picture
  That doubt nor stricture can ne'er call liar.

"It stands to show us how war has roses,
　　Its woes encloses with hedge divine
　　That cheers us ever, and how attended
It is and blended with motives fine.

" It stands to show us that, midst ambition,
　　The radiant mission of woman glows,
And that we find oft her kind dominion
　　Controls opinion and conquers blows.

" But when 'tis mentioned, this legend golden
　　Of dates all olden, will some a myth
Pronounce the Black Bear, and though not surly,
　　Hold, late and early, for Captain Smith.

"Tetehee? She married young Castelmain, heir
　　By right long and fair (his shield nought to
　　　　mar)
Of an English estate, and palaces wide-halled
　　His dusky bride called 'The Morning Star.'"

Our voyage ended, engagements previous
　　On errands devious sent us apart,
But muse I often on war's dread chances
　　And other lances that touch the heart.

OUR LADY OF LOURDES.

ON the third day the Vision spoke,
　　For, on the other days,
She merely had the rosary moved
　　As one in worship prays,
Or had the sign made of the cross
　　As one who heavenly powers
Seeks to invoke when lofty thoughts
　　Engross devoted hours.

"For fifteen days," the Vision said,
　　"Come thou, bring others, this
If thou shalt do I promise thee
　　Here and hereafter bliss."
The Queen of Heaven it was whose voice
　　Was heard thus in the dale,
But heard alone by one who, tranced,
　　Had pierced the senses' veil.

The first two visits children two
　　Alone with Bernadette
The supernatural niche approached
　　The Glorious Presence met.
This visit found with her adults,
　　But only two, who came
To seek the childish story's truth
　　Or fix upon it blame.

But, young or old, none heard the voice
    Except alone the child,
A peasant-girl of simple ways
    And innocence undefiled.
Fifteen times yet the child returned,
    For eighteen visits there
This artless child to meet were made
    By Her Divinely Fair.

How many came, and what words spoke
    The Glorious Vision more?
And what was done to show her words
    A seal eternal bore?
The next day came a hundred, drawn
    By rumor's mighty voice,
Then hundreds, thousands, came impressed
    With what heaven yields most choice.

A part of what the Vision said
    Was for the child alone,
Not all is for the ear of all
    That comes from God's own throne.
Sometimes she said: "For sinners pray,"
    And earnestly penitence urged,
Benignant she would not the world
    Should for its faults be scourged.

Asked of herself, she meekly smiled,
    Nor sought the world's applause:
"Through me Immaculate was conceived
    The Word of all things Cause."

This said she on that sacred date,
  The Annunciation, wise
In all the observances of the world
  As well as of the skies.

And in what year? In our own times,
  These latter days, it came,
In eighteen hundred fifty-eight,
  As if from Sinai's flame.
"My child," she said, "where dust is seen,
  There at the grotto's side,
Dig with thy fingers in the soil,
  And thence shall flow a tide.

"And eat thou of the herb there seen,
  And wash thee in the wave,
The parched ground shall become a pool,
  The sparkling waters save."
The child obeyed, dug, ate, and watched,
  The rock the Dame obeyed,
Where dust had been was moisture now,
  As erst in Horeb's glade.

And day by day the stream increased,
  Until its bathings gave
To thousands health, in miracles,
  'Mongst those who came to lave.
"A chapel and processions here
  I wish, that all mankind
May here for souls' and bodies' ills
  Health at their seeking find."

When, eleven days later, came the date
  Of Monday in Easter week,
Ten thousand people saw a thing
  Would strengthen faithlings weak:
For, 'neath the fingers of the child,
  As prayed she there in trance,
A burning candle she no heed
  Gave or by word or glance.

Altnough the flame remained there long,
  More than an hour's fourth part,
And, rising, through her fingers flamed,
  It hurt gave none nor start.
Came forth her dainty hand unharmed,
  From slightest scorching free,
As from the furnace came of old
  Of God the servants three.

And when, in all these interviews, time
  Brought in the grievous date
Called of the Lance and Nails, was seen
  No Vision early or late.
For sacred sorrow held in heaven
  The memory of the deed
Ordained that for a sinful world
  A stainless Lamb should bleed.

From February's days until July's
  These eighteen meetings spread,
Then, with a blessing given her Maid
  The radiant Vision fled.

Not fled, but vanished, gradually
 Its outlines turn to gold,
Splendor would come, and in its heart
 Its chosen Lady fold.

From June's to October's ruled the law,
 That is the law of man,
The local ruler put the place
 Beneath a local ban.
This, by the coast at Biarritz,
 The Emperor learned, and frowned,
And swift his lightning message threw
 The barricades to the ground.

And now are seen processions long
 Of pilgrims at the place,
Come to enjoy the promises given,
 And share this Lady's grace,
Come in great hosts, as armies come,
 From lands remote and near,
The niche, the grotto, and the church
 To view in love and fear.

And what's become of Bernadette,
 So favored and so famed?
A recluse was she for some years,
 Then heaven her presence claimed.
Her mission was fulfilled on earth,
 But always there at Lourdes
Her name a blessing will receive
 From every sufferer cured.

And long as from the Pyrenees' snows
   Rolls down to Pau the Gave,
The Paradise of Massabielle
   Men's praise and faith shall have.
Oft will they deem that Eden's bowers.
   Its primitive race sent forth
To hold these mountains claiming speech
   The earliest used on earth,

And that not idle was the strife
   For Christ that saved these lands,
Else doomed long ages' servitude
   To bear 'neath infidel bands,
Loved lands by sun and star caressed,
   As were none other's e'er,
Where nature's forms are unsurpassed,
   And awe reigns everywhere.

Much art thou favored, beauteous France,
   The eldest daughter thou
Of that fair Church the Lord ordained
   And spreads through nations now.
Through ages unto thee the trust
   Descended from on high,
Keep it, fair France, unsullied keep
   The legacy of the sky!

NOTE—The foregoing poem follows closely the admirable work of Lasserre, entitled "*Notre Dame de Lourdes.*"

THE BALLAD OF ROSALIE.

'TWAS 'mongst the hop-vined glens of Kent
  And poppied fields of grain,
The May-day sports were broken in
  By mighty drops of rain.

Swiftly the May-queen sought the roof,
  With all her blooming court,
And with the crown which on her brow
  Had laid the merry sport.

Wild rolled the clamor of the skies,
  The tempest fiercely howled,
Through dark clouds levin flashed, and then
  The blackened heavens scowled.

The patriarch of the cottage up
  The well-thumbed Bible took,
And sought to make the children hear
  Words from the blessed Book,

When came such crashing bolts that voice
  None in that hour was heard,
Sight e'en was blinded, only sobs
  At times the silence stirred.

Expected all to hear the crash
　　Would set their spirits free,
First wind, then forked fire, had torn
　　To shreds the nearest tree.

When, all at once, fair Rosalie,
　　The little four-year-old,
Said " Father, look! I see her come
　　Enclosed in gleaming gold!"

" See whom," the father said, " my child?"
　　" The angel, like to those
Are pictured in our Bible, me
　　She beckons as she goes,

" Her palm-branch waves she, and she means
　　I shall her follow, see,
See, how she nearer comes to earth,
　　And seems to call to me!"

The father looked, the mother, all
　　None could the angel see,
But in the blinding storm went forth
　　The little Rosalie.

And followed all, not doubting fear
　　Had crazed the beauteous child,
And caring nothing in such mood
　　For all the tempest wild.

Crash, crash, and blinding levin smote
  Behind them ruin wide,
The child rushed on in ecstacy,
  While all with terror cried.

And, in that moment, 'gan to fade
  The gold from out the sky,
And left sweet Rosalie's raptured ken
  The angel now so nigh.

And looked the terror-stricken crowd
  Behind them, and beheld
A burning ruin flat the house
  Whence they had been so spelled,

And all owned then the angel sent
  By heaven's sweet charity,
To draw them from the danger forth,
  Queen, court, and Rosalie.

NOTE—The incident whereon the foregoing verses are based may be found related in one of the earliest numbers of *Blackwood's Magazine.*

THE BATTLE FOREST.*

IN SEVEN PARTS:

1. TIPPIKANAU.   2. ELSKWATAWA.   3. THE WAR CHIEFS.

4. THE GROTTO.   5. THE WAR SONG.

6. THE CAMP.   7. THE VICTORY.

*** The first edition of this Poem was made part of the NEW YORK MAIL AND EXPRESS of the date of October 18, 1890. THE MAIL AND EXPRESS published, also, in pamphlet form, a second edition, in the month of November of the same year.

DEDICATORY SONNET.

To Mrs. Benjamin Harrison.

THREE eras, Madam, mark thy lofty name,
    Each, as the fruitful Wabash, Po, or Rhine,
    Mark, on the globe, where sheaf, or branch,
        or vine
Reward the worker and the summer's flame.
The initial era gave our Nation fame,
    Through the great document men were
        proud to sign,
    Wherein shone Liberty superb, divine;
    The second was the event to sing I aim;
The third the patriotic strife which brought
    Thy husband to the helm supreme of State,
    A pilotage he rather shunned than sought,
And which he holds with loftier mind sedate
    That thou art with him in the important seat
    For which thy traits make thee so fitly meet.

PREFATORY NOTE.

The following production aspires, perhaps too ambitiously, to the character of a National epic. Longfellow has probably approached nearer to the preparation of an epic than any other American poet, in his Hiawatha, his Evangeline, or his Miles Standish. The Hiawatha is a collection of the legends of the native tribes inhabiting the lands west of the upper waters of the Mississippi; the Evangeline is a story of the destruction of of a Canadian village, and the wanderings of two of its families, both of which suffered extinction; and the Miles Standish is the story of the founding of the colony of Massachusetts.

The Battle Forest embraces the story of the triumph of American civilization in its struggle with the strongest aboriginal force ever organized on the continent. Tecumseh, the highest product of the Indian race, an aboriginal Julius Cæsar, had planned a conspiracy embracing the entire United States. Leagued with him was the government of England. This league, embracing two hemispheres, was met by the vigilance, the ability, and the heroism of Harrison. The Battle of Tippecanoe was the first, as that of New Orleans was the last, of the great events connected with our second war with England.

The heroic measure is adopted, of course, as the suitable measure, and the rhyme as the invention and privilege of modern poetry.

THE BATTLE FOREST.

I.—TIPPIKANAU.

MUSE, aid this story of the forest wide;
    As moves the theme, be thou my favoring
        guide;
Here come in conflict races great of men,
Supply my memory slight, inspire my pen,
That men may sit attentive to a song
That rolls all echoes of this land along!

The scout, the interpreter, the efficient aid,
Well known to Harrison the place had made
Where stood the aboriginal force at bay,
At home, their Town, the shock of war to stay;
And, as the day wore on, the Indians showed,
Once and again, the hate that in them glowed,
And followed, lowering, all the army's path,
Concealing scarce their deep, consuming wrath.
But knew the White Chief well his mission high,
And, as he came to their entrenchments nigh,
Fear seized them, and they said, "We are for
        peace,
At least until to-morrow let war cease;

We would be friends and cruel bloodshed save."
" Agreed," the General said, and from a brave,
A Shawnee hunter, whom the White Chief knew,
Sought, as to camping information true,
And what he asked obtained:. " Westward and
        south
A creek is, with sweet waters for the mouth,
And 'mongst the lofty trees along its side,
Oaks, maples, elms, your men may well abide."

A halt the general called, and Dubois sent,
With Clarke and Taylor forward, aids intent
On prompt, intelligent service, to inspect
The ground the Indian mentioned, or select
Some other: " Here, meantime, stand we at rest,
And soon will know if truthfully speaks our
        guest.
Keep watchful eyes about ye, and what news
From straggling red men comes, that not refuse.
And, Captain Prince, take you an escort, go
In that direction where distinctly show
The skirting woods the course the river wends,
The river Tippikanau, see if tends
Our prudent progress thither; it seems best
Not on this Indian's word too much to rest."

When Prince returned, " Much marsh," he said,
" Toward the woods lies, and by springs is fed."

Came soon the reconnoiterers; content
Was with their words and pleased expression
            blent:
" Selected, General, as your aids, such grounds,
In this rare paradise of sights and sounds,
To seek, as may give rest, or strength, or war,
With haste, but care, we've looked the country
            o'er,
And find, not far, the favorable field.
The Prophet has his savages near, concealed
Beyond a swamp adjacent to his Town,
Built firm with logs and palisades, whence his
            frown
Is fixed portentous on the coming fight.
Around his head he claims a holy light
Rays from the Indian's God supreme, which
            brings
Assurance full of victory, as he sings.
Yet little saw we of his Town or braves;
'Neath it the Wabash dashes murmuring waves;
Our errand was to find fit place for camp,
Not rough, nor steep, nor flat, nor drear, nor
            damp.
It stands above the marsh a score of feet,
Is covered with a wood of monarchs meet
To save the men from flying shaft on shaft;
It tapers to the south, and gayly waft
A dimpling creek's clear waves November's
            leaves
Close on its west; its eastern side upheaves

Fair, fern-clad banks, turned by the marsh's face.
The lofty trees of brush but little trace
Have left to grow. Hence, safe's the way; there
        wains,
And men, and stores, and our artillery trains
Will have good place and good positions find
Should the red foe to battle be inclined."
Such Dubois' words were, spoken for those sent
By Harrison to find a camp where tent,
And steed, and wheel, and glowing hearts of men
Might rest from warfare past, or meet the foe
        again.

Then thus the tried commander: "It is well;
Let now the bugles' echoes rise and swell
Throughout the force, and through the cam-
        paign round,
That all the stragglers may in rank be found;
And let the march begin, you in advance,
That this good field we may not miss by chance!
There let the Almighty say whose right is best,
Let hear the forest heights His name addressed!"
Fife, drum and trumpet thrilled the expectant
        host,
Above them waved the flag, our country's boast,
Came on in order, infantry, cannon, horse,
The army moved in its appointed course.

From Cedar Bluff, an outside sentinel's eye
Could Harrison's last night's bivouac fires espy,
Where camped he lay, some miles from this
          famed field—
This lookout place could widespread surveys yield.
Approached it was, first by canoe, which drove
Three winding miles to where a lordly grove
O'erhung the river; thence a mile of steep,
Moss-covered cliff, whence freshet torrents leap,
By active climbing overcome must be;
And then a step led to the prospect free.
And, at this day, this dream of height and vale
Bears, not in vain, its name, Tecumseh's Trail.
Near where the sentry saw the curling blue
Ascend to heaven, now stands our famed Purdue,
While now bestrides the limpid Wabash, then
Remote and silent, far from haunts of men,
An iron bridge, which learning leads to parks,
Belt railroads, factories, and that scheme of Sparks
To make a Minnetonka here, and on
Its banks to show a rival of Boulogne.

Whence came the sentry's orders forth? The town,
Whose stretch of cabins on the airy crown
Of prairie, skirted far the Wabash—thence
Went orders forth for forays and defense.
Its ruler was Tecumseh, when at home;
His absence gave the power in this his dome,

His citadel, his capital, unto one
Who claimed of prophecy gifts. Him so alone
Tecumseh would not trust, but left decree
That, in his absence, peace with whites should be.
Injunction wise, spurned by the Prophet vain,
Who brought upon his people ruin's reign!

And why this town imperial loved he so?
Muse, tell us, of Tecumseh we would know!
It loved he that it meant the war he fought;
It built he for the advantage that it brought;
Its site strategic threatened and combined;
Vincennes it threatened, and the Ohio, lined
With teeming farms; and here tribes near and far
Might centralize for any destined war.
For 'neath its walls a limpid highway flowed
Which times primeval often gayly showed
Streamed o'er by rustic navies; which the lakes
United with the gulf; the portage breaks,
Alone Maumee and Wabash 'twixt, that line
Whereon the North, the West and South combine;
A place desired, the choice abode remote
Of pre-historic races; this denote
The tumuli, still seen upon the crest
Of bluffs that crown the Tippikanau, blest
With all associations that may count
To make them of all dreams the fairy fount.
Behind it, to the north, a country flat
A refuge furnished, if it might be that

Some Fabius might arise to win success,
To give some Hannibal untold distress,
In following through the swamps of Kankakee
The foe unsearchable, who might with glee
See quicksands swallow cavalry up, and wains
Sink deeper down for all a Hercules' pains.
Upon this highway, moons not far away,
Went forth an armament rich and bright and gay,
Four hundred youths in eighty stanch canoes,
Five warriors placed in each, of iron thews.
Ah! but to see them in their war paint, decked
In hues terrific, all with feathers flecked!
'Twas in the summer, and the natural brawn
Shone forth, and some had blankets on,
And some had hideous pelts with hideous tints,
Some guns, some clubs, some arrows tipped with
        flints
Or jasper heads, or agates polished gay,
Which they had brought from distant strait or bay.
And all their tomahawks gleamed and scalping-
        knives,
Threatening to faces pale and lilied lives;
And all the war-whoop sounded, often stirred
To this by mutual hint, or spoken word,
Or sign, or as a token of their hope
That they might soon with other warriors cope.
Their faces showed that steady, stolid pose,
Which on the boy by imitation grows.
At times they saw the river lashed by winds
All into foaming serpents; sometimes lines

Of silvery light the moon traced o'er its face;
Sometimes, by sun and calm's united grace,
Broke their swift keels the mirror of the waves,
The mirror picturing bison, deer, birds, braves,
The headlands painted and the azure skies
The inverted bluffs with varying tints and dyes,
And upturned forests shimmering in the breeze
And trembling with their wealth of lordly trees.
How played the naiads with their shapely guests
Within the billows pictured! Songs and jests
The nymphs could hear, as floated through their
        realm
Rude music's notes from every gallant helm.

There is a beauty in the early prime
Of nature seen not in the later time;
There is a freshness then, a choice perfume
That civilization hastens to its doom,
And, doomed, it ne'er can be replaced; the tint,
Mixed of the skies and earth's all-modest glint,
Fair nature wears, no art cosmetic yields;
And culture robs us of those perfumed fields.
Simplicity in character has more
Attractiveness than all a bookworm's lore.

And as the gallant navy stemed the tide,
And flung its waves far forth to either side,
Shone in the midst Tecumseh, marvelous star
Of aboriginal history; braves from near and far

Had heard his summons; he with pride
Surveyed his force; the privilege denied*
Made it more precious to his arrogant soul,
Gave solace to the mighty dreams of dole
His heart held 'gainst a hated, insolent foe,
For to the Long Knife† would this armament show
He deemed *his* wish no rule, no law for chiefs
Who sovereignty claimed above him, and who
   griefs
Might show, by hint; if not in rapine wide,
At least by this armada on the tide
Of this great natural highway that must here
In future float the Indian's bloody bier,
Or rise the theatre of his triumph; fear
Felt not his soul of all the future drear.

This quaint and antique navy came from streams
North, south, and lakes of many legends' themes,
'Twas walnut fired, or birch-bark sewed, or lin'n
Carved out by lazy labor, while a fin
Of ash at times flashed forth its silvery pearls;
Then dimples Father Wabash showed, as girls
When merry jests go round, or when is given
Some merited praise extols their worth to heaven.
And where the God might seek to sink the keel,
Was used the pine tree pitch the gaps to heal,
Or wax from plenteous hives in tulip trees,
Or gum one yet on varnished cherries sees.

---

*He was acting in disregard of the wishes of the Governor, Gen. Harrison, in approaching Vincennes with so large a force.
†The Indians so called general officers in allusion to their swords.

On bends, round points, gave forth these forest
      tars,
In honor of their admiral, fierce huzzas,
Or rippling rapids woke with cheer on cheer
Which from their coverts roused the startled deer.

Whence came the name of Tippikanau, word
To town and river given, and this day heard
As designation of a county?   Whence
The idea that gave the seat of power immense
That was to be, this quite peculiar name
By war forever linked with honored fame?
'Twas thus, the bard declares: the buffalo
These early fields commanded; here would flow
Across the State his legions, and their course
Being changeless made them symbols true of
      force;
And in the river gleamed the buffalo-fish,
The tyrant of the watery depths, whose wish
His subject sturgeons, bass, pike, muscallonge
Obeyed, all heedful of his vehement plunge.
On either element thus the symbol held,
On both it conquered and all rivalry quelled.
The northern tribes a boat call a cheemaun
(A boat's a ship, a deer grows from a fawn),
The Sacs keneu the great War Eagle call,
The bird supreme in sovereignty over all.
Tippi's the fish, Kanau the buffalo; we
Tippecanoe the inadequate name decree.

II.—ELSKWATAWA.

CAME shades of evening on, then night, the last
The Shawnee power should know; the luckless cast
Was thrown, within the Prophet's brooding mind
To prudence lost, to obvious warnings blind:
The law Tecumseh gave him he would break,
The dreary marsh his Rubicon he would make,
Heedless of all, and he would storm the gates
Which held behind them good and evil fates.
His choice was made, and now the high priest, shrewd
And bold and eloquent, with care reviewed
The assembled army of his race, all glad
To do him reverent honor, and he bade
That, while the outside sentries kept remote
A vigilant watch, all should convene and note
In council his instructions; then that all
Details of fight should to the war-chiefs fall.

Who was this lawless Prophet, placed in power
Thus recklessly, and destined to bring sour
Defeat and overthrow to cautious plans?
The Tawa towns, the Mississinewan bands
Acknowledged him as leader; and the praise
His fellow-chieftains gave when he would raise
His voice sonorous at the council-fire,
Took, in the way that personal traits inspire,

The form descriptive of a name, which said
This warrior has a voice of power and dread.
All this in Laulewasika was implied.
Then Penagashega, prophet honored, died,
And, as the Hebrew seer, who rose to heaven,
Transferred his mantle, so, divinely given,
The mantle of the Indian seer seemed apt,
Albeit this seer no flaming chariot rapt,
For Laulewasika's shoulders.   He now bore
The name of Elskwatawa, Open Door.

Why he thus changed, with change of office,
    name
Seems on our Muse to have no idle claim:
Some counsels he had held with black-robed
    priests,
Some sermons he had heard interpreted, increased
His scanty store of scriptural knowledge; so
That, not through mighty winds, he knew, nor
    glow
Of fire, nor quaking of the earth, the call
Came to the sacred seer, but still and small
The voice of Manitou descended soft,
Through zones empyreal, from calm realms aloft.
From some such idea may have come the change,
Fantastic, vain, and beautiful as strange.
The loud, clear voice of wrangling in debate,
The sharp punctilio in affairs of state,
Had had their use, their day, but now he stood
The edifice, the temple of all good,

The dazzling palace wherein all was stored
That yet remained of all his race's hoard
Of skill and wisdom, and the door wide thrown
Of that new union, which, if they would own,
There entering they should strength and courage
          find,
The dauntless will, the high heroic mind.

The assembled throng by one consent was still,
Pleased to give homage to his sovereign will.
Not more sedate grim ranks at Shiloh shone,
Nor iron squadrons glittering on the Stone.
A thrill, from deep, mysterious silence, ran
Throughout the throng, and then the sage began,
Or, rather, stood in pose to speak, and slow
His words to form before their readier flow:

" Chieftains and fellow-warriors, not to-night
Have I to hold forth arguments for the fight;
I know your native ardor prompts you; vain,
Perhaps, would be my efforts to restrain
That boiling mass of valor flaming high
I see in every cheek, in every eye.
No! 'Tis but to remind you of the cause
For which you fight I speak; I beg you pause
But just enough to let the Long Knife fall
Into deep sleep before he hears the call

Of vengeance; then the Seventeen Fires* shall
    know
What 'tis to have this army for a foe,
An army which the consummate flower is known
Of princely worth such as should save a throne.
And while we wait, let me in part employ
The time that must elapse before the joy
Of victory greets ye, to recall our claims,
Your claims and mine, and history, and the aims
Our race proposes to itself to try,
Beguiled by treaties oft and frauds, and why,
Before so many worthies of our race,
The tribe of Shawnees claims supremacy's place.
Supremacy claim we even o'er the whites,
In their own methods even of claiming rights:
By journeying from a land beyond our land,
And sacred marriage joining hand to hand.
Approached the Shawnee ancestry from far,
Dim shores remote, where rests the sun his car;
And afterward came from Californian coasts
To Georgian vales our aboriginal hosts.
All that claimed, voyagers Columbus, Penn,
Hudson and Raleigh, Plymouth's Alden, when
They sought possession afterward, took too late,
Usurping what we held of prior date.
A Georgian maid there was, the daughter fair
Of a high lord the King had given the chair

---

*The seventeen States at that time composing the American Union,
each State being regarded by the Indians as a council fire.

Of sovereignty o'er all that pleasant Fire.
She, when my warrior-ancestor her sire
Approachéd to treat of grievances long borne,
Felt all her soul with fiery passions torn
Of love for him the Shawnee chieftain; prayed
Much she her princely father; they were made
Husband and wife; my origin comes from thence;
Marriage of princely lines gives no offense
To either line.   No history can deny
That earlier settlement and that marriage tie.
The two, or either, make our rights supreme,
Rights which we hold as servants, for we deem
All honors held as held for you in trust,
To you we bow all humbly in the dust.
The heavy duty's ours to guard your lives
From all that, natural, supernatural, strives
To work ye harm, the ambush and the charm,
The evil eye, and ghosts, a grisly swarm.
Ah, brethren, that which us most deeply grieves
Is that you must expose your lives to thieves,
Thieves who, instructed by the Seventeen Fires,
Death's doom deserve, as traitors, murderers,
     liars!
And, furthermore, let me some personal things
Say, which, in this assemblage, will no stings
Behind them leave, for here I only friends
Behold; to them no faults belong, no sting ex-
     tends.
Me the Great Spirit grants to know the men

Who deal in magic—this I say again—
Me the Great Spirit grants to speak their names,
And you commands to purge their guilt in flames.
With his own hand the ancient prophet slew
False prophets at the brook: I look to you,
As executioners of my will, as well herein
As in all cases where is quest of sin.
So did ye with the chief who crossed my path,
Base Leatherlips, who fell beneath your wrath.
I, armed with this great power, name none else
        now,
To-morrow I shall read on each man's brow
Praise written or condemnation; so die first
By sacred wounds, ere by my thunders cursed.
But die we shall not, that same power divine
Has granted me to cast that spell of mine,
Taught me by dusky angels of his throne,
Around the paleface. It is I alone
Possess it of his prophets. I will sing the themes
Taught me by voices heard by me in dreams,
Voices of heavenly hosts above the stars,
Whilst you attack. The foe have thunder cars,
Guns great and little; none shall hurt ye; swords
In their hands held shall melt before my words;
And horses' hoofs shall harm ye not, repelled,
Made vain by me, by my enchantments spelled.
Did I not, when the Long Knife called me fool,
Ask Manitou for power the sun to rule?
Did not I, when it pleased me, gloom bring down
Upon the world; bid cloudless noon to frown,

And universal nature wrap in black,
Grieved that your prophet due respect should
　　　lack?
Ah, I can bring the moon down from her
　　　sphere,
Or rain of stars, fraught with abundant fear,
But these great prodigies would forests burn
And kill my people; I their love would earn.
Wâkan our northern allies mystery call,
Which o'er weak minds appears to cast a pall!
Mystery divine; on me no mystery preys,
Light, speech and power from heaven attend my
　　　ways.
Was it for nought I starved in forests drear,
Where met I the Great Spirit, and drew near,
Chilled, weary, worn, his messages to hear?
Recall what saw ye in the sacred cave,
Where heard ye, by me mastered, howl and
　　　rave
The spirit of evil, dastard, fool and knave,
While ye from him my strong will safely walled,
While him the sacred symbols dread appalled:
The flesh of the Great Spirit,* and the awe
All felt when fiery tongues descend we saw,
And saw the glittering snowy crystals down
Fall from that roof fit kingly domes to crown,

---

*A tangle of coffee-nut beans, lizzards' tongues and birds' livers, tied to
a cord, and wound in mysteriously from a pelt-screened sanctuary, that
they might be touched by the twelve apostles.

And, from the spiritual presence, light
Sublimely glow on gem-decked height on
      height;*
The gong of praise which to the faithful spoke;
The trump of war which far-off echoes woke;
Where, each with his red coal, my heralds came,
The sacred twelve, sent forth to spread my fame,
To spread abroad the rumor of your wrongs,
And preach my gospel, and intone my songs;
Three times ye knelt, three times ye bowed in
      prayer,
Three times ye hailed the sacred taper there.
Saw ye not, but to-day, an eagle wheel
Sedate aloft, while smote the thunder's peal
All summits of the forest and the heights?
The storm not moved him, nor its dazzling lights;
The sun, the cyclone, felt he neither, fear
Touched not his tawny bosom; nor does here,
Within my bosom, lurk of fear one trace;
I am this Eagle, I, in pride of place
Sail thus aloft o'er all the red men's Fires
That gleam in council wheresoe'er aspires
Our race to claim its rights; the Long Knife's power
In fort or battle dies with this good hour."
And then a look repressive of a noise
Applausive gave he, and made signs to boys
Recumbent on the ground, his acolytes,
'Twixt him and lads who held the pitch-pine lights.

---

*The results of fire-works, fulminating-powders and explosives. The
prophet had looked about him in theatres, as well as in churches and
caves.

Up from their place they sprang; the sacred wand
One held, the other, with a gesture fond,
Held t'wards the chief the enchanted skin tattooed
Whereon the sun and moon, in figures rude,
And stars, gave token of its use divine,
And, in due order set, curve, point and line,
Or dark or light, of mystic lore made sign
And heaven's interpretation and design.
That stern and staid impressiveness, like a mask,
Wore they, as did their chief, but still the task
Was pleasant, 'twas important, a high grace
Held firm upon their comely faces' place;
Great grandson, one, of Wa-pa-tha, the same
Who 'neath Penn's treaty tree gained worthy fame;
The other scion was of Georgia's child,
Le-moy-a-tun-gha, ever free and wild.
Not Ganymede, when stood he 'fore Jove's throne,
Rapt by the eagle on from zone to zone,
More radiant stood, with boyish honors bright,
While from him beauteous Hebe in despite
Turned her vexed eyes, what time the angry air
Of stately Juno showed her grim despair
That her own daughter should be thought of worth
Less on Olympus than a son of earth,
Than Wa-pa-tha's descendant stood impressed
With every charm that ever boyhood blest.
Nor Polycletus, e'en, nor Phidias' self,
More beauty placed in goddess, faun or elf
Than showed their swart limbs where might fail
　　　　　　to lap
The rabbit-robe, or frolic show a gap.

Not more devoted are the chosen sons
Of noble Roman houses 'neath the guns
Of famed Saint Angelo's fort on festal days,
When all its pomp and beauty Rome displays,
Nor on the chapel's floor in Holy Week,
Before the pontiff prostrate, mild and meek,
Than were those scions of that native stock
Which thus serenely faced the battle's shock.
Bore cunning leers enough their merry cheeks;
Indeed, within the last half dozen weeks,
Much pork had these same pious acolytes killed,
With all a Nimrod's high ambition filled,
Where flocks domestic roved in many a wood,
And boasted bears had furnished forth the food;
Perhaps some inkling theirs of Moses' law,
Or that in Blackstone they were not too raw
To learn that on tame beasts one may not prey,
But only on those *feræ naturæ.*

The skin was of the far-sought wapiti,
The large red deer which feeds in pastures free
Beyond Missouri's gates, where mountains rise
Whose rocks to skillfulest hunters bring surprise;
And, once the skin's prepared, it e'er remains
A flexible pelt, though wet with myriad rains.
The wand was iron-wood, tipped at either end
With gold refined, gold which the tribes pretend
Comes from Peruvian mines, or missions taught
Far in the West, with every wonder fraught.

The prophet took the enchanted wand, and threw
Sands from far western mines, diverse in hue,
Upon the sign-wrought skin the boys upheld,
And in the sand traced with the wand, as spelled,
Mysterious figures, hieroglyphs, designs,
Contrived to have much force with ignorant minds;
Then, all intent, the fateful markings read
In words half said, half sung, then solemnly said:
"The will of heaven is evident; the cause
Divine we fight for will not let us pause.
Not here to-night will I still further signs,
Well known, repeat; form ye your battle lines;
To-morrow will be need of prophecy none;
Ye shall the proof see with the rising sun.
Respond not by the war whoop to my speech,
Let sacred silence reign, lest noise might reach
As far as to the sentries the Long Knife
Has posted far towards our lines; the strife
Expired, then shall we have good cause
For joy, congratulation and applause."

He ended, and so fixed the habit was
Of rendering answer as a warrior does
That went to hundred lips a hundred hands
To form the challenge, but his warlike bands
Th' heroic chief kept awed by strict control,
And gave the example of his lofty soul.

III.—THE WAR CHIEFS.

THE war chiefs then withdrew to council,
    proud
That unto them was duty such allowed,
The rules to fix, the measure of delay,
And methods best of mingling in the fray,
And when, combined, should launch their war-
    like force
All 'gainst the encampment; they must fix the
    course
Each band should take, what chieftan each should
    lead,
What countersign, what signals, all should heed,
The front, rear, center, spaces and reserves,
The approach direct or on the flanks in curves.
What with the wounded must be done and dead.
No thought they gave, so ruled their Prophet
    dread.

Around they passed the sacred calumet,
Which tribes unite in friendly council met,
Which warlike leagues confirm 'mongst allies
    sworn,
Here heralding peace, and there denouncing scorn.

And 'mongst the chieftians was of pomp no lack.
There were White Loon, Stone-Eater, Winnemac,
Chiefs of renown; they were the leaders tried
Who in the field would guide the battle's tide.

Not few the auxiliaries were the Shawnees had,
With various arms, in various costumes, clad.
There Sacs were, Kickapoahs, Ottawas,
Pottawatamies, Chippewas bred to wars,
And Winnebagoes, Wyandots, Miamis.
And under chiefs of no mean grade were these.
The lofty Shawnee warrior, orator, chief,
Tecumseh, would my lines have lent relief
Had he been present, but the absent brave
Sought with rash counsels the lost cause to save,
And distant, midst the southern groves of pine,
Urged tribes remote to join his battle line.
'Mongst the Sac warriors were Tepaukee, grim,
And Onondaki; what was hoped of him
Comes from his name, Destroy Town; and were
            sent,
That might the Sacs his name well supplement,
With these, Sag-wa-na-te-kwish-u (a name
Which means, if here a trope may privilege claim,
In our own plain United States, unfurled,
The-Thunder-that-is-heard-around-the-world,)
And Ha-hah-kus-ka, the White Elk; and came
From Kickapoan lodges braves of fame
Wide-flaming; there Bout-sa-ca-ho-ka was,
The Wolf, and Paca Rinqua; and uprose,
For war vehement, Ottawan names:
Tho-wo-nau-wa, amongst them, was in flames
For instant battle; and the mighty bulk
Of Taupinibeh's slowly sailing hulk

Launched was by Pottawataman zeal; and led
Onoxa's plumes this festival of the dead.
The Chippewan bands claimed Waubanoosa tall
And Shamanetoo haughty ('twould appall
Ears pious to know this God Almighty means,
But blasphemy's the homage given by fiends);
And, too, the Devil Standing (name profane)
Mintongaboit; and in red war's train
Strode the old warrior Wassachum—affrights
His rendered name: 'tis First-to-start-the-Whites—
The Winnebagoan hero. Sent the Wyandots
Tyanumka, Terhataw, Tarhe; lots,
Cast late by valiant hands Miamian, brought
Him whom prompt victory crowned, where'er he
            fought,
Mashepesheewingqua, or Tiger's Face,
Into the lists; and Cantanquar; a grace
This aboriginal prince our beadroll lends:
His name's the Sky; much glory therewith blends.
He claimed, like Wattawamat, that the levin
His father was, which, from a stormy heaven
Crashed on an oak tree, on a mountain's height,
Amidst the appalling darkness of the night,
And from the riven oak the hero sprang
All at a bound, while fierce his weapons rang.

In ermine wrapped, with treaties' transcripts rolled,
Safe in some woodland sanctuary old,
Some grotto whereto comes no restless wind,
And nature's to the hidden treasure kind,

With chiefs Wyandot, had been given in guard
The Great Belt of the Union, that not marred
Upon it might be one sole hieroglyph,
One bead, one course of wampum, for belief
In this their symbol had a sacred hold
Upon their consciences, it was their flag, each fold
Of which of ancient lineage spoke and dates
　　　　remote:
But vain with them as with the Epirote
Were his loved symbols, when the hosts of Rome
Whelmed in disaster banner, hosts and home.

Two braves had sought concealment in the camp;
The crime the same that gave Ulysses stamp
Of strategy and valor.　None deny
This to a Greek; but, to a red man, spy
Would be the weakest word our tongues could use,
Unchivalrous, thus, the fallen to abuse;
Their Trojan horse a clump of alders mixed
With pawpaw bushes and the spicewood; fixed
Their backs against a lin'n and beach, two trees
Whose shadow aided them; they were Shawnees;
One Larshapahe was, the Tranquil Chief,
The other Tamenatha, Arrow-Sheaf.
Sour greeting they with honeyed greeting met,
Said they were guests of their white brethren, yet
A grave surmise the General had that here
His Brutus was and Cassius, and severe
His countenance was; his horse they had observed,
The General's height and size, they sure deserved

Short shrift, a rope or guns, but times of truce
Counseled the affair be treated as a ruse
Unpunished, and the humbled braves allowed
To seek their own camp with vexation bowed.

And braves were there from many a western
      vale,
From many a mount, and many a charming dale,
From tracts Canadian, where a mighty king
Sought on defenseless homesteads war to bring;
From Sainte Marie and shores Chequamegan;
From where, o'er mines Gogebic, deer herds ran;
From Pepin's Lake and Straits of Macinac,
And where the Chippewan hears his foes' Haha.*
There were they met upon the forest's verge,
Met what they claimed their God-given rights to
      urge,
Met to contest the mastery of a world.
Think what high force on Harrison's camp was
      hurled!
Think how, sublime, with heavenly armor dight
And weapon earthly, they had sought the fight!

Ah, why begrudge this spray of asphodel
Planted upon their graves? They suffering fell

---

*The Falls of Minnehaha, within the territory of the Dacotahs or
Sioux, the hereditary enemies of the Chippewas, and near the boundary
line, the Mississippi River.

For what they deemed their sacred rights, not
        less
Were sainted heroes ancient songs caress
Sincere in all the battles where they bled.
For these to native land were dearly wed,
An ancestry was theirs of no far strand,
Yet them invaded pilgrim band on band,
And soon the invaders masters were, and heaven
Seemed upon them to pour but limpid levin.
Suppose they did not use the soil, that waste
Laid tracks primeval whereon beasts were
        chased?
May I not with my own do what I will?
May I not nature love, each tree and rill?
May I not have of lengthening leagues a lawn,
And pasture there the bison, bear and fawn?

And when I praise the warrior, I praise not
Wild license, rapine, lawless scheme and plot.
May poet none Columbia claims as bard
Mourn States controlled by power's Pretorian
        Guard, ·
But may free, unbought votes, free, noble speech,
Be the rich heritage of all and each!
What is our civilization? Is't that scope
For malice may be given to murderers, Swope
And Goodloe? Or that hot Kincaid† may find
In Taulbee's blood help for his anger blind?

---

†On the trial, which took place after the above was written, Kincaid
put in, and sustained, to the satisfaction of the jury, a plea of self-defence.

All whites these were of station high and tone
Exalted, yet the first sad pair must own
They carried each for each the gun and knife,
Nor place nor time was heeded; and the strife
Came, with the last pair, while our statesmen
    laws
Were framing in the Capitol, and the cause
Of Christian civilization in its home
The insult felt, beneath Columbia's dome.

Used to the horse the Indian is, the lance
Is his to use, with trappings of romance,
But suffered not the marsh, the night, the trees,
This friend of man his battle-rage to ease,
And corralled stood the neighing chargers,drawn
Forth from the lines, until the day should dawn
With joyful tidings to be sent with speed,
Or grievous dole which no dispatch would need;
And ordered with their riders in reserve
To aid the line should e'er the footmen swerve.

Few in that throng of fighting men lacked dress,
The season mild made them content with less
Than claims the rigorous winter, but parade
Of taste and acquisitions many made
Fastidious, and the occasion gave them cause
Long in their savage toilets to make pause.
Stripped to the waist were many, breast, arms,
    nude,
And painted thick with horrid pigments rude,

While on their backs and sides were spaces
          strewed
With guns, bows, horses, arrows, there tattooed.
All o'er the warlike cheeks and necks was spread
A background of vermilion's brilliant red,
And stripes alternate, sepia, yellow, green,
To aid their barbarous guise, thereon were seen.
The hunting shirt of doeskin, leggins oft,
And moccasins frequent, of the buckskin soft,
Blankets some wore, and some the savage hide
Stripped from some denizen of the forest wide,
Or roamer of the endless prairie's range;
And, in costume exceeding weird and strange,
Some helmets wore of the red fox, and free
The pelt fell o'er the shoulders to the knee,
Or yellow wolf-skin, drawn on as a hood,
As if within a beast a hero stood.
So Aventinus, friend of Turnus, came
Tricked to the war (that war Ausonia's fame
Fixed changelessly) in shaggy vesture dread
A panther's full pelt furnished; o'er his head
The panther's face rose horrible, and shone
The white teeth of the beast above his own;
More hideous gear than Roland wore, or masks
By white-capped white men worn, when lawless
          tasks
Employ them 'gainst their neighbors, and the
          night
Is soiled with civilized crime against the right.

Of trinkets, rings, chains, amulets, some were
        seen;
The exquisite, or wild or cultured, glean
Will from the fertile fields of fashion brass,
Gold, silver, copper, chalcedony, glass;
And medals graced at times a lordly breast,
Some sacred, secular some, and worn to attest
Regard for him that gave them, king or priest,
Great father, trader, sachem, west or east.
The tomahawk, the rifle for the strife,
Some had, and hung or belted was the knife;
But others, wanting rifles, war clubs held,
Whereby was many a doughty foeman felled.
The bow and arrow found their famed experts,
Skilled to inflict with these arms mortal hurts.
Most richly were the three great chieftains
        dressed,
As of control supreme in fight possessed;
Therein priority was given them, since
Costume must always indicate the prince.
Shirt, leggins, moccasins fine, with beads were
        trimmed
Of larger size, with ruddier tintage; rimmed
All the edges were with brilliant red; and flashed
Pistols and dirks from leather belts, while sashed
Superbly were these chieftains, nor denied
Each one the polished rifle at his side.
Their tomahawks with new-given sharpness
        shone,
Glistened their medals large, full weird the tone

The little silver bells gave forth, which hung
One following each gray eagle feather strung
Along the beaded leggins, snugly dight
With thongs of wolf-skin for this final fight.
Knives round their necks in scabbards hung of
          hide,
Wherein their wives or daughters loved had vied
Effect to give with hedgehog quills and beads
And tinted glasses meet for bloody deeds.
Full-feathered were they, beautifully gay;
Upon their heads the eagle's honors play;
Each round red dot upon the feathers dread
Worn by a warrior means an enemy dead,
Or man or woman, means a herald sent
Before to the Valhalla, with intent
That there the record may be kept as here,
Grim rubric read of strife and force and fear!

IV.—THE GROTTO.

STOOD forth the face of rock in rugged lines,
    Whereon from trees above came clustering
          vines
Grape-loaded in their season, mixed with hues
That come from tribute given of early dews,
The varied glow May brings, and mosses, ferns
And simple flowers the year advancing earns.
Such was the grotto's face when nature smiled,
A pleasing nook, and ne'er severely wild.

The praise of Daphnis Roman shepherds sung,
In their Sicilian grotto, from the tongue
Of loyalty came never freer forth
Than hence in vain came praise of prostrate worth.

Thither, when closed the hearing, and began
The chiefs to counsel o'er their battle-plan,
Went forth the Prophet and his nieces twain,
Their chosen place of rendezvous to gain,
Their devious, dim and secret way to wend,
While threatened mists the starlight's reign to end.
Westward it was from where the encampment
       slept,
Or feigned to sleep, so near that it but stept
A sentry's foot on twig or bark that cracked,
The noise was easily by the hearing tracked.
Across a flat and marshy space the view
Took in the encampment's point, the red, white,
       blue,
And all the numerous fires that lit the skies
To render warmth and guard against surprise.

The grotto was not lofty; rose a bluff
Not steep, and half way up its face, enough
Had nature excavated of a space
To make a niche or cozy tarrying-place.
A niche made broad where might sit three or four
And, sheltered, hear winds roar, see torrents pour.

The floor was highly pitched against the back,
In front it had enough of level's lack
To make it quite convenient as a seat,
Whence forward fell the rested sitter's feet.
Thither had shaggy bison robes been brought
By menials apt, zealous to think of aught
That should be done, and mantles soft of mink
Invited tired limbs therein to sink.

Not unknown to the nieces was this cave,
Oft they it trusted their fatigues to save;
Distant not far from the imperial seat,
For strolling friends or lovers a retreat.
Oft thither they had walked, and there had sat
To pass the pleasant time in pleasant chat,
Or rest within its grateful, cool recess,
Their subjects such as many a white princess
Has often interested, gossip, dress,
Ambitions which all women alike possess,
The latest hunting party, or the dance,
Or some foray, defeat, retreat, advance.
War none the less had interest for these dames
Than for our veterans, or their wives or flames.
Modest they were and graceful; Indian lore
Of heroes of this race has precious store;
Prized women, too, were theirs, and peerless those
Whose fame now haunts our verse, and therein
          grows.
They Tawala and Tawalara were,
Descendant one of Puc-ke-che-no, fair

Historic name in Georgia's legends wrought;
The other child of Chee-see-ah-qua; sought
In all ill fates Tecumseh him, until
Death's bolt sent him a hero's grave to fill.
Mothers they lost in earlier years, reclined
Their hopes upon their uncle's manners kind;
The youngest, Chee-see-ah-qua's child, more care
He seemed to give, but loved alike the pair.

There sat the three within the grotto's shade,
The middle place the Prophet's, and arrayed
On either side the maidens were, and placed
So that Tawala his good right hand graced.
Clad simply in a robe of beaver pelts
The Prophet was, beneath which little else
Marked his costume than the accustomed guise
Of tunic, leggins, held by feathered ties,
And moccasins beaded; on his head he wore
A turban of rich stuffs, velvet and satin, gore
By gore, a present from a captain high
Canadian, who it sent with words to imply
That he should wear it as a king his crown,
So were his courteous compliments written down.
Rose from the midst an eagle feather broad,
That thereby more might be the observer awed.
Hung from his neck his medals wide, three, four,
Perhaps the beaver robe hid several more.
Showed plain, when summer's heat exposed his
        breast,
A couchant tiger, which the art confessed

An English sailor used, to please the chief,
A tattooed work of wondrous skill, not brief
The time it took, and which the Prophet wore
In pride of that keen name his brother bore,
For means Tecumseh India's royal beast·
In act to spring upon his gory feast.
No wand of sovereignty he held, or mace,
Or staff; into his hands with dainty grace
Tawala placed his pipe, an heirloom come
From times ancestral, and her little thumb
Charged it with fragrant sumach, and by dint
Of catching sparks on punk 'twixt steel and flint,
Put fire upon the charge; but yet he held
The pipe not to his lips, but sat as spelled.
And quietly by him sat each lovely aid,
Content to rest; since early morn had weighed
Upon their minds the public business; haste
Had given them scarce of rest a moment's taste;
And now a vigil long before them rose,
Cut off from friends, in face of powerful foes.
Dressed were they with unusual height of care;
Their uncle dreaded for them the night air,
And hints had given jupons to wear and skirts
Such as might save them from the season's hurts,
The softest fawnskins fitted to their forms,
And all that paraphernalia that protects and
        warms.
Short were their dresses both, but leggins meet
Gave them continuations to their feet;

To walk, to romp, to mount the pony's back,
Required their dresses length should somewhat
      lack.
A neat embroidery fair of beaded work
Leggins and moccasins had, nor failed to lurk
Within the needlework hints of Indian lays,
Which moonlight sung and birds and flowers and
      fays.
A scarlet vest the younger wore, there wound
Three onyx buttonrows sent from Puget's Sound.
Earrings were theirs, and necklaces, of gold;
Bracelets on wrist and upper arm; a fold
Superb of beaded wampum made the belt.
Envy thereof by all maids might be felt;
Would reach each string thereof a length
Might well of envy's rage excite the strength,
And unto other Indian maidens show,
As does among white dames the diamond's glow
A disposition costly things to wear,
With father, uncle, spouse, the expense to bear.
The elder cousin's costume sympathy knew
With something told a crisis onward drew.
She wore, this night, a cross of silver given
By a black gown, who gesture made to heaven;
A benediction bore the cross, laid on
By lofty hands Italian; she was drawn,
In deep, long musings to recall the time
And those glad Easter bells with chime on chime.
This symbol of an alien faith she pressed
Often upon the throbbings of her breast,

And high prayers muttered, with her eyes up-
        turned,
From priest, interpreter or prophet learned.
For ribbons had the elder girl slight care,
But England's present showed the younger's hair,
Far down her back her glossy tresses flowed,
And through the waves bright knots of color
        glowed.
Else headgear none was theirs, except a plume
Of snow-white swan's down fastened by a comb
Of tortoise-shell danced Tawalara o'er,
And one rich ornament her cousin wore.
A flexible coronet of gold held bound
The abundant hair her comely temples round,
The abundant hair whose rippling waves
        deserved
To be the Crown's betwixt and Leo's lights
        observed.
Drousset's young gift, a souvenir of the dance,
It had adorned the unfortunate Queen of France,
To history known by Rohan's necklace given,
Fair Antoinette, by murder sent to heaven.
A cedar spray the elder maiden held;
Placed midst the feast it gives delight, and
        quelled
Are evil spirits when 'tis burned, by rise
Of its sweet incense upward to the skies.
A cloak the youngest wore with ermine fringed
And made of tails of foxes purple tinged;

A turkey-feather fan within her lap
Hung from her belt, thereby held from mishap.
The elder cousin boasted ermine full,
Whereof the white flecks shone like whitest
    wool.

With all, far, near, they general favorites seemed.
It had been noted Harrison them esteemed,
And had at Fort Vincennes them presents made
Which them it pleased at high feasts to parade.
Not only were they social stars, but well
At home they stood, nor on them censure fell
That they reserved their pretty, taking airs
For company, and, outside of that, were bears.

The ladies of the fort had given them gay
Things pranked with lace and things to make
    crochet.
These looked they on with female smirks of
    grace,
But laid them by in one or other place;
Not consonant were these things with their staid
    ways,
Nor fell they into this and that dress craze;
And deemed they angular these ladies fair,
Nor liked their shades of eyes and face and hair,
And when these fair ones came into their dreams
They ne'er forgot their effeminate little screams.

Demure they were, these maidens of the wild,
With looks, of course, constrained, and seldom
        smiled.
I do not speak of spikenard and ginseng,
Of sassafras bark and slippery elm, the bang,
And other similar frivolous things the sex
The gallant verse to pass unnamed expects;
But know I well that many a pale-faced maid
Helps the petroleum and the tolu trade.

These princesses claimed half a globe to own,
And yet the imagination sees them thrown
All day 'mongst dirty pelts or forest leaves,
And sad neglect which every housewife grieves;
Domestic lives they led serene, and care
Their cabin showed, 'twas not a lynx's lair.
Not Muses e'er upon Olympus' slopes
By whatsoever poet sung, in tropes
All musical and resonant, e'er were seen
To dip their radiant limbs in Hippocrene
With more of grace, with more of modesty, clad
Than were these natives of the woodland, glad
To seek in Tippikanau's waves delight,
And take the place of Naiads turned to flight.

Much they discoursed, much hath the legend lost,
Hope, joy were with them at the first, but tost
At last were they upon a troubled sea,
An angry flood, and nowhere seen the lea.

Dread came and waned the murky, lingering
    night,
Then hurtling horror's clang, and trembling fright;
As heard they cries of pain, despair and death
To breathe they scarcely dared, or think of breath.

The Prophet, when a boy, the chief had seen
Of chiefs, great Washington; and with his keen,
Swift glance, that son renowned of Gaul adored,
The hero of two worlds, he whose true sword
Flashed radiance far o'er fields historic red
With patriot blood on Freedom's altar shed.
Of these he talked; of these and Shawnees famed.
Much Madison he, the ruling Father blamed:
"The paleface thinks no longer comes a war;
Bookmen and lawyers now rule nations—awe
Will rule their souls when rise the native bands,
And, midst red slaughter, seize our plundered
    lands."

His nieces, too, while he his pipe enjoyed,
With all the misty future's happenings toyed,
Their games, pranks, journeyings and exchange
    of gifts.
As struggled clouds in heavy, thickening rifts,
"Ah, uncle," said the younger, "what a time
We'll have at the Four Lakes! And when we
    climb
The rocks at Mackinac! Or Pictured Portals seek!
On them in vain big storms their angers wreak!

Then the Dacotahs, too, their Thousand Lakes
May us invite to visit, there where breaks
The Father of Waters into cascades fair,
Which fill with rainbows all the brilliant air!
I well remember now that pretty song,
Which once relieved a tedious journey long,
Trilled by a maid from Waves Sky Tinted; so
Upon the moonlight from her lips 'twould flow:

> I will be the belle of Minnehaha!
> I will be the belle of Minnetonka!
> Let me sail upon thy waves, White Bear!
> Let me breathe thine Island's sacred air!
> Dance and music, ye are joys divine!
> Friends and summer, be ye always mine!"

In musings died away the charming voice,
Musings were times which were to her of choice.
The seer smoked on, his thoughts were with the
        past
And future; rolls a ship without a mast;
The silver cover fastened with a click
To hold another charge of killikinick;
Tobacco oft sent him a southern friend,
But lest it might his nieces' nerves offend,
He seldom used it; he that would be great
Must yield at times in small things sans debate.
And then the elder cousin sighed, and said,
The while she held impatiently her head,
And patted restlessly upon the floor,
And glanced upon the sombre Open Door:

" This afternoon, as I my usual stroll
Took, past where waves on our loved islands roll,
With me Cakimi sent her restless boys;
What pleased me wearied her, their ceaseless
   noise;
No quail, no squirrel, their quick eyes escaped,
Nor towering tree with hanging grapevines draped.
Above a patch of flowering water-flag,
A kingfisher I saw all easily drag
From their sweet circuits tawny butterflies.
Herein, O uncle, is it danger lies
And threatening to our cause? Or may it be
The flies are they, the happy birds are we?"

V.—THE WAR SONG.

" HIST! do I hear the charge? . . . No! Wait!
  The time has not yet come to unlock our
   hate;
Yes, 'twas but some sly fox or wolf, which draws
The enemy's line of fire-heaps, or has cause
In some wild wings above us changing skies.
Or could it be from heaven some meteor flies,
Or comet madly whirling in its sphere?
Ah, crazed am I with joy and racked with fear,
At this high moment, and sustained by hope
That now at last we with the paleface cope.
Go on." "Yes, uncle; know you, ran my mind
On Uncle Tecumseh, ever good and kind?

A glorious day it was when he returned
From a long tour whence he had honor earned,
Plumed forth for war, as you remember well,
And we closed round to hear what he would tell;
And, first, before him set the wild rice, fish,
And tempting things delicious dish on dish,
And buffalo marrow, and rich pemican,
And we, sure, deemed him rather God than man."
"Yes, child," the Prophet kindled at her speech,
"Tecumseh's merits had the loftiest reach.
You know De Chouset said, the interpreter,
He who the Long Knives said could never err,
He had no easy task to follow forth
Things full of force and philosophical worth,
And lofty flights of eloquence divine,
And golden truths from every gleaming mine,
Tecumseh's mouth would utter; deep and wide
The interpreter's learning was, but like the tide
The Father of Waters sends when deep snows
　　　　melt,
Were forceful words Tecumseh's, treasured, felt,
As should be words of those the heavens endow.
Ah, this is sweet, my darlings, victory now,
While speaks Tecumseh in Tulaura's groves,
(I sometimes think of men as beasts in droves).
He, by my couriers, will the victory learn,
And we proud wreaths illustrious here shall earn.
Ah, Tawalara, you will find it true,
What I have preached, that in the beginning
　　　　grew

All Indian tribes from ours; for ages knew,
In his unbounded ken all nature through,
The Great Spirit only the Shawnees; his brain
Their ancestor produced, of Godlike strain;
From him we are all descended; gave to birth
The French and English, following us in worth,
The breast of Manitou; while from his feet
The German race came forth, as seemed most
      meet.
The Master of Life is with us at this hour;
He will, this night display his sovereign power.
To-night the Union is established; here
Shall meet its parliament, called from far and
      near;
Here shall the center be of all debates,
Hence shall go forth laws unto all our States.
Here we will found an empire fixed and free;
Here shall Tecumseh rule, sustained by me;
The white race, with their fripperies and their
      smirks,
Smiles gracious, wherein rueful danger lurks,
Shall, like the white waves, rocks impending
      spurn,
Dash into spray, and not like waves return.
Back, back, beyond the memory of old chiefs,
Or old tradition, rests our title; griefs,
Wrongs, murders, lies, all have not quenched our
      love
For this dear land; the reigning stars above,

Kehaukee, Pauwan, Talauree, declare
The crisis come, the dawn's deliverence near.
Yes, stars in which our foes affirm their faith,
And then deny; a God with them's a wraith.
And what a race of hypocrites they are!
They have their days for groaning, and they mar
E'en these with silly laughter and gay routs;
They have their days for laughter, wherein spouts
Blood from the veins of furious rioters, dazed
With long-drawn games, and all confused and
        crazed
With fire-water, which they drink and drink
Till ceases heart to feel or mind to think.
Corrupting, horrible, debasing vice!
To drag *us* there's their favorite, deep device.
They preach the things we need no preaching for;
They practice what they please; an open door
Is ever ready for the approaching lie.
One of their Black Gowns heard I, who could vie,
Whene'er to his red children he would preach,
E'en with Tecumseh in felicitous speech,
Open the book he carries, written in heaven,
And show the dangerous fire-water should be
        driven
Forth from the world; he had his secret flask,
And, in the same discourse he said: ' Each mask
Ye give the soul discard; 'tis plainly shown
Herein ye should not laugh, nor dance, nor groan;
Reverent, not joyful, thoughtful be, not sad;
An ancient king said,'Laughter and mirth are mad

And sorrow vain;' he heard his friend was dead
And shook the forest with his moanings dread.
Him gave I from my herd my finest horse;
He let the reins of merriment have their course."

Hurled from his coveted heights imperial down
To bear the red man's contumely, the frown
Of chiefs full fed with envy, and their lies,
Sowed broadcast, and his suffering people's
   cries,
He's not the first whom black ambition's lure
Led to betray a cause past hope of cure;
He's not the first whom mad vainglory drove
To try the thunderbolts of jealous Jove;
He's not alone 'mongst leaders of the church
Who saintly purity with statecraft smirch;
Judge him just as he was, a spiritual lord,
With crozier armed, and miter, crown and sword.

Now ceased the talk, nor cast down nor enthused
The Prophet sat, and o'er this idea mused:
The idea that whatever man may feel,
He should the emotion steadfastly conceal.
This idea governed all the tribes, east, west,
North, south; on all their minds 'twas pressed.
"Ye all," the God Hay-o-kah said, "should live
Calm lives, like mine, lives undemonstrative,"
The Apollo he, who from the earliest days,
Wore midst the Muses aboriginal bays.

A dispensation 'twas of gracious Fate;
They felt no rising of delight elate
At sight of this fair land around them spread,
They felt no sorrow when their hopes were dead;
At least they gave expression none to all;
Each thwarted joy, nor would be sorrow's thrall.
Somewhat alike to this is the high thought,
With old romance and antique feeling fraught,
Whereon is based the finest art of Greece
(And shall in this her rulership ever cease?)
The thought which gives their Gods a high
          repose.
No Grecian God emotion's traces shows,
No Grecian God is thus made Fortune's toy,
Nor chain confesses of or grief or joy.
Thus is the aboriginal native free,
The highest type is his of liberty.   .
Free as the Gods, thus his ideal high
Mounts radiant planes, e'en climbs Olympus' sky.
Emotion?   Yes, the fire is burning there,
But unacknowledged; when a Hecla's glare
Lights the horizon, then, in sullen wrath,
Volcanic fires assail the white man's path.

And now the elder princess, pondering still
Ancestral state, of silence broke the thrill:
" Rich hues shall have our totem!"   For no lars
By mighty families old, recalling scars
In strifes Ænean with the Rutuli,
Or later, gained with Nelson on the sea,

Or given by infidels rash in some crusade
Godfrey or Cœur de Lion famous made,
With feeling greater or more lofty 's viewed
Than by these red men were the legends rude
That held them to the past. "Ah, t'will be
      sweet
To see you, uncle, every honor meet!"
Ah, dear, dear girl, the sapphire-crested throne,
The diamond crown, are not for thee to own,
But meet thy jubilant hopes sat muttering Fates,
And dark Defeat sits at thy future's gates!

Then in a voice caressing, low and mild,
The Prophet spoke: "Ah, list to me, dear child,
You women spoil the prophets; through the
      town
You sing their ceaseless praises up and down,
Until mere tyrants they become, and prone
To say, and do things better let alone.
Hereafter I would hear but just the truth,
This I expect from you not lacking youth;
Yes, let detestable flattery come from men
Uncandid, and from tottering dames, and when
This bitter war is over, praise me not.
Praise I eschew, 'tis oft so overwrought.
Let us now think of all the risks of war,
Wounds, stress, resistance, watchings, strugglings
      sore.

For my part, were I wounded, death outright
Would be my prayer, or else a wound that's slight.
A slight wound honor brings, renown and friends,
A wound severe to lingering tortures tends."
"But, uncle, you assured them none should die,
Then your philosophy will scarce apply."
"Yes, so I did, the heavens have so declared,
But that Long Knife who leads our foes has
        marred,
Perhaps, by magic, all my sovereign plans,
Putting the right beneath his wrongful bans,
This to correct, to disenchant my men,
Soon as the signal's seen, sounds in the glen
That song I practiced oft on Georgian streams
And in that fair Ohio's vale where gleams
The Auglaize, that bright and rippling river, near
Where leaps, a fountain there, the Wabash here,
And on the heights we oft have climbed, we three,
Our Cedar Cliff, romantic, wild and free.
Oft Taupinibeh, Pottawataman King,
In speech profound, but e'er untaught to sing,
The ruler of this realm and other realms,
Whom justly every earthly honor whelms,
He whom De Chouset called Latinus, oft
Nodding to me as to Æneas, soft
Flattery, too, my brother giving, when
Him he declared Achilles chief of men;
Oft Taupinibeh would his peace-pipe take,
Brought from the Red-stone Quarry by the Lake,*

---

*In the Côteau des Prairies, just beyond Lake Travers. Lake Travers
is the source of the Red River of the North.

A source that gives its color to the flood
That northward pours its foaming gouts of blood,
A souvenir of the time he tarried there
As umpire of debates that taxed his care,
And me another give Dacotahs sent
In kind return for hospitality lent,
And say 'Come prophet-king, dismiss delay,
Enough has been our waiting, let's survey
From heights Janiculan ('twas De Chouset's word)
The maze of valley, forest, prairie, bird,
Star, cloud and sunshine that proud height affords,
O'er lands where a new Troy shall claim us lords.'"

The words scarce spoken were, the signal came,
A brand whirled circling, spitting sparks of flame.
As from the monks of Irenarion's shrine
Who, sleepless, sung the unceasing chant divine,
So rolled upon the night that voice which erst
Had made its owner honored as the first,
The best, of his tribe's orators; alas,
That honors must be lost, and praises pass
Far forth to others! Rolled the song and grew
Full and more full, nor trace of weakness knew:

    Strike, brethern, strike! Strike, braves!
      Strike, strike, with anger warm!
    Drive, drive your foes as waves
      Drive swift the midnight storm!

Forth, brethern, forth to war,
  The war of right 'gainst might!
Smite, smite the pale-face sore,
  O'erwhelm them in the night!

O, not Tecumseh's fame
  A prouder wreath shall bear
Than shall your every name
  When men tell what ye dare!

Watch, watch, from rock and bush,
  The foe that watches you!
With vigor onward push!
  Ye are many, they are few!

Stand, stand, for all your race!
  Stand for the young and old!
Meet, meet them face to face,
  O, warriors true and bold.

Soak, soak the field in blood!
  Drive club and axe and knife!
Let bullets pour a flood
  Of death upon the strife!

And came, in regular turn, as interlude,
Between each stanza of the strain, the rude,
Emphatic, earnest refrain rising high
And rolled along the weird and darkling sky:

Strike, brethren, strike! Be brave
Strike, strike! The good cause save!

From time to time came messengers to give news,
At first all roseate were the announcements; hues
Of dole come rarely at the first, but grow
The lingering clouds, then comes the crash of woe.

One of these messengers was Teewalah, vowed
Unto the younger of our maidens; proud
His record was 'mongst Ottowan warriors; grace
Ruled all his limbs, and dignity his face.
Not more intent was Peleus, when he saw
The Centaur bringing to the coast, when bore
The Argo past his isle, the beauteous boy,
To give sad fates one moment's gleam of joy,
Than was the Prophet when this brave came near,
Brave by fond woman loved and sacred seer;
For here was Elskwatawa's venture, here,
For his craved Golden Fleece he sought the mere;
Here shipwreck was before him, and beyond
Would hide him fate's contempt and folly's frond.
A glance passed 'twixt the lovers, ah, how sad!
And sad the words, in semblance only glad!
Their mutual loves erst pledged, would fail forlorn
Beneath the white man's burdening weight of
        scorn!
Home, city, empire lost, and prestige gone!
Would bring all this, alas, the hastening dawn!

Or, rather, let us think calamity naught
Changed in their souls with mutual homage
        fraught,
Their mutual faith an amaranth's fadeless flowers
Retaining all their bloom neath sorrow's showers.

And spoke her elder cousin: "Ah, how strong
The sulphur-smoke! Uncle, will it be long
Before our braves announce the battle won?
See, there are signs the night's long race is run."
Ah, sorrowing child of fate and sport of woe,
The morning dawns, but not for thee its glow!
For thee is no nepenthe's balm, dethroned
Thy life hath lost the queenly state it owned!

Loud o'er the forest rung the bugle's notes;
Loud o'er the strife cheer followed cheer, as floats
Wave after wave, when dash upon the shore
The jubilant billows crested o'er and o'er.
Those notes, those cheers, they knew their mean-
        ing well,
And heavy on their hearts their music fell.

Then came a messenger running, 'twas Twalee,
Betrothed to Tawalara. "Flee, oh flee!"
His first words were, and then his voice assayed
To tell the fight was over; that arrayed
In glittering harness steeds sent down from
        heaven,
Mounted by giant riders wielding levin,

Had driven the red men back, and that defeat
Was utter, and all bands in full retreat.
But not one word . . . . sobs only came
From lips hot with the battle's smothering flame
And whips of furies seemed to sting his soul
Burdened with love and sunk 'neath destiny's
      dole.
Naught said he, but the three him understood,
They asked no speech from him in that pained
      mood;
He dashed sad tears from out his eyes, sad swea
 From off his brow; dismayed their eyes had me
His and his loved one's; he had not the power
The Prophet's eye to meet in that dread hour,
And, as the messenger left, his head inclined
Deeply towards the girl in gesture kind,
And "Nenemoosha, sweetheart," said his lips,
With somewhat else which from the legend slips,
Alas! it was their latest greeting, sped
Through that true heart a trooper's charge of
      lead!

VI.—THE CAMP.

THEN was this Battle Forest nature's child,
  'Twas nature's paradise, and not a wild.
There blows a breeze incessant from the vale,
But rises never to a dangerous gale.

Strike, where the Prophet's ancient capital rose,
Frosts from Pike's Peak†, and hail the north wind
      knows,
But where the dead are gathered 'neath the shade
Of sheltering oaks, the heavens repose; invade
Their peace no storms by battle's besoms brought,
By mediation are those green mounds sought.
But still aggressive warfare there its ranks
Displays, deploys, for now on Burnett's banks
Faith has its citadel, religion's cause
Supplies with prayer the battle's loud huzzas.
The snares of Satan and the attacks of sin
Here warriors meet; the din's a sacred din;
And earnest pleaders, jealous for the Life,
The Way, the Truth, preach near the field of
      strife.
The field of strife remains intact, its fates
Opened to all God's civilization's gates.
There, close beyond, the village rises too,
And but a few miles southward comes in view
Domes, spires and turrets, showing where La-
      fayette
Shines like a gem in precious bordering set.

No eucalyptus there in torrid heats
Leaps to the skies, nor rank Sequoia meets

---

†The principal force of the Pacific and Pike's Peak current, traceable
through a series of valleys, the Columbia, Snake, Salt Lake, Grand,
Arkansas, Osage, Missouri, Wabash, is directed upon the site of the Prophet's Town, by the conformation of the Valley, and by the same conformation is diverted from the Battlefield.

The wandering eye, but lusk rich branches reach
From noble growths, the sugar, oak and beech
And hickory, symbol of unyielding will;
From walnuts of both hues fays fruitage spill;
And, in the valley, limns the graceful plane
Upon the view its tintage not in vain;
And climbs the lofty poplar heights divine,
Caressed, like Virgil's elms, by flower and vine.
Yes, growths are there for which the borrowing
        tongue
Of England has no name, which must be sung
In tones Algonquin whereto Hesiod dear
And loved Theocritus might lend an ear.
A plane tree by the prattling brook stood; vast
In was in burly bulk, and hollow; cast
Thereon contented looks the troopers oft,
For saw they there a swarm of bees aloft,
And rightly judged that this wild colony's home
Would rich stores yield of well-filled honeycomb.

Surprised the Dryads watched the unusual scene,
Meek, modest maids, midst sprays of eglantine.
Remote, beyond the din of war's array,
Beyond the grotto's ribs of mossy gray,
Satyrs and fauns, the sons divine of Pan,
Fled trembling from the military plume, and Dan
Silenus lost his leering, laughing looks,
And himself changed to echoes soft of brooks;
Fays, fairies, all the sylvan troop, dismayed
The hint their sturdier brethren gave, obeyed;

I know not whether Bacchus left the scene,
Perhaps could tell some contraband canteen!
Full well I know that Pan was there himself,
Friend, one would think, of every woodland elf,
And heard his terrible voice those native men
Them drive in flight confused through fog and
      fen.
Oft thrills of sympathy the embowering trees
Expressed in moanings to the midnight breeze,
Some aboriginal Phaëthusas there,
Or Dryopes, might stir the midnight air.

Take now the map Columbia shows, and pass
From Wabash banks, beyond where mountains
      mass,
To California's strands and Oregon's wilds,
Aye, climb Tacoma's heights and seek defiles
That lead to Saint Elias' peak, and there
See Asian seas whose shores our standards bear!
How many thousand millions does it add,
With mines, with vines, with emerald herbage
      glad,
To our resources wide, to our domain
Of acres bearing all all lands attain?
How many hundred millions will it rear,
Trained man to love and God alone to fear?
So many acres has this forest camp
Gained to our flag; so brightly burns the lamp
Of knowledge, faith and labor in the souls,
More rich, more wise, than any 'twixt the poles;

So much renown ne'er haughty Argonauts
    nerved
'Gainst royal Thebes, where victory they de-
    served.

Plodded the weary sentinels on, and heard
Only by dusky wolves the silence stirred,
The dusky wolf at times a covering pelt
'Neath which a spying Indian crept and knelt.
The white-tailed deers' eyes glistened in the glare
The watch fires cast upon a background, bare
Of aught but ghostly tents and foliage black
And starlight mixed with cloudy rack on rack.
The migratory birds who sought the balm
Of southern skies startled the scented calm
With clang on clang aerial, as obeyed
Their ranks their captains' orders on them laid.
Not in the open field the Indian fights,
He plans surprises, ambuscades; when nights
With dubious moons are found, then lurks his craft;
Or, by a sudden, swift movement, he will waft
His force round to a point not guarded; truce
With him means stealthy opportunity; loose
Is his regard to promises made a foe;
Not Punic faith could strategy's windings know
More intricate than knew the Shawnees, shrewd
To feign, to lull, to hesitate, to delude.
But history joys to tell that no tribe more
Than did the Shawnees intellectual power

Possess, and statesmanship and eloquence rare.
Of these Chief Cornstalk's an example fair,
And eminently Tecumseh is, whose bright
Exalted mind enjoyed superior light.

The night capricious was; at times seemed near
The brilliant winter orbs, distinct and clear,
At times withdrawn; and when the General stood
Consulting with his aids, the musing mood
Came on him, when the sky all radiant beamed,
And in their might the constellations gleamed.
"See, there," he said, "yon oak an opening fair
Gives to observe the miracles vast of air!
Through its broad leafless branches may be seen,
And through that walnut's, all the Giant's sheen!
Mark belt and sword! Stand here again! How
　　　wins
The Hexagon's beauty on one! There the Twins
Are, and Capella! One can easily scan
Procyon, Sirius, Rigel, Aldebaran,
All radiant round the Martial Star, a dream
Of starry splendor in the night supreme!
Just when we reached camp I the planet saw
Far west toward the sun; peculiar awe
Surrounds that heavenly orb; Tecumseh's gaze,
Which seems alert as well of nights as days,
One evening at the garrison, when it shone,
Just after a rich sunset, all alone
Upon the sky, watched its entrancing rays,
Then thoughtfully said—that man has pious ways—

'Ah, on the robe of Manitou a bead
Of wampum 'tis!' and bade me give it heed.
Who can forget the singular threat he made
To Tustinugee–Thlucco if delayed
Should be that chief's adhesion to the league,
If, as we say at cards, he should renege?
The threat was, and he made it good, that, day
And date he gave, he, in Detroit away,
Would stamp upon the earth, and thereby make
The Creek chief's capital, Toockabatcha, shake
To its foundations; this he really did,
Helped by that earthquake called of New Madrid.*
Tecumseh inspirations had of the divine.
Mind I right well his lordly presence fine
And air superb, when him I once besought
To seat himself in council: 'No,' he said, 'is
              brought
My life from him, my father, yonder sun;
From this my mother, earth, my life was won,
Upon my mother's bosom it were best
I should repose!'   And, it must be confessed
That, on the velvet grass there, he a pose
Of grace insuperable took; and rose
Acutely in my mind that learning old
Whereby in myths heroic we are told
How giants of primeval times on earth
To Cœlus and to Terra owed their birth."

---

*A slight anachronism, but one of only a few weeks. The date of the battle of Tippecanoe is November 7, 1811; the date of the earthquake shocks called of New Madrid is of the succeeding month, December.

Responded Clarke, who envied much the name
Tecumseh had of special power with game:
"A mighty hunter, too, he is; they say
He has shot down his thirty deer a day."

" The night grows darkling, soon the Pleïads
          seven
May rain or mist send from this glorious heaven.
You've heard that story of Alcmena's breasts?
Don't let the cavalry, boys, forget their crests!
The galaxy is so-called from galax.
Out in the brush there's one of those damned
          Sacs!
Through yonder hackberry I just caught his eye!
Go, try to take him, he's a dirty spy!"

Deem not the bard absurb if here he note
Movements the army would not know by rote.
For knew their leader much of learning old,
Of pages rich with poesy's bright gold;
And, by the light of science, Virgil scanned,
Homer and Milton, nor kept Dante banned
From his thronged shelves.   And after him came
          a war,
Which made of hearts so many sadly sore,
Whereby the Union of our States was saved
Intact by those who Mars' red thunders braved;
And he who merited the most in strife
Knew, best of all, this bright, ethereal life,

This wondrous maze of world on world piled
 high,
Their ways, their names, their laws, the how and
 why
Of all their being: Mitchel was his name,
Name which among the darlings ranks of fame.
The secret march he knew, the charge, the dash,
The levin that sends from a clear sky its crash.
Heroes he taught renowned, at Huntsville's walls,
How to redeem a nation's million thralls,
How to cut foes in twain and peace compel,
How fields to win and heaven to search as well.
Alas, he lived not till the victory came!
Heroic, chivalrous, bright with every flame
Of learning and of eloquence! Came the pest,
The yellow southern plague, and took the best
Commander of that army up to heaven.
May often such to our loved land to be given!

VII.—THE VICTORY.

Then thus kept on the General to his aids
And other officers of various grades:

"The approaching winter sets the birds to flight:
They travel southward now; 'tis plain, to-night,
The noise their clattering pinions make. The
 brant,
Pishnekuh, I am sure I hear; and can't

We almost see the green-heads, keen of eye,
The mallard ducks? Ah, but these birds are shy!
Say, Waller, might their traveling not suggest
To our red friends to lose their usual rest?
The robins, surely, and the bluebirds, too,
Are almost near enough to be in view.
And there's the plover, with his 'Dee, dee, dee,
Kildee!' He seems to say 'Kill ye, ye, ye!'
Or is't an augury 'gainst those rascally reds,
Who deem it brave to kill men in their beds?
What do they call the robin? Opechee?
And bluebird? Owaissa? I mind the glee
With which that pretty niece of Elskwata—
Wa's, one time at the fort, showed when she saw
The birds come to be fed on the parade.
Yes, what attention then her uncle paid,
The solemn savage, both those artless girls!
T'was when I gave them, Wal', those Roman
        pearls.
But ah, to-morrow we may other wings
Not only see but hear; the owl now sings,
To-morrow vultures may seek you or me;
But pray to-night, boys; prayer will make us free
From hesitation in our country's cause,
For God will not desert her arms and laws."

A pause ensued; the words had touched the souls
Of those brave men. At times communion holds
The man aroused with God, while nature priest
Is in her forest temples. Talking ceased,

Until the stanch commander speech renewed,
While round him stood his officers thought-im-
        bued:
"An Indian deems it right to gain by fraud;
Ne'er by a qualm of conscience is he awed.
Well I recall the fights of ninety-four,
Their ways on the Miami, how they tore
All compacts all to pieces, 'Watch them, boys,'
Mad Anthony always said, 'They make no noise
More than a snake does, and like it will strike,
So trust alone to musket, sword and pike.'
And then our force and discipline stun his mind,
And this to offset are his lies designed."
The night was far advanced, the vigil long
Led back the General to that hero strong,
The barrier of the West, the frantic foe
Whose heat in battle rose to furnace-glow.
But then this hero, though in battle great,
Failed to allow a reason having weight,
A reason urged by all Tecumseh's strength
Of genius and of eloquence, that the length
And breadth of all this continent was one land,
Flawless as broad, and permanent as grand,
One land inhabited by tribes diverse.
Therefore, Tecumseh, censured as perverse,
Labored to effect a union of these bands,
Labored to show the whites how many hands
Held title and dominion over all.
The States' rights theory, covered with the pall

Of dire defeat in our late civil war,
However much it had been praised before,
Tecumseh deemed pernicious, and maintained
The whites could hold no land unless 'twere gained
By universal cession; every tribe
Must have its share of the dishonoring bribe
And put its seal of sanction to the deed.
Strange that his reasoning white men safely plead,
Reasoning which stood the storm in time of need,
And which a war's dread sanctions made all heed,
Should, 'mongst the Indians, have met failure; sad
That fate treads nations down, and clad
In terrors supernatural are the fields
Where nation, tribe, State, every faculty yields
Before divine necessity! Holy Writ,
In simple terms, for truths celestial fit,
Records that Jacob's heritage spoiled their foes;
Came miracle after miracle aiding those
Who sought from lands long settled forth to drive
Their former owners; heaven has seemed to strive
At Plymouth and at Yorktown to extend
To invading chiefs all favors of a friend.
From unseen sources unseen floods of power
Come down to deluge battlefields, and lower
Dull clouds of doom, with storm and horror black,
O'er hosts by Gideons driven with feigned attack.
Yes, we had taken these rich Wabash plains,
Part of the Indian national domains,
From out the jurisdiction of their chiefs.
This was the ground of all Tecumseh's griefs,

Of all Tecumseh's sorrow; tribes but few,
The Kickapoahs, Weas, one or two,
Had signed the compact; they, remote, alone;
These little States illegally thus the throne
Usurped, and gave great spreading tracts away,
Which not to them belonged: the hastening day
Of retribution with Tecumseh came,
With twanging bowstring, stealthy deaths and
      flame.
Great tracts the whites claimed where the Wa-
      bash curves
Through wooded bluffs, and where tracts called
      reserves*
Show that the Pottawatamies and the Shawnees
      guard
Gave to their gifts, and sought thus to retard
The ultimate absorption of their parks,
Great natural gardens, through which log-
      wrought barks
Made easy voyages, with fish below,
And, near, wild turkeys, bison, buck and doe,
Nibbling the fat things that the valleys know,
Where cresses, berries, grapes and pawpaws
      grow.

---

*By the treaty of Saint Mary's, October 2, 1818, the land on which the Prophet's Town was situated was reserved to the Indians. The entire reservation is a strip six miles long, from the mouth of the Tippecanoe southward along the Wabash, and in width an average of a mile. It is known as the Burnett Reservation, the Burnetts having been the descendants of Cakimi, an Indian princess, sister of Taupinibeh, principal chief of the Pottawatamies, and wife of a French trader. Indian Treaties, 1778 to 1837, p. 253.

Now came the alarm; successive shots were
      heard;
The camp at once with fevered frenzy stirred;
As signal dread of danger, the long roll
The startled air shook, shook the startled soul;
The tents were emptied, men took place in rank;
Sounds of command came through the vapors
      dank:
"Attention, battalion, form ranks, form ranks,
      dress!"
And: "Hurry there, men, take arms, take arms,
      press
The line full forward." "Look out on the flank!"
"Here on the front, hug the bank, hug the bank!"
And "Form the new alignment, march!" "Re-
      ceive
The enemy in front in two lines!" "Relieve
That corner with fixed bayonets!" "Stand, men,
      stand!"
"Music to the center, fife and drum and band!"
"Attention, company, to the right wheel, march!"
A wheel the army formed, its tire and arch.
"Platoon, attention, ready, take aim, fire!"
A stream of death came from the smoking tire.
The exigency some men brought half-dressed,
With half-oped eyes, and dreaming slumbers
      pressed.
Forbes, like the classic hero, in his shirt
Sought his command, and Orcus fed ungirt.

And rose the Long Knife's orders on the breeze,
While flashed gun, sword and epaulet 'mongst
    the trees:
"Close up, my brave boys, we can whip them!"
    "Mark,
The red devils hope to break our ranks there!"
    "Parke,
Drive now with all your force!" "Taylor, attend!
Go, Spencer tell, down at the field's far end,
To hold his Yellow Jackets† well in hand."
"Go, Hurst, and tell Wells I want him to stand
Till freezes over hell, and he shall save
His company, the bravest of the brave,
And all now here; else, Hurst, boy, we are gone,
He, I and Floyd and Daviess, Owen and Croghan!"
"Ho, Tipton, run there quickly, quench those fires!
From Decker and Baen take what the work re-
    quires,
Get water from the creek, and throw a guard
Well forward, you will find the service hard."
"If Boyd his customary coolness keeps,
And that his valor caution not o'erleaps,
He'll throw an avalanche upon them, sure,
To give their appetite for fight a cure."
"There Barton and Geiger must hold firm as fate;
Their rifles' aim is wonderfully straight;
Their horses, too, are brave Kentucky stock,
Like men they stand, firm as a mountain rock."

---

†A volunteer force, commanded by Spencer, was so called from the color of their coats, a light drab. The name sometimes given to a wasp or hornet.

"The line keep, Cook and Peters! Push those
    reds!"
"What from the creek? The Indian line, see,
    spreads!"
"Baen, Prescott, forward! Firm! Hold the left
    flank!   .
Red devils see in force now mount the bank!
Down on them! Have a care!" There on the left
Blaze Warwick's rifles, suffering and bereft
Of their fine leader; and there Spencer's dead,
And his lieutenants both.   O time of dread!"
"Robb, from the center come thou, and give aid,
Let be by slaughter slaughters dire repaid!"
"Take, Prescott, of the Fourth United States,
The place by Robb made vacant and his mates."
"Poor Owen is fatally wounded, and is rash
Jo Daviess to excess; the man has dash
And zeal to put great Lucifer's self to flight,
But he the lines must keep, or die this night."
"The Prophet I don't see."   "No, he is perched
Upon a bluff near, like a woman churched.
The infamous old rascal's singing songs
He says will soon redress the Indians' wrongs."
"Well, let him trust that horrid twang; a lull;
Yes, I can hear its harsh monotony dull,
It must these pious red men much console."
"Take care, there's Dirk; that darky's soul
Is stained with treason, but he's pinioned there,
Like Caiaphas' self nailed on hell's pavement bare,

As shows the Inferno we at Greenville read.
(List to that Prophet with his dronings dread.)
But Dirk would move e'en Satan with those eyes,
And I'll forgive his treason and his lies."
"A gap now in the sky Andromeda shows,
Midst constellations mirroring boreal snows;
And Perseus; he white, she black, (by the bye,
The fates at last have spread a clouded sky).
He saved the girl from Juno's wrath, and drove
The dragon back and broke her chains, and love
So wrought on him he married her; I doubt
If this be so. From these old stories out
Must half be stricken before you have the truth."
"Yes, the court martial, when his tender youth
Is taken into the account, should free the boy—
I know a cabin where 'twill make much joy.
Yes, Snelling, I am glad you speak for Dirk,
He's wild, but still all right if kept at work."

"Well, General, are you safe yet?" asked an aid,
The while the hero, ever undismayed,
Heard roar and crash, and saw, in ceaseless flood,
All round him flow the boiling, mutual, blood.
"Why, no; but—only a mere scratch, my coat
A bullet hole has; so has my hat; just note
How near to Charon's ferry I; and here,
Take Taylor's mare, she's wounded, bring me
        Deer."

"Here, here, they come! Strike, Wilson, that
    snake down!"
"Ah, thank you for that service, Ensign Brown!"
"He gave me that same look once at Vincennes,
The time Tecumseh gave us trouble." "Friends,
Let's all be steady." "Close up there, brave
    men!"
"I see the dawn, and with it, peace again."
"Go see if they are strong enough there, Clarke!"
"Those slumbering logs again are kindling!"
    "Hark!"
And close beyond the encampment's east line,
    "Charge!"
Was heard along the entire embankment's marge.
"I hear their jangling deer hoofs, 'tis *their* sign,
To charge along their whole demoniac line.
Those Yankee plowboys surely will stand firm,
For bravery's, in their home, no idle term." ·
Wheeling they come, with gallant swing, the
    same
That throws, on holiday scenes, from fireworks
    flame.
Flaming they wheel; flame, wheel, the order
    made
To be o'er all the field as law obeyed.
The bayonets of the infantry drive back,
At last, the riotous fiends, and quell attack;
The irresistible dragoons the marsh
Fill with the bands that fly that tempest harsh.

The exultation of the White Chief voice
Sometimes attained; was sometimes mute by
    choice.
"Ah, those are brave men!" "There's Bartholo-
    mew!" "Fame,
Blow thou through all thy trumpets name on
    name!"
"Hargrave and Wilson! Barton! Brilliant Scott!"
"If braver men exist I know it not!"
Yes, there are victories sung in olden lays
That were not won with greater claim to praise,
Cæsar none prouder for his cohort claimed,
The first cohort of his tenth legion famed.
Nor Frederick, when he saw the cannon plow
His favorite regiment's ranks at red Torgau.
And here were men, among the national troops,
Whose fathers fired between the fences' loops
At Lexington, and on the hill of Breed
Met glorious wounds, rejoicing there to bleed
With Warren, and at Bennington shed lives,
And Saratoga, for our babes and wives.

But how depict the battle! If the day,
Midst sulphur fumes and dust of the affray,
Lends terror to a scene of mutual strife,
What must the murky night produce when life
Hangs on the uncertain edge of troubled dreams,
When deep-prized sleep is broken by the screams
Of maddened demons; when the secret ping
Of the chewed bullet, and the deadly ring

The poisoned arrow gives, come to the soul,
The while sounds ominous forth the dread long
          roll
For all to spring to arms, and comes a rain
Of orders from the leaders (some profane).
The task is idle; this e'en Homer tried
In vain; he gives, instead, one homicide
Upon another, tells how many slew
His hero Hector, how Achilles flew
Here, there, intent, in mourned Patroclus' cause,
To make his list of dead his friend's applause.
Words cannot paint the scene, the deep, intense
Reality no speech can compass; fence
Is here to genius; here it finds its bound.
E'en colors can't paint fire, and this is found
On art's own easel, this Van Schendel knew,
Most skilled of all e'er light on canvas threw.

Only the poet can the evening's scene
And morning's paint, the mighty sheen
Of arms reposing or preparing, smiles
That wait the coming battle, or sad miles
Of wounded stragglers, groans suppressed or given,
And prayers for death or water thrown to heaven.
The deepest things and highest all outgo
Whatever flight of song, whatever moan of woe.

Rose o'er the field the voice of conflict dire,
Mixed rifle, hatchet, sword and knife and fire,

Club smote on musket, musket smote on club,
Smoked hot the wheel of fight, tire, spoke and
       hub,
Yell answered yell, the bubbling war-whoop wild
Defiance bore from every forest child,
And screams defiant gave foes, teeth to teeth,
While victory yet gasped in her sulphur wreath.
The death-groan startled all that horrid air,
Aloft the red fiend flung the trophied hair,
His tawny brethren grim the bloody ground
At full length struck with dull and sickening sound:
Was thickly strewn the ground with feathered
       chiefs,
Ah! who can tell the weight of that night's griefs?
Griefs, joys, in war or peace, contrasted stand,
And joys awaited now that conquering band.
The struggle's fierce contention held them yet,
The rapture, and the frenzy, and the sweat.
They could not, at the first, be made to know
That, in the cause all-glorious, such a blow
By them had been dealt out, by them was fixed;
Doubt yet was with their pride of battle mixed.
The regulars stood, machines of death, all cool
To deal out slaughters still by prescribed rule.
The volunteers, ecstatic and all nerve,
Burned to rush forward, nor could yet observe
Upon the General's face his high repose,
Repose vouchsafed to him who duty knows,

And knows the victory come, and clamor hears
Of plaudits given down through the lengthening
        years.
So Harrison felt, such things he saw, foresaw,
And knew himself a rallying cry of power.
At first he had no voice.   The event had come;
It found its chosen hero meekly dumb.
The bugles sounded, waked the regular up
To drink of peace the rich, abundant cup,
Relaxed fixed duty's forms, and bade the heat
In boiling veins of raw recruits retreat,
And bade the leaders of the fray provide
For wounds, for death, and for their glory wide.

What are the vestiges of this hard-fought field?
What yet remains by time still unconcealed?
Where are the veterans? Eighty years have
        passed,
Save one, and over all the stirring scene is cast
The glamour of romance.   But we may pause,
And ask the rise, the spring, the philosophical
        cause
Of that event: Whence came it? Whereto tend
Did it? Does it instruction's wisdom lend
To themes of nations? Was it force? Or law?
May moralists thence a healthful inference draw?
Was it ordained by Mars from olden times?
Or from the mist came it to deck these rhymes?
A few old men the veterans are, then youths;
A line of graves marks history's steps; the truths

Divine contended for remain; the new
Race brought in conflict with the old; renew
Herein their meaning the repeated signs
Of given ascendency; the pleasant lines
Kept for the one, and for the other woes,
Contempt, oppression, ribaldry, lies and blows.

Great battles are the pivots whereon turn
The points of destiny; the sepulchral urn,
Vine-wreathed, and spread with sweet memorial
       flowers,
Has brought in arts of peace; the haughtier powers
Fought down with sacred force, and crushed the
       strong,
And saved the weak from many a hideous wrong;
Has served to inaugurate the rein of law,
And tribes of men from brutal ignorance draw.
There was the Milvian Bridge, by which increase
Was given of glory to the Prince of Peace!
There was Soissons, which drove imperial Rome
Forth from fair France, of rising art the home;
There was proud Waterloo, which peace restored
To Europe, slave of an aspiring lord;
There was our Yorktown's siege, whose bugles
       blew
Far forth fair fame to patriots tried and true;
There was our Huntsville's capture, which in
       twain
Cut armed rebellion, impious, rash and vain.

The highest consecration is of blood,
The highest sacrifice, the richest good;
So history all, remote and recent, shows;
This through the plan of man's redemption flows.
The best blood of our land has soaked this soil;
It sealed the record of unselfish toil.
There is a feeling which controls the man
More than all creeds, opinions, interests can;
It is the feeling that the patriot calls
To duty's ranks, and cheers him when he falls.
With reverence,then, tread we these sylvan shades!
With reverence, cast our glance along the glades
Which, in the battle, heard the hot huzza,
The rush, the crash, the struggle heard, and ah!
Heard cries of pain from wounded men, and deep,
Soul-sickening sobs that led to icy sleep!
Yes, this is consecrated ground; to it
We owe all forms of ceremonial fit;
We owe the polished shaft that seeks the sky,
Ornate with praise to meet the expectant eye.
There let the laurel and the cypress twine,
And mortal memories mix with thoughts divine!

SATIRICAL POEMS.

PROFESSIONAL SUPERCILIOUSNESS.

I.

FRIENDS sought for me a Doctor of learned
    ways,
Enough to cure a colic or a craze,
Or hypocondria (each of these things pays)
But when a case of inflammation came
That burnt my bowels as 't were with very flame,
His medicines hurt me, and friends sought a dame
Who poulticed me without, and tea'd within,
And all the Doctor could do was to lift
High eye-brows at the dame, to show how miffed
His royal highness was, and with a grin
Admit (wool-gathering in his learned maze)
That "Peritonitis is most hard of cure!"

II.

I sought a brother-lawyer, and would know
If I could him employ against my foe,
If I could hire him barkings to bestow
Upon my case: "No, no, it may be tacked,
That mortgage which Wasp holds!" Alas, he
    lacked
Some information he had never tracked:

The tacking doctrine, in its curious course,
Went never out of England, but its place
Kept there, unlike the Rule in Shelley's Case,
And when I told him, his high legal horse
He mounted, and the beast smote blow on blow,
But found he books than me had studied fewer.

III.

A reverend clerk I begged to render aid
In forming a benevolent band, and prayed
That he to ours would add his presence staid:
He turned upon his heel.   I afterwards learned
Why thus we had been so unworthily spurned,
We who for charity's ways so deeply yearned:
It was because my good companion had
Some days before some trivial slackness showed,
A pater missed, or late to chapel strode,
And so, with manners so exceeding bad,
This clerk, who of his office mockery made,
Wronged grievously a man whose heart was pure.

PHILOLOGY IN THE PULPIT.

THERE is a rule the Church lays down,
   Which certain pastors break:
The Church of Rome then gives a frown,
   And I, for her dear sake.

The rule is, that the Scripture should
  Be to the people read;
And, that it may be understood,
  And they therein be led,

The plain vernacular should be given,
  The Douay Bible, where
Meet English-speaking people heaven
  Aspiring to in prayer.

And further that each pulpit must
  Such word of God contain,
Whence pastors, in their sacred trust
  Should read, and thence explain.

But pastors sometimes think their art
  Lies in philology,
Or that they may translate in part,
  In part trust memory.

Flat, bungling reading thence us greets,
  The inverted Latin crawls;
The Greek, if Greek they read, defeats
  Their skill, and feebly falls.

THE FAVORITE HOBBY.

WHAT is the reason that the temperance cause
    On so much piety and eloquence draws?
Is it that they who preach it never drink?
Is it that non-teetotalers never think?

No, 't is a hobby that the pious use,
A stalking horse no eloquence can refuse,
The Pharisee finds thereon his fancy free,
And license grants his steed Hyperbole.

COLD WATER.

By night she groaned, by day she dosed, and all
To no effect, and made call after call

On druggists three and doctors four, and why?
She had a wonderful affection of the eye.

The more she drugged, the more the doctors posed,
The more she felt she was not diagnosed.

At last to me she said in drear despite,
"How *shall* I get again my ruined sight?"

"Polly," said I, "the way is plain, give o'er
To every doctor running and drug-store,

"And wash your eyes with water, night and morn;
Then you may hold these quacks and fools in
scorn."

"Cold water?" "Yes, cold water, since the day
That Satan tempted Eve has rolled a spray

"From fountains, cataracts, rivers, sent to cure
Mankind of hurts by medication pure.

"The medicating power in nature placed,
Of this be pleased to try a little taste.

"The faculty's slow, six thousand years have flown,
And to them yet cold water's power's unknown."

The maid my admonition heeded, laved
Her lustrous orbs, her battered eyesight saved.

POLITICS.

"THE State is equally balanced," said a sage
        And potent chairman of our paper age,
"And therefore, now, as sure as rats is rats,
We must buy, sir, twelve hundred Democrats."

"Twelve hundred, at two each, is twenty-four,
And trusted men will need, each, how much
                        more?"
"A hundred trusted men: two thousand, sure,
Will be enough these chattels to ensure.

"Five thousand say this makes, we'll double it,
Such vessels leak always a little bit;
The seive may fertilize the land somewhat;
An agent's pocket is a sombre grot."

Ten thousand, then, is raised, and joyfully come
The host of patriots at the tap of drum,
Joined by the purchased troop, and happily so
The Union grows, and laws and ventures flow.

II.

Suppose one voter in the twenty sulks:
This may plow navies down to trembling hulks.
Suppose another of the twenty votes
The opposition ticket, and thus gloats

In treachery o'er the party he should aid:
This may mean navies in the bottom laid
Of roaring seas, and prospering navies borne
Above the throngs of drowning seamen lorn.

What may produce this lack of duty sad?
One man may do it, if of manners bad,
How high soe'er may be his mental force:
Manners of failures often are the source.

What is the remedy?   It resides in this,
The guarantee of high political bliss:
That, whereas the one party may control
The government, its course, in part or whole,

Its policy, is by the other ruled:
One may manipulate the helm, but schooled
It must be by the other, and the breeze
May hulks destroy whose maxims rule the seas.

III.

From voting I would bar the young and old.
No voter before thirty should be polled.
At seventy all should lose the right to vote,
For some men at that age begin to dote.

What would I do with women?   They should be
Within these ages at full liberty
To use the ballot.   Some would never claim
To have reached a time of life which every dame

Is cautious of admitting.   Cicero said
When him a gossip to the subject led:
"I know that lady to be twenty, why?
She has for twenty years past said it, I

Believe a person who so sticks to truth,
And thus retains her ever-blooming youth."
Woman in every age remains the same,
To-day's shrewd girl succeeds the Roman dame.

IF.

L OVED the Laconians brief and sturdy
    speech;
They language used without regard to show;
Came once upon them threatening to make
            breach
Of sacred bounds the Macedonian host,
And Philip's messengers, in martial glow,
Reported grim the conqueror's haughty boast:
" If I your country enter, I'll destroy
Palace and temple, and make of the past
Your city Sparta."   They felt no annoy;
The messengers had pictured them aghast:
They answered, undisturbed as by the waves a
            cliff,
And all they answered was to quote the boasters'
            " IF."

A BRILLIANT WESTERN GIRL
ABROAD.

A BRILLIANT Western girl abroad
   Men, women, of all ranks had seen,
Peasant and villager, slave and lord,
  The high, the low, the great, the mean,
  All stages that exist between
    Royalty and Democracy.

'Neath tatters she had virtues found,
  'Neath costly robes deceit and guile,
But, in one class, the perfect round
  Of great and noble, low and vile,
  And all that comes 'twixt either style,
    Royalty and Democracy.

And as the girl conversing stood
  Upon a steamer's deck, her craved
The captain of the steamer good
  To know whom deemed she best behaved.
  She heard, and this response vouchsafed:
    "The British Aristocracy."

The Captain was an Englishman,
  And felt his pride of country rise,
But drove too far his questionings when
  He asked who gave her most surprise
For bad behavior? " They, likewise,
  " The British Aristocracy."

AMERICAN INDEPENDENCE.

OUR boasted independence, year by year,
  Implies at English claims and ways a
    sneer,
And yet the English language 't is we use
In setting forth our independent views,
And mix with it abundance of rude noise
From Chinese crackers furnished to the boys.
The tongue is yet a slave to England, then?
Yet foreign trinkets rule boys, women, men?
Yes, while we love our native land the best,
As leader of all lands e'er poet sung,
We find in adventitious things a zest:
'T is sport to abuse Old England in her tongue,
And dig some aid from each barbarian nest.

THE CRITIC.

I.

HE wrote and wrote, and then he labeled it—
What? " *Criticism*," product of pro-
foundest wit:
·But candid minds in it no wit could see,
And deemed its fitter label "*Ribaldry.*"

II.

" Then criticism, sir, you don't respect?"
" Yes, friend, I do respect the thing and men:
But ignorant and pretentious fellows, oft,
The clogs and sills of great machines are found:
So Catholic Rome has, in her great employ,
Men lacking modesty and learning both,
And English literature, surely, owns a race
Of heavy, lumbering, creatures, fixed to uphold
The tons of worth that rise above their weight."

III.

To be moved by any critic,
Thou must first respect the critic:
Thou must love or hate the critic.

Speaks he of thee sweetly, fairly,
Thou may'st think he wisely, fairly,
Follows gossips speaking fairly.

Speaks he of thee rudely, coarsely,
Thou may'st think he blindly, coarsely,
Follows blowhards speaking coarsely.

Be thou of thyself the master.
Slights, then, come to thee their master,
Praises find thee, too, their master.

THE BOOK TRADE.

I.

I called for Munday's Poems, and the brilliant
          book-monger,
Having the chance to appease in me, as would a
          cook, hunger,
But intent, chiefly, he, on adding to his bank
          account,
Looked slowly through his shelves, and slowly
          then a blank amount
Of information gave from his speech gained, as
          follows
(He had not learning quaffed in dangerously
          vast swallows):

"*Day* poems of any special day I cannot find, sir,
Month poems complete and almanacs we have
got, mind, sir."

II.

Occurred in a provincial town that piece of
mockery;
Another's enough to crack a shelf of crockery,
And happened in that place of trade its denizens
call "N'Yawk."
Of course an uncouth westerner may, or short or
tall, be awk-
Ward in a roaring place, a metropolitan city,
But that none there knew better, would from any
man pity
Bring on the best of their booksellers, who ne'er
once knew, sir,
That Cowper rendered Homer; 'tis, or I'm a
dunce, true, sir.

A MODERN COMEDY.

STROPHE.

"O WE have so much poetry sent us,
Send us no more, it will dement us!"

ANTISTROPHE.

"'T is plain you must most dearly *love* it,
You *save* it all—you print none of it!"

BETWEEN THE LINES.

A POETICAL TRIBUTE INTERPRETED BY A MAT-TER-OF-FACT PERSON.

ANOTHER noble woman's soul has left this
world of change,
[An artful female fiend.]
None other e'er was so beloved, so kind, so
sweetly meek;
[so despised, so sour, so full of freak!]
A Christian purer you'll not find, where'er your
path may range,
[A spitfire bitterer!]
A neighbor kinder, lovelier, in vain you'll wildly
seek.
[A gossip hunting so for news!]

II.

Farewell, dear friend, while, bowed in grief, a
a city all laments;
[Go, traitress sly, while in content a dozen cronies grin!]
Farewell, alas, bright social light, and idol of
the heart!
[Go thou unmourned, dark social blight, and stifler of, etc.]
Maiden divine, tears flow for thee, so void of all
offense,
[Old maid perverse, tears have we none, which might have plenteous
been,]
Thee youth and age alike deplore bright, mark
of death's pale dart!
[Thee youth nor age deplore, but gladly from thee part!]

THE SWELL HOTEL.

I SING the Swell Hotel: O Maids, descend,
　Immortal, from your heights, and me inspire,
And teach my thoughts with fitting words to blend
　As I touch daintily the alimentary lyre!

The American tavern, be it understood,
　Is what my satire reaches: we are proud,
Too proud to imitate examples good,
　To look to Europe is not here allowed.

In France or England, ladies keep the place:
　They meet you at the threshold, and a smile
Of courtesy is a dearly-coveted grace
　The stranger feels who's traveled many a mile.

A rabble, here, of porters, boys, throng round,
　They gloomily sieze your satchel while you
　　　　gloom,
Sign, sadly hear the tapped gong sound,
　And are escorted to a gloomy room.

Called to account, the hypocritical clerk
　Says "We are full just now; to-morrow night
"You shall be changed." Dear sir, 't is but to
　　　　work
Your patience; he'll ne'er make the outrage right!

At dinner comes a forest dark of coons,
  Whose greasy ooze gets on each tardy dish,
Plate, knife, and cloth, on forks, and chairs, and
        spoons,
  And finds its way into both flesh and fish.

You sit with hunger mad, fatigue and chill;
  The coon a cold plate brings you tardily; then
Permits you to remain in posture still
  Ten minutes before he shows his face again.

What comes then? Food? O, no, a bill of fare,
  A hideous fraud, now known as "the menu":
Enough the devil from realms below to scare,
  And on it absolutely nothing new.

'T was stereotyped before the coon was born;
  The heading's new, that's all, the hash the same,
And cheap-bought stuff, potatoes, squash, and corn,
  For hunger's pangs enough, if it e'er came!

And *then* the food, to you quite desperate grown?
  O no, a knife, and fork, three spoons, another
        fork;
You look at these, while thoughts of murder
        moan
  Your breast within, exceeding hard to cork.

Now nearly thirty minutes in your chair;
   One sip of *something* warm you'd think were
      nice;
And yet no food: you almost tear your hair:
   He drops into your tumbler lumps of *ice.*

And then the wretch his disappearance makes;
   But, after a while, returns with comfort's cup?
No! with a solemn look your patience breaks
   He fills with water that same tumbler up.

Food comes: all bad, soup horrid, and beef tough;
   Potatoes spoiled, bread sour, peas old, beans
      hard;
Of pie and corn-starch you'll soon have enough;
   The pudding's some canned puzzle fried in lard.

You call for fruit, and hardly know the same:
   Apples the size of filberts, oranges stale,
Dry, wilted grapes your keen disgust enflame;
   For English walnuts—these, you think, can't
      fail.

In mingling England herein we should pause:
   To her we should make due and prompt
      amends:
The nuts are mildewed, bitter, what's the cause?
   'Tis this: their age, four years, to rankness
      tends.

You think of coffee, saw it you there, perhaps,
   Where all is printed, in stiff stereotype:
You ask the Lord, as your poor tongue it laps,
   If He such sin as this from souls can wipe.

Such meals repeated are from day to day;
   You pace the gloomy corridors back and forth;
The insolent clerk still bids you stand at bay;
   You seem to ask "Is life the living worth?"

Fops throng around, at times a dame flits by;
   These people meals take at unusual hours:
And can you tell me, please, the reason why?
   By day they sleep, the night exhausts their
     powers.

At last you ask the "Cashier" for your bill,
And pay three prices, while in secret grieved.
The American people like a gilded pill:
   As Barnum says, "They love to be deceived."

THE TWO FIFTIES.

I.

"IN this are fifty dollars, I'm in drink,
   A most unfortunate vice 't is, don't you
     think?
Maudlin it makes one, see my poor eyes blink,
A boiled owl I, or else the missing link.

Now take this white envelope, mister clerk,
And kindly lay it in your safe aside,
Should I be robbed 'twould mortify my pride,
And I should be forever after guyed."
He took the white envelope with a smirk.

II.

The guest departed, sought a crony gay,
And whether 't was the merry month of May,
Or dull November, that I cannot say,
The night, I know, they turned quite into day;
And when the guest returned to that same clerk,
'Twas long before the guest could catch his eye,
And only then half caught it, for a lie
The clerk gave forth: " No money, sir, have I
Received from you," he said with that same
        smirk.

III.

And then the guest a skillful lawyer sought,
And by his clever tact and shrewdness taught,
Another white envelope took, and caught
A passing friend and to the hotel brought,
And in his presence handed to the clerk,
First counted by his friend to know 't was right,
Another fifty in an envelope white,
And by the friend sealed up, all right and tight:
The dignitary took it with a smirk.

IV.

The guest, alone, now to the office went,
And said: "That little package, please." It
  came.
One fifty was reclaimed, and felt no shame
About the other fifty, for the game
Was not suspected by this robber lame,
This unsophisticated hotel clerk.
But yet remained deposit number one
In jeopardy, and yet to be undone
The roguery whereby the same was won.
The face felonious held its usual smirk.

V.

Together now repaired the guest *and friend:*
They made demand, which made the fellow stare:
"I gave you your envelope, gave it where
You stand this moment; do you want a pair
Of fifty dollar envelopes? Impudence rare!"
Thus to the guest insisting spoke the clerk.
The friend struck in: "Hand out at once that
  cash,
A white envelope, do you want the lash
The law provides to hurry laggards rash?"
It came, but, O, with what a sickly smirk!

THE FORK.

THE Fork is a Fetish in Fashion's realm,
   Or, rather, in our day, no Fork exists:
A spoon, with tines four-fold, has taken the helm:
   The ancient Fork may go whereto it lists.

Poor Crœsus! Cæsar poor! Elizabeth poor!
   And e'en Victoria in your earlier days!
Ye would have been sent scorned from Fashion's
         door
   Had ye, in our times, shown your vulgar ways!

No! If a man all heinous crimes commits,
   . And adds, to homicide, perjury, robbery, theft,
He may find charity; but if he sits,
   Of homage for the new Fetish bereft,

At any stylish table, let him sink,
   Despised, disgraced, beyond all depths of shame,
A social outcast hovering on the brink
   Whence come Plutonian steams and screams
         and flame.

ALPHONSO THE THIRTEENTH.

Alphonse, the Spanish king of four years old,
  Grasped with delight a savory drumstick great.
      Advance
He saw a knighted servitor, quaint and cold,
  Who said: "Kings eat not so." Of recent date
      This thing was.

The king with greasy lips and fingers looked
  At his reproving minister's querulous face
      Askance,
And firmer still his baby digits crooked
  Around the leg, and said with royal grace:
      "*This* King does!"

HEROISM.

AT the age of thirteen, in the last week of the
      war,
He fiddled in a regiment, and is a hero evermore.

WEATHER-PROPHECY.

(A SATIRE.)

WHEN Nicodemus came to Christ by night,
  The Incarnate Word, illumed by Infinite
    Light,
Said: "Like the wind the spirit is of man, the
    sound
Whereof is heard, but which nor course nor bound
Hath men may scan, for comes the breeze divine
Whence men know not, nor can they, blind, assign
Its course unsearchable; for 't is controlled
Now, as through ages dim of old,
By laws, decrees and statutes framed above
Where Infinite Force holds sway and Infinite
    Love."
Yet comes the almanac-maker, and says, "I
Will tell you true whence come the winds that fly
And where, throughout the year, athwart the sky."
And sits arrayed a "*scientific*" corps,
Who seek to advance a day, and scarcely more,
Advices of the weather: all are vain:
These things the rash conjecture fails to attain.
Comes still the storm as come the gifts of God,
Wends still the wind controlled by His own rod;

And I may stand upon my homestead's sill,
And watch clouds, sun and air, and breeze, and still
I cannot, nor can clown or sage, three hours
Into the future, tell the weather; powers
Which it control no man can know; is given
To none to search the secret things of heaven.

CONTEMPORARY CRITICISM.

A LADY said no use to warn her
   Against that giggling Mister W * * * * *
And said another: "Of that beau G * *
   I have to say that he *is* bogus."

RETRIBUTION.

MOURNED Banker Needlenose his favorite
     cow,
   Him it had cost a right round sum in cash,
And he would like to know the where and how
   Of its removal, and give crime the lash.

He need not have sought far to find the thief,
   He had an enemy in poor Harry Vance,
A man whose theft was sanctified by grief
   For blood sucked from him at each frequent
     chance.

Ah, yes, he held 'gainst Needlenose a grudge,
   And grudges, for hard, grinding, twisting ways.
In these things we must not too strictly judge,
   Vance was at heart as good a man as prays.

And after waiting for some time the thought
   Her owner seized to offer a reward:
"Perhaps she's strayed; and home she may be
      brought;
   And I for this five dollars can afford."

"Five dollars," thought Hal Vance, "I'll easily
      earn,"
   So he a day took for a trudge to town,
And said to Needlenose "If you would learn
   Where is your cow, pay me five dollars down."

In vain expostulated Needlenose,
   And friendship privilege pleaded, and all that:
Whereat in Hal's breast secret anger rose
   And gave to all these pranks denial flat.

At last reluctantly the money came,
   And Harry calmly pocketed the V,
And he a lookout had for further game,
   As in this narrative we shall presently see.

"Now that's a good man, drive her up, my friend,"
   Thus with fine flattery Needlenose him fed.
"Hell!" said bluff Harry, "that thing's at at end,
   For that fine cow is as a door-nail dead."

"Dead?" said the man of money, with surprise,
  "And dead from what?"   "Perhaps from
            poison-vine,
Besides from her foul, sickening odors rise
  Would even make a tan-yard watch-dog whine.

"And let me tell you, sir, the neighbors round
  Insist that I shall call on Lawyer Whiz,
And have you to the coming circuit bound
  Because a nuisance that dead carcase is."

"O, well, now, neighbor Vance, you must so kind
  Be as to bury the dead cow, 't will cause
You little inconvenience I'm inclined
  To think, so, Hal, this little trouble take."

Much like that Norman duke who would not bend
  In homage at a hated master's word:
"No, sir," said Hal, "I don't at all intend
  To save you from the penalty you've incurred."

"Not if I pay you?" "O, that makes the shape
  Of that affair a little different, risk
There is my family may not plague escape,
  Or I, how shrewd soever I, and brisk.

"But I'll incur the danger if spot cash
  Right now is paid to me, two dollars more,
I'll then a job do that is certainly rash,
  And you'll escape a prosecution sore."

He got the money, thus his five increased
　Made seven, which when he afterwards told,
"And here your profits," said his crony, "ceased,
　But you your foe had very nicely sold."

"Yes, sold, but still the profits ran along,
　For I was planing for a margin wide,
I thought there might be nothing very wrong
　In pocketing three dollars for the hide."

THE JUDGE AND THE LITIGANT.

THE litigant pursued the judge, here, there,
　　The judge heard his long stories with
　　　　unrest:
"Why don't your counsel give this thing *their*
　　care?
These stories should not be to me addressed."

"Ah, I've the judge on my side, on the stair,"
　Thus said he to his counsel, "he me pressed,
·'Why don't your counsel give this thing their
　　　　care'
Mysteriously." And he suppressed the rest.

THE UNJUST JUDGE.

THE judge who sits upon a bench and dares
  To rule unjustly may be counted brave,
Because he lays for confidence no snares,
  And buries honor in an open grave.

But he who plays the saintly hypocrite,
  Or by a church backed or a secret ring,
Must down to hell's profoundest boiling pit
  Of blackest tar be sent to rule and sing,

Because not only does he manners break
  By his pretence of righteousness assumed,
But he, put there fair fight for law to make,
  Sees vanquished law in her own halls en-
    tombed.

Backed by a church ? Yes, I knew such an one,
  And him ecclesiastical power maintained
Until he joined another church, and run
  Was then his course: just censures on him
    rained.

—

THE JUDGE'S CHARGE.

THE judge's charge was clear and plain,
 It meant his side the suit should gain;
But hours he waited and report
The jury none made to the court.
" Go, bring them in, and we will see
What may their trivial problem be;
Perhaps some technical word of art,
Or else some juror over-smart."
The bailiff went, filed in the array,
The judge the silence broke to say:
" A verdict, gentlemen, have you found?"
The foreman spoke, and somewhat frowned:
" Your honor, we are eleven to one."
" And tell me, pray, who may he be.
Perhaps he does not clearly see
The points the court made in its charge,
I may repeat them more at large."
" No," said the foreman, " naught can change
Him in his fixed opinion strange;
We've argued long, he takes a pride
In arguing always on your side."

REPROBATION OF THE UNSAVORY.

'TIS pleasant to meet with a thinker,
　Or a safely moderate drinker,
But deliver us, Lord! from a stinker.

MARCO LOMBARDO.

MARCO LOMBARDO owned a fame wide-
　　spread,
　'Mongst men of noble purpose, earnest thought,
And honor followed him where'er his steps
　Him amongst men of this description brought.

But sometimes was the philosophic sage
　In ignorant circles found, who knew not worth,
Their frivolous minds would not in twelve
　　　months give
　To one sincere, ennobling, sentiment birth.

A wedding-party given amongst the gay
　The occasion was which claimed his presence
　　once,
There arrogant Pharisees were, Philistia-bred,
　Whereof.each one was proud to be a dunce.

"Ah, Marco," said a type of this same class,
  "You have no wedding-favors, cloaks nor
      scarfs,
While I have seven, by Jove, I'm loved, you see,
  While of the crowd you only earn the laughs."

"Friend, I observe this thing gives you surprise,
  Not so with me, these people have your ways,
Suit them your words, your attitudes, your style;
  Wear you herein the undisputed bays!"

THE BALLAD OF ISABEL WHITE.

CAME to the beer-shop Isabel White,
    A beauteous child of seven,
A tin pail in her dainty hand,
    She seemed sent down from heaven.

Rolled from the symmetry of her head
    The loveliest golden curls,
Her ruby lips, her pearly teeth,
    An angel's or a girl's.

Her breath the lily's fragrance had,
    Her foot a fairy's pose,
And o'er her dimpled cheeks there ran
    The radiance of the rose.

O, teach me, God, these souls to love
   So lately from the skies,
Let me drink in the innocent light
   That comes from children's eyes!

Let me the jubilant laugh enjoy,
   The music of a voice
That, driving meaner thoughts away,
   Bids me with them rejoice!

Ah, Oreads meek, ah, Nereids gay,
   And ye, coy woodland sprites,
Your various charms the human girl,
   Concretely fair, unites!

With weaving step and trusting gaze
   She on the counter placed
Her metal pail, the while I thought
   Was Hebe e'er so graced!

Then spoke she to a smiling man,
   Pomatumed o'er, who wore
An apron white, and seemed to say
   "You have been here before!"

"Mister, my mamma says if you
   Will fill her growler, she
Will have my papa pay for it when
   He comes down after tea."

The man a moment feasted on
  The marvellous beauty there,
Then filled the growler with the best,
  And gave it her with care.

The child, in turning, met her pa,
  Who said: "A lemonade!"
The child demurred, and sweetly thus
  The admiring host she prayed:

"O, Mister Man, don't give him, please,
  Those sickening temperance drinks,
They all our trouble cause at home,
  My dear, good mamma thinks.

"For pa, when he has drank of them,
  Is crosser than a bear,
He never speaks a pleasant word,
  Go to him I don't dare.

"But when he has his toddy strong,
  He loves us all, and cakes
He brings us home, and us to see
  Dear Uncle Tom he takes."

The apron white a tender heart
  Held underneath its folds,
He looked inquiringly to White,
  But he opinion molds,

The politician, stood at hand,
    Intent new votes to make,
He knew friend White a partisan,
    And thought in charge to take

A convert from the opposing ranks,
    A gain in precinct six,
For every gain in voting counts,
    And sometimes also sticks.

"Come, Mister White, let me your child,
    A second give, and move
That you this time at my expense
    The worth of toddies prove."

Alas, then, W. C. T. U.,
    For your stanch proselyte,
He drank the toddy, and one more,
    And left with footstep light,

Left with the angelic child, who said,
    "Now, pa, that seal-skin sacque
I'm sure you'll buy dear, good mamma,
    Nor on your word go back."

"My child," he said, "from this day forth
    I temperance will observe,
I will avoid each false extreme,
    Nor from good teachings swerve,

"You shall have toys, your mamma clothes,
  Myself respect of men,
And you shall learn, at home, at school,
  To love your pa again!"

THE LAIRDS OF LYNNE.

O WOULD you know the Lairds of leafy
    Lynne,
Beyond the Tweed, far in the north countree,
Then listen to the lay I bring you here,
  And men of manners diverse ye shall see.

There was the ancient Laird of mickle might,
  He all his lands and tenants watched full well,
And many a season brought him treasures heaped,
  And with his thrift his treasury still would swell.

All could he watch, and keep in limits strict,
  Except his crafty steward, Rab Macleach:
Rab, spite of all the good Laird's care and pains,
  Would tenants equally and Laird o'er reach.

And came the ancient Laird at last to die,
  And thought but little of his reckless heir,
Except that he would all the treasure waste,
  And strew both land and gold upon the air,

" My son," he said, "when all is gone ye'll sell,
  Sell for a paltry price your heritage,
But be it so, only that Idlewild
  Ye will not, let me earnestly engage.

" And I now thee an ample reason give:
  In that lone cottage thou a friend wilt find,
When friends none else are left thee, and therein
A cure will be for all thy madness blind."

The last rites o'er, and scanty margin left,
  The new Laird summoned all his jolly freres;
With rout and music shook the ancient manse,
    Flowed costly wines, and fled the frowning
        Cares.

And wealthier still became the shrewd Macleach,
  Much of the wasted gold his pocket found,
He steward still remained, while state the heir
  Kept as upon a throne a sovereign crowned.

All pressed to greet the bounteous Laird's sweet
        ways,
  Gay smiles him met wherever he appeared,
Before him glowed the world in brilliant sheen,
    Bowed Beauty bright, bowed manly Valor
        keen.

Alas, alack, friends fell away full soon,
　Men smile while Fortune smiles, but when the
　　　sun
Lacks lustrous golden rays, frowns take their
　　　place,
　And him they worshipped once they meanly
　　　shun.

"Help me with what I need for these my debts,
　Good ancient steward of our house," he said,
"You shall my gratitude forever have,
　And shall with usury large be all repaid."

"Not so," the steward said, "but thou shalt have,
　For all thy land good store of shining gold,
I will thee give a price." He named the price
　And stood for answer with a look full cold.

Full cold the price struck on the young man's
　　　heart,
　Not half was it of what the land was worth,
And stood the wolf before the young man's door,
　And 'twas the last of all he owned on earth:

The last except the nook of Idlewild,
　This thought Macleach of value none, and so
Not in the bargain was the sylvan nook,
　Naught did the steward of the friend there know.

A natural hesitation made the Laird,
   But, after somewhat murmuring, gave consent,
Laid earnest down the steward, and prepared
   A writing witnessed of their joint intent.

The rioting and feasting brought back friends,
   At due times came the payments spent e'er
      seen,
But not at home the revelings now were held,
   The steward now held state as Laird of Lynne.

And one sad day the young Laird in his purse
   Had only pennies three, one brass, one lead,
And copper one, and silver none was there,
   And therefrom long before all gold had fled.

"And now," he thought, "my pleasant friends
      will lend,
   Full surely, somewhat to repair my state."
So trustful was he, that he deemed that these
   Would help him out with readiness elate.

Not so. By some turned from their doors away,
   He was by others scorned without a blush;
Such jibes and insults suffered he that seemed
   Their heartless treatment must his courage
      crush.

" Ah well, ah well," said now the heir of Lynne,
　　See how ungrateful are these fellows base,
They who have passed so merrily their time
　　At my expense of gratitude show no trace.

" Ah well, I will to Idlewild repair,
　　And seek the friend of whom my father spake,
The depth of satire was it that in death
　　My father should such a proposal make.

" But yet aught other place to me is closed,
　　A hermit I must be for all my sin,
Herbs and a crust hereafter will provide
　　The wasted table of the heir of Lynne."

He went, and sought the long-abandoned house,
　　O'er hills, through vales, past rippling rills,
　　　　went he,
Until before it, in the lonely glen,
　　He stood, and wiped a tear from either e'e.

The door hung swinging on one rusty hinge,
　　(The other broken) and before it grew
A tangle wild of dank, unsightly weeds
　　And briers, and not one violet's eye of blue.

All that he saw therein showed comfort none,
　　No cheerful hearth, no bed, a stool, no chair;
Hung from the ceiling old a stout noosed rope,
　　Whereon a legend grim quite raised his hair.

"Since all is lost, unworthy heir of Lynne,
  Make trial of this cord, and with it end
Thy sorrows all!" These words alone his voice
  Could frame, but these said all: "Welcome,
      my friend!"

The stool a platform made; the neck-tie fixed,
  Down from the stool he leaped, intent to die,
But, tumbling as he tumbled, came a board
  Drawn by his weight from out the ceiling dry.

.Showered on him gold from out the loft above,
  Gold sent in mockery by the Fiend he thought,
But no, it was as pure as from the mines
  Of Ophir or Pactolus e'er was brought.

"Gold, I have read," he thought, "came down
      from heaven,
  A tribute given by Jove to Danäe,
But where read we of golden showers sent men,
  At least on such a squandering wretch as me?"

Natheless he promptly sought the floor above,
  Rats, bats, and wasps, and spiders held the place,
Together with great stores of golden coin,
  Which he surveyed and counted with good
      grace.

Then made upon his knees before his God
    A solemn, earnest vow the heir of Lynne,
That he would mend his wayward life and forth
    From that good hour a prudent life begin.

First in a trusty place he hid his gold,
    Except some pieces in his pockets stored,
Then sought the ancient homestead where he
        found
    The steward pranked-up as its sovereign lord.

And with him sat his sovereign lady dear,
    He Laird, she Lady of the House of Lynne,
And round them Lairds of high and low degree,
    'Midst feast and festival, laugh, and jest, and din.

He of the golden shower came forward mute,
    And hailed him all with kindly looks and fair,
All save the Laird and Lady, who thought ill
    Their feast should be invaded by the heir.

"Macleach, I ask from thee no favor great,
    Excuse me that I break in on your cheer,
If you will loan me forty pence I not
    One other moment, Mac, will linger here."

"Away, thou thriftless loon," the other said,
    "Be on my foolish head a blighting curse
If I thee lend one groat, I know thee well,
    And thou shalt have no aid from out my purse."

"For charity, sweet madam, hear my prayer,"
　　Then to the Lady bent he his address,
But this great personage her wide mouth ne'er
　　　　oped,
　　But only at the folds picked of her dress.

"Now by Saint Fillan's holy bones," said one,
　　"I don't, Macleach, this treatment understand,
I'll lend him forty pence, and more, and ye
　　Had from him a great bargain in the land."

Then straight again invoked on his own head
　　Curses divine the pranked-up Laird, and cried:
"A bargain! No, it me a loser makes,
　　I wish the purchase all were set aside.

"And here, before ye, Lairds and Ladies all,
　　I offer, if the youth will take it back,
To give him back again his worthless tracts,
　　The price a thousand marks of mine to lack."

"I take the offer," said the youthful Laird,
　　"And pay, as earnest, golden crown on crown,
Be witnesses ye all, and let a scribe
　　Write now, at once, the fixed agreement down."

'Twas done, the next day poured the gold on Mac,
　　And Madam Mac no more of Lynne was
　　　　queen,
But lived the Laird of Lynne in modest state,
　　And led in quiet peace a life serene.

A steward new ye may be sure he had,
  And soon a wife, a lady new of Lynne,
Who daughter was of that brave Laird who
      shamed
  Him who so short a time Lynne's Laird had
      been.

DANTEAN PROTESTS.

DANTEAN PROTESTS.

I.—CRITICISM.

HOW shall I voice my deep and strong disgust
 For all the petty tribe of critics pleased
To say high things or low of Dante's verse?
The high things raise him to an undue height,
The low him bury in a noisome grave.
Men speak of Dante who his lines ne'er read,
Men write of Dante who suppose that all
He wrote was the Inferno, leaving lost
His journey to the stars and his approach
To that empyrean seat, God's judgment-throne.
Some deem him but a common lover lorn,
Some make him founder of a novel faith,
Not deeming pure esteem his love illumed,
Not caring that Christ's Church was his delight.
And who's to blame?   The commentators first
Who ignorant twaddle wrote instead of sense,
And next the unskilled translators who have failed
To grasp the ideas he wrought into his rhymes,
And last the rogues themselves, whose scope has
   missed
The man, his times, his object and his words.

II.—METAPHOR.

False phrases run in books, false metaphors pass,
Analysis should weed plantain out of grass,
And send the counterfeit coin to junk-shops base,
But grows the plantain, speeds the metaphor's race.
An instance much in point which thus has fared,
And has wit, beauty, science, learning snared,
Seems one of recent fashion, but not less
To be condemned, whatever be its dress.
This the cathedral metaphor may be named,
And currency it have given wise authors famed.
This methaphor curious let us analyze,
And see from what it has its probable rise.
Dante three-fold division gives his song,
To these do rhetoricians manifest wrong,
For architectural metaphors' narrow scope
Fits illy in with faith and love and hope,
And infinite thought comparison will not bear
Even with a church which holds a bishop's chair.
The first division Dante gives is Hell,
Where every horror sounds and demons yell,
More gently termed the lower world, and planned
To include Elysium, with its worthies grand,
But Christian never, and the allotment next
Is Purgatory, which the ancient church
Alone makes doctrinal, and which i' the lurch
Is left by those same rhetoricians sage
Who metaphors use whose force they do not gauge.

The third is Paradise, God's choice abode,
The regions bright with stars and angels sowed,
Deep, deep, aloft among the systems bright,
Far, far, along the infinite planes of light.
Considering these things let us see how fit
These tropes when we consider them bit by bit.
The metaphor false runs in this idle way:
The Comedy Divine to a Cathedral may
Comparison have, because the Inferno's lay
The vestibule suggests, the Purgatorio hint
Gives of the mid-placed nave, and that sweet glint
Of glory in the Paradise fits the place
Whence sound the tidings of redeeming grace.
The vestibule the ancient place of ghosts!
The vestibule the abode of Satan's hosts!
Slight praise is this to gentle people meek
Who therein pause the holy vase to seek.
The auditorium, where sound dronings long,
The place where saints praise God with fervor
            strong!
And, last, the apsis where the Calvary stands,
And Christ comes bleeding, side and feet and
            hands,
Compared to heaven, where angels' harps and
            tones
Cheer, in their joy, the dwellers in its zones!
Ah no! the Poet's rhapsody sounds in thought,
Sole in comparison therewith can be brought
Infinity's self, nought else can furnish forth,
As equal to the occasion's call in worth,

As not disparaging it, comparison due
To what embraces all, far, near, false, true.
Cease, idle critics, cease: celestial wings
They need who would attain to heavenly things,
And Terraced Mount and winding Banks of Styx
Refuse alike the rhetoric of your cliques.

THE DIVINE SATIRE.

THE DIVINE SATIRE.

I.—PARABLES.

MATTHEW XIII, 34.

HE spoke in parables, aye, and more than that,
  Satire divine upon his syllables sat:
Satire divine which took of scorn the place,
Satire divine which, while it moved in grace,
Yet used the tones of noble, patient grief,
Grief, scorn for men, of whom Himself the Chief,
Took to himself the blame, the care, the cure,
He Beam Divine from God's own lustre pure.

II.—CANA.

JOHN II, 3.

WHAT was't at Cana's feast but satire's play
  Made water wine, and made him pleased
    to say
Unto his Mother: "Woman, what with thee
Have I to do?   Upon my mission me
An hour supreme awaits, then may'st thou near
Weep, plead, but all in vain, on Calvary drear."
Ah what a satire on the soul of man
Which, unlike God, cannot the future scan!

And satire here deserved is found 'gainst those
Who would the use of God's own gifts oppose
And laws which Nature made, and Nature's God,
Seek to reverse at a fanatic's nod.

III.—BETHANY.

LUKE X, 38.

AT Bethany, too, what was't but satire's shaft,
    When Martha sought her sister's aid, and
      laughed
Our Lord at her just claim, and, strangely "Go,"
He said, " work on, and let thou Mary so
Embrace my feet; 'tis best; whilst empty sloth
At this inopportune moment holds us both."
Ah! What a lash it gives the clergy's ways
Who sit fed fat with sickening women's praise!

IV.—JERUSALEM.

MARK XIV, 58.

WHAT was't but satire spoken to the crowd,
    Who jerred his sayings as absurd and proud:
" Make thou this temple, men, a ruin mere,
Whose building was a miracle: not a year
Will I require, nor month, to make it new;
In three days, men, and without aid from you
Or any man, I will restore it, willed
By me into new state, and with all worship filled."

Ah satire keen! The riotous multitude,
By flowery tropes controlled or threatenings rude,
So told that they themselves should break the walls
Of God's appointed Temple, and the thralls
Of prejudice and passion ope the way
Which led unto the Resurrection Day!

V.—PETER.

LUKE XXII, 31.

WHAT was't but satire when, to Peter, " You,"
He said meaning the apostles all, " not true
Unto me are; you Satan hath desired,
With fell ambition 'gainst my mission fired,
To sift like wheat; but, Peter, I have prayed
My Heavenly Father that He give thee aid,
And, aided, turn thy brethren from the snares
That Satan sets; be wheat, enough are tares!"
Ah satire on the preacher's frequent lack
Of practice, and the insidious fell attack
Which Sin reserves for soldiers who the guard
Appointed are to keep, and who retard
Sometimes, by their example poor, the pace
Of men intent upon the heavenly race!

VI.—CLEOPAS.

LUKE XXIV, 13.

WHAT was't but satire, when the Temple New
Of God's Own Majesty quite nearly drew,

Upon the highway, to disciples twain
Who walked perplexed, in doubt and dread and
    pain:
"What news, my friends, know ye in these dull
    times?"
"Dull times! And canst thou, stranger, not have
    heard
With what deep grief the hearts of all are stirred,
How one to whom we looked to lead our race
Has into danger fallen and dire disgrace,
Nailed on the cross, and three days in the grave,
He whom we hoped all humankind would save!"
But when at Emmaüs arrived, and raised
His hands were in His Heavenly Father's praise,
Above the bread at dinner, then they knew
Was with them God, the Risen and the True.
Ah here was satire lips divine applied
To all who would the guise of man, as guide
Seek, for their estimates of character, worn
Not on the face, but in the bosom borne!

VII.—SAMARIA.

LUKE XVII, 17.

WHAT was't but satire when Samarian fields
    Him, Master of all forms of power that
    wields
Or saint or seraph, and each lofty height
Of knowledge, e'en in its empyreal flight,

Heard ask, as one might ask in questioning doubt,
Intent to solve some puzzling problem out,
"Where are the nine?" as t'wards him meekly
     came
The leper, sole of ten, to praise his name.
"Where are the nine?" Response came none,
     for saw
The man his Lord, and stood, held dumb by awe.
Ah, knew not then the Omnipresent God
Where walked the nine, He by whose sovereign
     nod
Each system shines, each silvery planet rolls,
And who all matter and all motion molds?
The nine were of the Lord's own people, they
Refused their debt of gratitude to pay,
The stranger came, and homage gave profound,
And thus o'erstepped his narrow nation's bound.
"Where are the nine?" The stinging satire rings
Where'er Redemption's voice its tidings sings,
The satirist He who said the prophet true
Shall to his home and kindred vainly sue,
And praise exalted merit nobly earn
From lands whose souls its radiant mission learn.

VIII.—JOB.

THE BOOK OF JOB.

AND what but satire is it shown in Job,
   That earliest breath of music on our globe?
There friends came round a sick man full of pain.
Intent him for his foibles to arraign,

They narrowed down in argument sour the laws
That governed God, and scarcely gave Job pause
To say he honored God, but thanked not them,
A man renowned for patience moved to phlegm.
What then?　The wisdom of the ancients given,
Approached a youth, Elihu, as from heaven.
The course the ancients took he showed was false,
But yet continued their ill-timed assaults,
And, like them, urged a man all racked and sore
Gay, cheerful, songs of jubilee forth to pour.
All vain the human aid, the human arm,
All bitter with impatience and alarm
The tortured man, and angry each with each
The arguers, as leech will rage 'gainst leech,
Came from the whirlwind's breath the humbling
　　　　voice
Of God himself, He who all blessings choice
Gives at His will, and at whose will the unjust
And just alike fall prostrate in the dust,
And to the frenzied Job declared His might,
His mastery, His providence, and His right
O'er men and demons, fate, and sin, and hell
And all the pains that goad and prides that swell.

SONNETS.

WHAT IS A SONNET?

WHAT is a sonnet? 'Tis a little bell
    Which rings, on paper, melodies of the
      heart;
Its silvery tones no terrors rude impart
In tinklings clear its quick-wrought numbers
    swell
And reign in realms where fairy echoes dwell.
'Tis heard in sweet philosophy's paths, where
    start
Tear-drops, full oft, when, free from guile or art,
The touched emotions own its Sibylline spell.
Huge bells there be which storm or danger clang,
Or with the epic muse sing fame and arms:
Our little bell such numbers never rang;
Its carillons' peals bring only love's alarms,
Like that which from the altar sends its sound,
Or that which says your guest your door hath
    found.

THE MISSION OF FRIENDSHIP.

ARISTOTLE IX, ix, 7.

WHAT is the mission of friendship, and what
    Is the source of its power? Wherein
    does it move

To lighten the load of us mortals, and prove
More lasting than love?   Whence divinely are
      brought
The forces wherein our emotions are caught?
Where in the nature of man is the groove
Wherein with such pleasure such fond prompt-
      ings move?
The *heart* is our oracle here, not the lot
From urns, old or new, of ambiguous rhymes:
Its mission is happiness, sympathy's aid
It seeks, and is strongest where contrasts exist.
It has thrills which are heightened by differing
      climes,
Or when feature, or mood, or station, or grade,
Make dear unto me what in my nature's missed.

INTENSIFIED.

BY station are men's traits intensified.
    Take the professions: let the preacher
     stand
A sample forth: how is his arrogance fanned
To ruddy ardor!   Or, if lacking pride,
How does humility send his praises wide!
And then the man upon the mission grand

Of soothing human suffering: is he planned
On little bases of deceit, or tried
His nobler traits in crucibles divine?
A mousing charlatan he is, or, great
In wise simplicity, a welcomed friend.
And then the advocate, law's learning's mine:
Hear him or bark in some small, mean debate,
Or, with angelic fire, worth's heights defend!

THANKSGIVING.

STANDS Candlemas for Saturnalias lost,
    The leaping priests who gladdened Roman
        streets
Give place to hymns processional and the sweets
Of high communion with the sacred host,
And all that reverence loves and prizes most.
Gregarious, sure, is man; his nature meets
The fine ethereal sense, which fondly greets
The eternal and the heavenly; 'tis the boast
Of every nation that it has its days
Of frolic and of worship; e'en the sad
And introverted Puritan finds at last
A vindication in that joy which rays
To-day throughout New England proud and glad
That she with thanks can glorify her past.

WORM, CHRYSALIS, BUTTERFLY.

SOMETIMES I muse a paltry worm is man,
    Changed by drear Azraël to the chrysalis
        state;
And next a butterfly bright at Heaven's high gate;
And thus conciliate I the eternal plan,
Formed when the counsels of the Word began,
With suffering here, and sin, and lowering fate,
And charity's laws divine, and earthy hate,
And this our threshing-floor cleansed by God's
        own fan.
The worm is but a ghost, a spectre, mask,
It comes from out the dust, but soul-possessed;
A timid, eager child the chrysalis is,
A girl who smiles her father's smile to ask,
Like that fair vision Adrian's last sigh blessed,
Then at His knee is hailed as always His.

THE SACRED OFFICE.

CHRIST left to men the Golden Rule on
    earth,
Which, followed, would bring back the Golden
    Age,

And named a Church, as shows the Scripture's
        page,
But in his clergy was of grace such dearth
That one à traitor proved, who, in its birth,
Would strangle God's behests, and jealous rage
Of deadly foes against its Life engage.
And many of his preachers, since, lack worth,
Ill-workers in the Lord's great vineyard, base
Laggards when called unto His Marriage Feast;
Showing of His meek spirit scarce a trace,
Selfish, and rude, and gluttonous, they would
        smirch
The fair, sweet fame surrounds His Bride, the
        Church;
Angelic some, the name some earn of beast.

THE PLEIADS AND ORION.

JOB XXXVIII, 31.

CANST thou, vain man, that glittering scene
        restrain
The Pleiads furnish in the autumnal sky?
Or bid Orion's wintry girdle fly
Dismissed from heaven towards some earthly
        plain?
That glittering scene my changeless laws ordain;
My laws, too, by that measuring girdle try

All depths, all space, or low or wide or high;
The twinkling Pleiads shall forever rain
Sweet influences down, and, dancing, shine
Like fairies prisoned in a silvery net;
The giant's studded girdle shall apart
Its mighty trinity, fixed in poise divine,
Hold, while my myriad systems rise and set,
High-sphered, nor based on human pride or art.

ANTARES.

O STAR of summer, gleaming from the East,
    Worthy to lead the advancing season's
        march
Illuminating far the empyreal arch,
Whence hath descended the supernal feast
Orion's cortège gave, by thee increased!
Through thee we learn of him would rivers parch,
Through thee of antique jealousy which would
        search
For punishment dire all worldly leavening yeast.
And lo! thy beams are poetry: far along
The perfumed heavens they bear the Arthurian
        name
Arabia boasts: for, in the dates remote,
In prowess shone, and shone in lofty song,
Like Charlemagne gone, like Tennyson too, a
        fame
Full worthy in thy crimson beams to float.

GALAXIA.

ALONG the summits of the sky I sought
　　Star piled on star, the constellations wide,
And that rich belt of myriad suns I tried,
The paths whose silvery tints Orion caught,
The path whereto their golden sandals brought
Gods, demi-Gods, and heroes, when, in pride,
Up to that throne where shall all men be tried,
They praises sung with loftiest homage fraught.
The ultimate far judgment-seat divine
I saw before me, saw Alcmena's breasts,
Her son, the child heroic, and saw stored
In all the gems that all the pathway line,
Things teaching of those infinite dread behests
Announced to her who bore the incarnate Lord.

THE FAUN OF POLYCLETUS.

THE faun of Polycletus be my theme,
　　Theme dating back to storied times of old,
When men in marble wrought their thoughts of
　　　　gold,
And lustrous Art made sure each brilliant dream,
Concrete and clear to shine along Time's stream!
Ah, Phidias! far beyond thee did unfold

Thy skilled disciple beauty's lines and mould;
Aye, far beyond thy Gods his boys I deem,
Boys which the glory crown of old renown,
Beauty which shines in gait, in eye, in curl,
And mould which makes us know man's form's
       divine;
For, though the myths have laid their laurels
       down
Before the throne of Jesus, He the Pearl
Of all the Ages, yet their splendors shine.

THE KNIGHT OF SANSOGNA.

FELL Lancelot to battle with a Knight
    Well named as of Sansogna; all of true
And noble knighthood this one lacked, and knew
Only to challenge anyone who might
Furnish a foil unto his armor bright.
But now from smitings on this Chloreus flew
A flame of sparks, and heavy breath he drew
To say: "A pause! Who art thou? Let the fight
Stand still a moment!" "I am Lancelot,"
Responded briskly then the indignant brave,
And in pursuit straight lifted up his sword,
But "Pardon!" said the dastard, "I am not
Afraid of thee; thy sword aside I waive;
The name I yield to of so great a Lord!"

FATHER, SON, AND HOLY SPIRIT.

THREE persons in the Adorable Trinity are,
    And three in my friend's family too are
       found:
There is the father in whom traits abound
Of goodness infinite, with nought to mar
His rounded character seen near or far;
There is the son, to whom instruction sound
Has given a philosophical high ground
Of contemplation, whence from star to star
He views the dome celestial; and then Rome
No worthier saint can claim than may claim those
Who own the spirit sanctified of her
They name as mother.   Bless their radiant home,
Thou Trinity High, a home where piety grows,
And rustling wings of angels leave their stir!

WHAT IS IT, SISTER?

TO SISTER BLANDINA.

SOMETIMES methinks religion's but a thing
    Of putting on of airs: there is the priest
Omnipotent o'er all, and there the minister least
Of all his congregation; style e'en forms a ring

Within the sacred altar; praises sing
The choir to God, but money is the yeast
The leaven whereby pew piety's increased;
Its lubrication makes the censer swing.
Where is the lofty sense of right and wrong?
Where is the quiet life that shuns display?
Is it among the nuns all white of face?
Is there the beatific ardor strong
Where Saints Franciscan shun the public way,
Pageant and pomp and velvet, plumes and lace?

TO' DANTE.

POET divine, or, yet, in terraces meek
    The effulgent Cross of southern oceans
        lights,
Or, throned where Seraphs, in empyrean heights,
Close contemplation of the Highest seek;
Thy heaviest woes from wrath · that factions
        wreak,
Thy keen resentments voiced in melody's flights,
Safe thou from Minos and infernal rites;
On whose behalf was Beatrice moved to speak
With Virgil's shade, his aid expert to pray;
On this thine humble follower's task do thou
Look down benign! Since went thy soul its way
From out the western wave hath risen, and now

Hails thy great Muse, a realm more wide than
    Rome's,
And give thy themes their thoughts its studious
    homes.

WHEN GIRLISH CURLS DANCED 'ROUND THY FOREHEAD FAIR.

TO A. Y. S.

WHEN girlish curls danced round thy fore-
        head fair,
I paused sometimes upon the street to gaze
And wonder o'er thy wealth of charming ways,
And deemed some heavenly radiance filled the air;
And when, with school girls' tasks sedate, would
        wear
Thy face new beauty, I would think what lays
Of happiest bard could paint thy glory's rays
That left for added traits nor thought nor care;
But now that years have brought thy summer-
        time,
The triumph of thy spring's surpassed, while climb
To ripe abundance thy perfected gifts;
And may thy russet autumn view thee blessed
With all good things that e'er the good caressed
While slowly God thee to his bosom lifts!

THE BIRTHDAY.

FEB. 9, 1887.

NATURE is kind: she gives, in winter,
    gloom,
That round it she may shed a halo bright
And stars that sparkle through the darkling night;
Midst accents rough of daily care to bloom
She grants sweet flowers of song; then, glad,
    assume,
Midst song and beauty, skies a brighter light,
And earth a ministry holds of high delight,
Which leaves for weak regrets nor cause nor
    room.
While Alice reigns the winter flees, the power
Of frost o'erwhelmed concedes the genial hour;
Before her beauty Nature hides her face;
Before her voice the minstrel's lute, the fame
That waits on art where'er its pennons flame,
Seem idly tame; all lack her power, her grace.

TO A. L. K.

ADAH, as often as I see thy face
    A dream I see of stately loveliness!
Louise—it suits me well thus to confess—
When looking round the world for forms of
    grace,

I think of thee, all unadorned by lace,
Or trinketry, but in the guise would bless
E'en Psyche's self, whose smiles oft thee caress,
Thee clothed with every charm adorns our race!
And let me own thy majesty of worth,
Thou moon full-orbed amongst the lesser orbs;
And let me claim thy casual word or thought,
Word, thought, exceeding treasures heaped of
   earth;
And let me bend—this still my soul absorbs—
In worship at thy shrine, divinely sought!

TWO EYES I SAW.

TO C. H.

TWO eyes I saw, and they were sweetly bright,
 Two eyes which answered radiance to my
  own,
Two eyes unrivaled in whatever zone,
Two eyes which gave fair features what the night
Which Luna rules gives to each lofty height.
O were I privileged to assume the tone
A lover knows, and mount love's lofty throne,
I could fond tintage give to my delight! ·

But such is not the privilege I possess,
My privilege is to worship from afar,
But while I worship I can give my voice
Some plenitude of license, as of right,
And say that never came, with power to bless,
My heart within, such orbs, each like a star.

TO E. B.

SEPT. 1, 1889.

BEAUTY, and modesty, and worth, their light
  The lady gave who made my journeys sweet:
A pensive beauty, for the gifted meet,
And modesty serene, and worth whose bright
Insignia lead to every lofty height.
I would that she were born my vows to greet,
And with like heat my passion's heat to meet,
But Fates may not thus severing paths unite.
Her mind sits calmly in its starry plane,
She holds Diana's rule, nor gives
Aught save mild scorn to gentle Cupid's bow,
Whose shafts have caused her sometimes love's
              fond pain.
I know not where a lovelier lady lives,
A privilege 'tis her castle's wood to know.

RESCUE BY AN AMERICAN LADY
OF AN AMERICAN LADY.

SHAME on our boasted times, that they count
   men
Who treat with tiger cruelty a wife!
But heard I of a mingling in that strife,
For sought an Angel the vile husband's den,
And brought her ward to heaven's own light
   again.
The story is of three lands rich with life:
The one where sound the drum and stirring fife
Pæans to Liberty; the next where glen
And sea and mountain boast imperial themes;
The third where Herrmann's lofty glory dwells.
The bride and her deliverer were apart
A thousand leagues from where their native
   streams
And plains and mountains weave their mystic
   spells,
And wove in alien lands this history of the heart.

THREE SCORE AND TEN.

The seventieth wedding-anniversary of Mr. and Mrs. John Tallman,
of Tappan, New York, Oct. 16, 1889.

WE read that years three score and ten
    Were given mankind to live on earth,
To live in sadness and in mirth;
We see, alas, how often men
Regret that race none run again,
Or, looking forward, reach from birth
Few years indeed, and little worth:
But here are friends who thrill my pen
With *marriage* lasting seventy years!
O wedded bliss how long drawn out!
O wife and husband greatly blessed!
O time, filled full with smiles and tears,
And hopeful days, and gloom, or doubt,
Now waiting only Heaven's behest!

EPITHALAMIUM.

SEPT. 18, 1889.

BE it our prayer that God may speed them
    well,
William and Alice, in their wedded life,

He man adored, and she beloved wife!
May this of each sweet, jubilant wedding-bell,
As on the air its pleasing accents swell,
The prophecy be, and may the loyal strife
Of mutual duty ne'er feel severing knife!
This say, my son, and say thou this as well:
That, as the years grow long, may love grow
      too,
And graces grow, as grows the fragrant vine
Around their cottage-door, and friends increase,
Until all blessings that e'er marriuge knew
Shall bless their honored names, and joy be
      mine
In oft observing this fair scene of peace!

THE FEAST DECLINED.

THANKS for your invitation let me send?
   And, at the same time, this avowal make
Of my dislike for parties? For the sake
Of pleasing you or any other friend
I might my strong disinclination bend
To meet the occasion, might of cheer partake
Which should appreciative praise awake—
At your house things ambrosial without end;
But then I should be sorry for it the next day;
For posing, talking, looking wise and sweet,

An evening through, even in *your* presence
       bright,
Would be a tax my health might grudge to pay.
Besides, there are very few I care to meet;
And so, my frank regrets you'll own are right?

TO DOCTOR HOLMES,

ON READING HIS "CHANSON WITHOUT MUSIC."

NO other bard, like thee, dear, radiant Holmes,
    Can lyrics sing in English, French and
       Greek,
And mix these in a sovereign song, where seek
We not in vain the sterling words of Rome's
Triumphal arches, forums, fanes and domes!
With other bards it were an idle freak
Of venturous humor, which full soon a-leak
Would spring, and founder; e'en the admired
       tomes
Which come from antique Europe's laurell'd
       coasts
Of such an Argo sailed bring rumor none:
No, 'tis not in fame's lofty trumpet's boasts
That of this polyglottic feat the peer
Has e'er been seen beneath the fruitful sun,
One rounded thus, and mixed of smile and tear!

FOURTEEN LETTERS, FOURTEEN LINES.

1891.

A LANDSCAPE when we see that's truly
      charming,
Aglow with tints that make it all entrancing,
Fond looks we send upon its colors glancing,
Or be it glimpses rich confused with farming,
When sad clouds frown not on it for its harming,
Or gaily there a cavalcade's advancing,
Where laughing dames and knights curb coursers
      prancing,
Such beauteous view no lurking foe alarming,
Long, after gazing, do we muse admiring,
Us, as of Arcady, a gleam enthusing,
Recalling traits Narcissus dazzled peering:
But one may look upon a face where tiring
Will ne'er eyes own, and charms despair of losing
Than antique myth or glade far more endearing.

TREFOIL, QUATREFOIL.

FULL sweetly shimmer on the scene, thou Sun,
    O summer's Sun, above the field of dread,
Unclouded, gild the grave where heroes bled,
Reversed the scene that gloomed when sword
      and gun

Light gave the land from night's big battle done!
Each form of ill, each savage vision, fled,
Alert leads beauty where grim courage led,
Frowns yield to smiles, by each their victory won,
Contrasted on this field of clover-blooms.
Lay let us ne'er aside one lofty thought,
One aspiration for the great and good,
Voices surround us from heroic tombs,
Evangels come of peace through struggle brought,
Rings still the war through this majestic wood.

Tippecanoe Battle-field, July 5, 1892.
The above sonnet is to be read as an acrostic.

THE AMETHYST.

SWEETNESS of manners, this the amethyst
   Is held to signify in sentiment.
And when the thunders down from Sinai sent
Confirmed the array of gems that should a mist
Of beauty give the breastplate, in the list
This gem was found; hereby was plainly meant
How soberly unto his duties bent
Should be the pontiff. And its radiance kissed
In Sagittarius all the sparkling skies;
And sacred, said tradition was the gem
Unto Adnachiel, he whose pinions rise
In lofty heavens where glories Gabriel,
Those realms where angel with archangel vies,
And where all amethystine souls may dwell.

POEMS OF THE WAR.

THE VETERAN.

AT fifteen strode he in the war,
      In glowing arms and vesture clad,
That heightened all his visions glad,
And made a hero of the lad,
And patriot to his bosom's core.

The march, the mess, the picket-guard
      Each found him gay, elate, superb;
      Naught could his temper's poise disturb;
      Sometimes his zeal the men would curb,
Lest strategy's aims might thus be marred.

Rich Mountain saw him climb its steeps,
      Until from out his wounded thigh,
      Torn by a shell that climbed the sky,
      Came blood that him to death brought nigh
And showed him why 'tis history weeps.

At Huntsville, yet with that wound wan
      He rushed upon the unguarded town,
      Rushed with his comrades, like a frown
      That came from Fate with terror down
Through roseate skies at break of dawn.

And stood he where war's bloodiest rule
   Round Gettysburg poured shot and shell
   And heard the words through slaughters fell,
   The prelude to that storm of hell:
"Wait now, and let the cannons cool."

And saw at Chickamauga gore
   Incarnadine the stubborn field,
   There where the lost cause would not yield,
   Although each smoking gun that pealed
Wide rents in its sad banner tore.

In other battles, too, he fought:
   A Shiloh shell tore through his face,
   Where scars he wears yet, as a grace,
   And of that grand career a trace
Which stars upon his shoulders brought.

At fifty past his vigor holds,
   But as he looks adown the past,
   He sees the war's ranks thinning fast;
   His beard shows streaks of gray at last,
And grief sometimes his thoughts infolds.

The plumes above the heads that rose
   Of brave commanders sink in death;
   Those who survived the gory heath
   Where many a hero yielded breath,
Have gone to meet in heaven their foes;

The world to him is changed, and rude,
   Sometimes from younger men he hears,
   Words which him sink in secret tears,
   Him whom counts Glory 'mongst her peers,
Him treated with ingratitude!

Slowly his sun sinks in the west;
   The good will thank him, and the blood
   That for his country poured a flood
   Will unto Fame's pure amaranths bud
Above his ashes wept and blest.

GRANT AT SHILOH.

APRIL 6, 1862.

STURDY foes on Shiloh's field
   Stood, and neither side would yield;
   For the prestige wide and great
Grant, the iron hero had
Only made their zeal more mad,
   Trembled courage, thirsted hate.

Days had battle raged, and out
Grant was venturing as a scout:
   He too far alone had passed
'Neath the bluff, where hissing wings
Death-borne, sent their summoning stings
   Thick and merciless and fast.

Sabbath afternoon, alas,
'T was saw men in battle mass,
   Saw grow heaped the death-rows red:
Elsewhere chimes were sweetly rung,
Sabbath scholars sweetly sung
   Hymns divine, and prayers were said.

Fear none Grant had, nor was rash,
Duty's sense had held the lash
   Over caution, and his steed
Had him carried onward far
Where the heavy brunt of war
   Men met spread o'er hill and mead.

He a picket countersigned,
And the twain, as brave as kind,
   Saw before them peril spread,
Saw the signs whence peril grows:
Yet no multitude of foes
   Could have given Grant aught of dread.

Now his steed he turned, but,—God!
Dropped the picket on the sod,
   Headless from a cannon-ball!
Said "Poor fellow" he so used
Bloody scenes to view, and mused
   But a moment, that was all.

"Who commands this regiment, sir?"
Then he asked of one whose stir
   Showed him there to hold command;
"I do, General, as relief
To its wounded colonel.   Grief
   Meets us here on every hand;

"Fifth Ohio Cavalry; killed
Sixty; Headley's life is spilled."
   Major Ricker's voice he heard;
Came then, and without retard:
"Let me have a bodyguard,"
   Order honored at the word.

Captain Curtis quickly out
Wheeled his company, and about
   Safety now the General clips,
But, before 't was done, with hot,
Hissing frenzy, struck a shot
   The cigar from 'twixt his lips.

"Lightning," said he, cool as ice,
"Strikes the same place never twice,"
   And, as though 'twere quite of course,
A cigar came from its case,
Of that lost to take the place,
   While around him formed the horse.

On they rode through cannon-crash,
On they rode through cavalry-dash,
   Caring but to save their chief,
Caring but for duty's call,
Duty 'neath the sulphur-pall
   Of that reeking field of grief.

TO COLONEL WILLIAM C. WILSON.

THERE be some gems of speech too seldom
      heard,
Gems which should radiate in a sphere more wide;
There be some fortunes follow on the tide
Of high resolve; and oft the spoken word
Is as the air the pathway of the bird.
These thoughts came to me, not to be denied,
When I perused, and re-perused, with pride
Thy speech, my friend, wherein again to gird
The historic blade of battle was thy cue,
And make a chieftain welcome to our vale,
And strengthen bonds of comradeship divine;
And, as I read thine eloquent words and true,
Methought our people, surely, will not fail
Full heed to give to such high claims as thine.

SHERMAN.

WHEN from Atlanta reached his march the
        sea,
Savannah fell, the ornament of the coast,
A jewel superb, his conquering grasp within.
"This city give I thee, a Yule-day gift,
And, with it, seven full score of heavy guns,
All shotted, and large store of powder and ball,
And cotton one score and a fourth of thousand
        bales,"
Thus flashed he to the people's worthy head,
The illustrious chief whom martydom soon sought.
Flashed back response: "Well done, thou hast
        our thanks."
And asked bronzed veteran or meek refugee,
In pride or wonder: "Sherman, whither now?"
The gift, the question, bore the solstice-date,
The sun upon his southward course had paused,
And Sherman, not afraid to match his might
With any star in heaven, e'en Phœbus' self,
Responded: "Hither I southward came, as came
That orb whose glory gilds our arms, the sun.
He stands a moment ere is changed his course,
And so do I, and then my course with him
I take, as takes he his, towards the north."

And as flashed further north the mighty orb,
So northward Sherman passed, and met him hosts,
As met pale armies iron Charlemagne,
To sue for peace and friendship at his hands.

IDYLS OF THE WEST.

THE TREE AND ITS ROOTS.

A PROLOGUE.

GREW in the Orient all the balms of life
    And all the lore; a vigorous tree; and there
The trunk and lofty, leafy crown remain;
But have swept onward to the Occident,
As race hath followed race, ambitious all,
And crumbling city city fair, by turns,
The roots that held the baby bole aloft
Until the sustenance supports the tree
Comes not from that small pristine garden-plat,
That Eden wherein the saplings earlier frond
Of suckling beauty perfumed land on land;
But,—all the moisture drained of regions old,—
Drink those same roots, extended t'wards the
        West,
From lands erst savage, filled with culture now:
Aye, those same nourishing roots have swept far
        forth
Across the lands Atlantis ruled, and strike
New shores Columbus found, then bleak and
        drear.
Tiber's, Seine's, Thames', successive nourishing
        floods
Increased the frondage brave, so Lalla Rookhs,

Vatheks, and song, and history, and romance
Which erst Euphrates fed, and Nile's fat ooze,
And Simois' waves; and, later, tap those roots
The waters rich the Charles and Hudson yield.
Will reach the mighty progress further shores,
Until, the Father of Waters' self, attained,
And streams Pacific, send this nurture forth.
The minstrel shall suggestive murmurs seek
In lofty groves, born where the snowy crests
Of mountain rivers send to either sea,
Cañons and crags and plains, or white or green,
And where burst forth the scalding geyser's floods
From secret depths; new Alps, new Juras; tales
Strange as the legends of the deserts old,
And full of hazard as the Pyrenees' heights,
Or all the glens and cliffs the Apennines claim,
Shall grace the annals of the new-found world.

Be it our task to give some echoes form
Which else might be neglected, tales which speak,
Like Alden's, or Evangeline's, of home;
Which court not all the barren lands grouped
            round
The tree's huge breadth and height, but utter
            forth
Facts, words, philosophy, which treat old forms
And instances as yielding now to those
Which later come as symbols in their stead,
And gild the tree with fruitage of the West.

HUMOROUS POEMS.

AN INCIDENT OF THE COURT-ROOM.

THE court had called the bar for motions o'er,
    And opened had the docket for the day;
But, now and then, his honor t'wards the door
    A glance inquiring sent, as though to say:

" The criminal cases have priority,
    And therefore should the state's attorney first
Be heard in motions, I expect to see
    John Miller soon into the forum burst."

" You're late, sir," said the Judge, as oped the
        door,
    And came the attorney in with busy port,
" But we have waited for you, since no more
    Important business is before the court."

NOTE—The Judge was the Hon. David Turpie, prior to the incident,
and again, after it, a Senator of the United States.

ASHEEM AND CHOACE.

" ORDER, keep order," said the judge in
        court,
" Disorder in this room has reached its *asheem*,
No more confusion of this rowdyish sort
Must happen here, much as this hubbub may
        seem

The proper thing to counsel in their sport,
And I will stop it here now, quick and short:
See, sheriff, strictly, you no more grace
Give thus to talking, walking at a high pace,
Or, at each moment, giggling with a grimace,
I only hold the joker, and can throw ace,
We must at once bring order out of *choace!*"

GOOD ENGLISH.

A CELT and Teuton were opposed
    Attorneys in a suit,
Huff on the bench, and, sitting round,
    The usual audience mute.

The suit was of a trivial sort,
    But one a jury claimed,
B*h*m was the Teuton, of grand port,
    The Celt was R*l*y famed.

The sheriff called the jury-list,
    And read, upon the roll,
A quiet clothing-merchant's name,
    A certain Jacob Joel.

There Jacob sat, averse to serve,
    He first refused to budge,
" Axcuse me," then he said, " I no
    Ond'stand goot English, Judge."

The Judge, a wag, first gave a shrug,
  Quite in his usual style,
Then, " No good English, sir," he said,
" You'll hear upon this trial."

So Joel, compelled, assumed the box,
  With one consent all roared,
But not a sign of merriment showed
  The two attorneys bored.

ON THE NEW COURT HOUSE.

PRELIMINARY ADVERTISEMENT—The poet, in reciting this lengthy, and of course, fatiguing poem, devoted to sensibility and philosophy, imagines himself in view of the lofty and elegant half-million edifice, and in his best Homeric attitude reaches forth the hand (the dexter hand) and proceeds thus :

A Thing that is Fine should have a Fine Name:
I therefore call this the Temple of Fame.
  END OF THE POEM.

APPENDATORY NOTE—The announcement " End of the Poem " is supposed to have a soothing effect upon the stretched attention of the auditors (or auditor, as the case may be).

THE BALLAD OF BLUFF SUMNER.

BLUFF Sumner had, in some wild mood,
  His neighbor's cattle penned,
And snort up, when the neighbor sued,
  A snort the sky would rend.

'Twas in the early days, when roamed,
    Wide on the prairie grand,
O'er miles of waving sward, fat herds
    Known only by the brand.

Steers, with initial T, not his,
    In number seventy-seven,
He drove from section, town, and range:
    On this was brought replevin.

The case was flagrant, so much so
    It made some people stare,
But others said, "That's Ned again!"
    And gave it little care.

But Sumner, lawless, owned the law,
    Before him shrunk the judge,
And every juryman did his will,
    To 'scape his grinding grudge.

For raw the county was, and votes
    Were by his word controlled;
It made a precious difference when
    His herdsmen's votes were polled.

In caucuses he was powerful,
    Conventions feared his nod,
Men treated he like cattle, and
    Them ruled with potent rod.

But much of equity's force he knew,
  And lawless was in sport,
And, in this case, he only sought
  To have a scene in court.

The case was tried before Judge Mills,
  Of the Benton Circuit Court,
In the commission of the peace
  The judge had been up-brought.

In such a suit much argument,
  Of course, was lavished round,
And this ex-justice Mills's brains
  In dire confusion bound.

In awe of Sumner's lawyer most,
  He judgment gave for him,
Whereon the other error prayed
  Unto the Court Supreme.

This Mills refused. " Is this the court's
  Decision? " asked the bar.
" *If this court understands herself,*
  And she thinks she do, it are."

Sumner, while roared bar, jury, crowd,
  Said, with the occasion gay:
" Let Templeton have the judgment, I
  The costs will willingly pay.

" And let me say, judge, if in law
　　I were as you are short,
I would not suffer myself, sir,
　　To sit and hold a court."*

---

*Summer would have applauded the waggery of Sir John Millesent in the anecdote related by L'Estrange. Millesent was a lawyer of rare ability, and being made a judge, he was asked one day how he contrived to live in peace with his brother judges. " Why, in faith," said Sir John, " I have no way but to drink myself down to the capacity of the Bench."

JUDGE DEAN.

SAT in his ermined state Judge Dean
　　With lengthened law-suits sore,
While on his docket to be seen
　　Were twelve sad cases more.

The law the worthy judge well knew,
　　Knew lawyers' ways and clients,'
And, in these cases, had in view
　　A clever piece of science.

" Not through these cases will I hear
　　The citing of bad law,
And jibe, and taunt, and fling, and jeer,
　　Low joke, and loud guffaw,

" But guilty every wretch shall own
　　Himself, and waive all trial,
The lawyers, e'en, with humble tone
　　Shall own their clients' guile."

" Stone," said he to the sheriff, " which
   Of all the dozen's the worst? "
" The worst, I think, my Lord, is Fitch."
   " Him, then, I'll try the first.

" You tell him, Stone, to guilty plead,
   And I will easy be,
I think this will the others lead
   To leave their fate to me."

" I thank your lordship for this chance,
   His wife and blue-eyed girl,
When they know this, for joy will dance,
   Now plunged in sorrow's whirl.

" Last night their sighs and moanings stirred
   The echoes of the jail,
And afterwards in my dreams I heard
   The shrieks of phantoms pale.

" I'm sure his wife's a lady, sir,
   And has seen better days,
And of the child's sweet face no blur
   Disturbs the enchanting rays."

" Bring them all in at once," he said,
   " Array the full dozen, all;
I wish you'd see, Strong, that of dread
   Their modicum is small."

The twelve appear. "Fitch, what's your
        plea?"
    "I guilty plead, my Lord,
And hope that you will mercy me
    Be pleased, sir, to accord."

"Your life may, prisoner, not so slack
    Be as it seems to be,
'Tis said that Satan's not so black
    As we him painted see.

"Three months your sentence is, and let
    Me hope that when 'tis run,
Your old companions you'll forget
    And their example shun."

"What plead the others?" Then ensued
    A whispering 'mongst the clan,
All pleased to find the judge's mood
    So favorable was to Dan.

There were young Diggs and Donnegan old,
    And Rattler, Rawles, and Rugg,
Gray huge, Green slim, and villainous Fould,
    And Mulligan, Cowles, and Crugg.

Make no mistake, the clients these,
    And not the lawyers were,
Let us be just to Sergeants Breeze,
    Day, Hay, and Gay, and Blair.

" We're guilty all, all plead the same,"
    Came from the wretched throng,
Their lawyers, e'en, were rendered tame,
    And joined, too, in the song.

Then came upon the judge's face
    A frown, severe and deep,
Of his good humor not a trace
    Seemed there its seat to keep.

" Prisoners, your many criminal deeds
    Me my strict duty teach,
I follow where my duty leads,
    And give ye ten years each."

" Sheriff, the sentence of the court
    See that thou execute."
Forth went the eleven with rumpled port,
    And sad, and grim, and mute,

But round the neck of happy Dan
    His wife and daughter hung,
While tears down rugged faces ran
    From rugged natures wrung.

LINCOLN AND THE BRITISH MIN-
ISTER.

ONCE in a while most curious things there be
　　Which men supreme in fame and state
　　　think on,
An instance came well certified to me,
　　As characteristic of our great Lincoln.

It seems a high lord came across the sea
　　(This you may answer by a smile, or call facts)
Accredited to this land of liberty
　　(I had it from a witness, Schuyler Colfax)

And sought a suitable opportunity
　　To hand in his credentials to the President,
Accompanied by a speech of comity,
　　In settling down as British Minister resident.

The speech made, Lincoln said with brevity:
　　"Your name we'll easily recall, Lord Hart-
　　　ington,
It makes a rhyme, you know, so perfectly,
　　With that of our Mrs. Partington."

SAINT PATRICK PREACHED BEFORE THE KING.

SAINT Patrick preached before the king;
　　His voice had ring, his eloquence rose;
He lifted up his staff, and down
　　　It came upon the royal toes.

Uprose the king, convinced, but pained;
　　The saint explained it was not meant;
The rubric called for no such thing;
　　'Twas but the vehemence of the saint.

BRUNETTA SCRUPULOSA.

BRUNETTA Scrupulosa went to church
　　To make confession for imagined sin.
She had done nothing to provoke rebuke,
　　But feared she had, in thought, or deed, perhaps,
　　And, possibly, had suffered some relapse;
Her habit, too, had been this quiet nook
To seek against the world's disturbing din.

There found she one who never in the lurch
Left duty any which his station brought:
The Reverend Doctor Michael John O'Doyle.
   To him Brunetta made her foibles known,
   To him made ample promise to atone
For wrongs to heaven, and begged him, in the moil,
To help her grasp the great reward she sought.

Full many a time had he Brunetta heard,
Bowed with regret and trembling with remorse,
Make similar mention of her faults divine,
   Full oft had he judicial answers given
   To aid her on her trembling way to heaven,
And, citing holy precepts line on line,
Encouraged her through all her prayerful course.

But now disturbed his judgment just one word:
Brunetta asked, "Good father, can I *paint?*"
"Why, yes, my child, make thou the canvas glow!
   When perfect in the art I will require
   You in the church place, where may all admire,
Worthy, perhaps, of Fra Angelico,
Proof of your skill, a seraph or a saint."

But sweet Brunetta was ill-understood,
And, dealing ne'er in ambiguity,
And seeing how was lost her actual drift,
   She quickly said: "Good father, 't is my face!
   May I 'Invisible' use without disgrace?"
The avowal almost gave her heart a rift,
And woke the kind priest's curiosity.

He knew his penitent of all that's good
A miracle, and deemed some strange offence
Lay wrapt in this mysterious, curious prayer,
  He therefore said: " Come with me to the light!"
  Her face, erst black, was beauteous now and
      bright:
Permission gave he to the questioning fair,
And drove her with an added blessing thence.

HUMORS OF THE CAMPAIGN.

A LYRIC OF ERIN.

1884.

" 'RAH fur Blaine!"
        Says Cragin;
" 'Rah fur Logan!"
        Says Hogan;
" Let's be rallyin'!"
        Says Callahan;
" Cheer 'em hearty!"
        Says McCarthy;
" America Go Bragh!"
        Says Meagher;
" No! *Erin* Go Bragh!"
        Says McGrath.

RUM, ROMANISM AND REBELLION.

1884.

" RUM, Romanism and Rebellion, Mister
        Blaine,"
Said Burchard, "all our history's annals stain,
Them every Christian soul must view with pain.

" Of these portentous evils huge the worst
Arises from indomitable thirst:
Rum of all evils is the most accursed.

" And Romanism follows next in suit,
No tree in Erebus bears more hateful fruit,
Of many minor ills it is the root.

" And almost equally base Rebellion frowns
In many of our treacherous northern towns,
But in the South of course it most abounds."

Blaine heard the strange alliterative blast,
And smiled, and gayly through the occasion
        passed,
But, when he read the specials, was aghast.

The election came, and Cleveland won the day,
For not a thirsty soul would say him nay,
And all the allies rallied to the fray.

THE CONSTITUTIONAL CONVEN-
TION.

1850.

TO frame a constitution for the State,
　　Met sages, each a representative Hoosier,
And while there were discussions often wise,
　　Things otherwise would frequently amuse you.

Came to the capital a man of brains,
　　A reverend preacher, Alexander Campbell.
" To make the prayer to-morrow," preachers two
　　Said " let's invite him; it will nothing trammel."

"Consent!" came back the universal voice,
　　Which pleased the mover, Reverend Mister
　　　　Badger,
Of Campbell's church, and, like his master, shrewd
　　In things polemical, and ne'er a cadger.

Could scarcely have a more incongruous name
　　The other: Pastor Wolf he was; a shepherd
Among a flock of lambs, this preacher mild
　　Might just as aptly have been named a leopard.

The incongruity struck a brother sage,
  A great man with the little name of Pettit,
A scoffer, too, but in a gentle way,
  Who, seeing the drollery, more than halfway
      met it.

"I see," he said, "how fitting 't is we send,
  We who misrepresent the sovereign masses,
A wolf and badger to arrange a scene:
  A camel praying for a pack of asses."

IGNORANCE.

IGNORANCE of fact's a good defence, if
      true,
And if not true, and sworn to, it will do:
Ignorance of law excuses none, and gone
Is that man's cause who in its net is drawn.
Two bright, keen men these sound truths each
      in turn
Illustrated, each had somewhat to learn.
One, Watkins, was an editor, he sneaked
A lottery advertisement in, and wreaked
Just vengeance on him one who held the post
Of village postmaster, Ben Sims, the boast
Of social and religious life, but most

Of learnèd and political circles.   Well,
The editor, arrested, went pell-mell
Into the swearing business, said he knew
Nothing at all of things notorious; flew
The prosecution, in this mode, to wreck;
But on Sim's record Watkins found a fleck:
Some weeks before, when Christmas presents
       rained,
Sims had his record all too plainly stained
By taking from his clerks a present; caned
He had been in good style, an ebony staff
Gold-headed and inscribed, and Sims would
       quaff
The incense thereon graven, and would laugh,
Clear down into his boots, with soul-felt glee
When he this stick would rap 'gainst palm or
       knee.
What said he when the editor demand
Made through his columns he should forthwith
       stand
Dismissed from office as the penalty
Printed in black on white for all to see?
What shrewd defence was then forthcoming?
       This:
That true the law's plain terms were such, but
       miss
It clearly did the case in hand, because
Sims, every moment conscious of all laws,
Had not accepted this same ebony wand,
Had always told his clerks so, nor had dawned

This idea on his mind after he read
Keen Watkins' article, but that, instead,
Immediately upon the cane's receipt,
Cancelled the gift had been, as was most meet.

ORION OR O'BRIEN.

ADDRESSED TO JOHN O'BRIEN, ESQUIRE, OF
SAINT PAUL.

IS there a constellation of Orion?
    Or have men missed the letter B, O'Brien,
And turned one E into an O? 'Tis tryin'!
And then, the apostrophe; there's no denyin'
Stars moan through all the heavens for this loss
            sighin'.
A glorious name comes not by fraud or buyin',
And ignorant ages have the heavens been eyin',
And precious loss to Erin this see I in,
And sometimes ask myself the reason why in
The name of Goodness men should be so pryin'
Through telescopes and opera-glasses spyin'
The spangled fields of heaven, when there's a
            cryin'
Injustice done a royal race, which, high in
Historic fame, no hero fears nor lion.

ORIGIN OF THE WORD TORY.

Came from pedantic times the name of Tory.
  Some foreign witling, in his way sarcastic,
  Deeming his cue called for a term bombastic,
  Of England's King spoke as the Alpha Tauri,
Comparing thus the Johnny Bullian glory
  To that of stars, all in a method plastic
  Which learning mingles with allusion drastic.
  This student's name has not come down in story,
But all his promptings must have made him curious
  To find all terms legitimate or spurious
  Which warring Albion's friends might render
      furious.
Brittania at his punning irony wondered,
  And then the name adopted, which has thundered
  Wherever states have leagued or armies plun-
      dered.

SIMPLES AND SYMBOLS.

I.

" JOHN, do you have the simples bad as ever?"
    A lady asked me as we drove to church.
  I thought she would my claims to sanity smirch.

And yet the carriage-wheels o'er gravel and
stone
Such rattling made that all except the tone
Of her fine voice reached me through some endeavor.

II.

Thought I unto myself, the name of "clever"
Some English friends applied unto me once
But now I think I'll own I am a dunce.
So, with meek hesitation, said I "Yes."
My looks betrayed me; came, with greater
stress,
"John, have you faith in symbols, now as ever?"

ABSOLUTELY PURE.

"LORD, make me pure," the child sighed
forth,
A girl scarce six years old,
"O, absolutely pure, dear Lord!"
While she her eyes uprolled.

Her mother heard, and much was piqued
To know the reason why,
And asked the pious child the cause
Of uttering such a sigh.

" Than our newspaper," she replied,
 " Was gospel never truer,
And baking powder, it tells me,
 Is absolutely pure;

" Perhaps that I will public praise
 For merit have, some day,
And for good baking powder's worth
 Is what I humbly pray."

PHUNNY CRAFT, BEE BANE, AND BOLIVAR ROBB.

PHUNNY CRAFT, Bee Bane, and Bolivar
 Robb;
The first two,—ladies; and the last,—no snob,
Nor mixing ever with the groveling mob,
But cause full often of the love-sick sob.

And would you know who was this Phunny
 Craft?
A solemn maid she was who never laughed,
And who with love of Bolivar was quite daft,
But whom Cytherean wings refused to waft.

And who the last, the innocuous, sprightly Bane?
Alas! She tattle talked through street and lane;
Robbed flowers of honey never, but would fain
With little effort a good husband gain.

THE DAINTY HOUSEKEEPER.

"STOP there," she said, and crossed the floor,
And stood inside the wire-screen door,
" Your feet are large and clogged with dirt,
They would my dainty kitchen hurt.

More real estate in Omaha
Upon a man's feet I ne'er saw,
Were you a Rocky Mountain bear
You could not give me such a scare!"

She took his bunch of butcher-meat,
And then he beat a quick retreat,
His eyes a-gog, his senses low,
While she went back to sweep and sew.

PEARL.

A YOUTH, the dandy of the hotellerie,
Prompt to bestow his patronizing ways
On prandial maidens primp whom he might see
To guests distributing eatables on trays
Extended,

A new girl noticed, spruce, alert and shy,
  And thought: "Here is another; now I'll show
My knack at talking, even though thereby,
  After continual nagging she may grow
        Offended."

So, as a dish of rather dainty hash
  She placed before the sovereign of the hall,
" My dear," he said, "tell me your name." A mash
  He sought, and insolence with his manner all
        Was blended.

" Pearl," said the rosy maid with reticence fine;
  Replied he: " I suppose one of great price?"
" O no," she said, "the sort are thrown 'fore
    swine."
  All laughed, and he to silence in a trice
        Descended.

CONCORD.

"COME see me, friend, at Conquered," kindly
      said
To me the incomparable sage of Concord; whence
I gleaned that, by pronunciation led,
Peace comes from victory gained—peace? har-
    mony!

Heard I, before, of quite a clipping strain
From Saint John of Seven Oaks, and readily
      thence
Inferred that one was welcome, when he said:
" Sinjon of S'nooks, my friend, come thou, and
      see!"

NEW YORK.

THROUGH busy streets once called of Am-
      sterdam
  We took one day a friendly, social walk;
I found my friend disposed to rout my calm
  By using constantly the word " N'Yawk."

And as there passed us on the trottoir's marge
  Man, woman and child, I heard the self-same
      talk:
'Twas ever the same courteous manner mild
  Spoiled by the gulping way of speech:
      " N'Yawk."

I had abroad heard used their Lun' and Ween,
  And said I'm sure if British men may balk
Upon their town, and Austrians so demean,
  Why may not New-York Yankees say
      " N'Yawk?"

TERRE HAUTE.

"WHERE do you live?" He answered with
      much care,
Like one who on his spoken French could dote,
But of the double R regardless, "Tare,"
And ended with a daintily-spoken "Hote,"
                      Tare Hote.

"Where do *you* live?" The man a maid to marry,
    Who might his views of matrimony suit,
Sought on the Wabash, and with readiness,
    "Tarry"
Was his response, to which he added "Hoot,"
                      Tarry Hoot.

"Where do *you* live?" The maid with fun was
    merry,
A coquette brown as any beechen nut,
Her dimples moved, and giggling came forth
    "Terry,"
And with a pretty little simper, "Hut,"
                      Terry Hut.

" Where do *you* live?"   Saint Mary's graduate
        ne'er a
Good chance could lose to call an oat an oat;
She answered: "Sister Eugénie called it 'Terre,'
And therewith taught us also to say 'Haute,' "
                    Terre Haute.

SAINT LOUIS BURNS, AND HOW.

I.

A MOST irreverent proclamation makes
      The interior of my fire-place, used now
For Natural Gas: severe as burning flakes
    On Phlegethon by Dante seen, or pains
    On purgatorial terraces felt, where stains
From souls nigh pure are wholly burnt away:
    SAINT LOUIS BURNS, AND HOW.

II.

But closer scanned, an E develops there;
    A forky tongue of gas has, like a plow,
Almost erased it, as the laboring share
    Gives shaping new to tufts in violets dressed
    On vernal fields; and, in the fire-clay pressed
The earlier shape gives pause to our dismay:
    SAINT LOUIS, BURNS AND HOWE.

THE MASQUERADE.

"'TIS all I osk, O gront it me,
    I only osk one glonce from thee!"
Entronced all other voices fell,
Enchonted by the singer's spell.
The lover La Belle Fronce had seen,
Had possed thence through gay scene on
      scene,
And loncers donced with Italy's queen.
His idol, Fronces, had been, too,
Abroad, where clossic bonks her drew,
And ronks, seen brought in gay review
Upon the Donube, and she said,
Since thus the advonce his voice had led,
And in romonce her dread had fled:
"O Olbert, foncy, I you tosk
To bosk in glonces, I unmosk!"

VASE.

I.

I BOUGHT me a vase,
    And it came by the cars,
'T was not like papa's,
It resembled mama's,

It received some hahas,
Just as good as huzzas,
The marines and the tars
Would have thought it the Czar's.

II.

Tom gave me a vase
Bright, summit and base,
And on each side a face.
One beauty in lace,
One pride of the race,
One holding a mace,
One wherein of grace
Was more than one trace.

III.

But a theme for all lays
Is, Stella, your vase
Surrounded with rays
Of beauty would daze
One not used to a blaze.
On it I oft gaze
As on Fanny's sweet ways,
And it has my praise.

ENGAGED.

A N unsophisticated maid,
  Engaged to tend the door,
A caller meets, on street parade,
  A wag and something more.

" Tell Laura, Lillian Liptrap's here,
  My card I need not send,
Her pleasant voice I seem to hear,
  Quick on your errand wend!"

Responds the servant oddly, " Miss,"
  Then, stammering, "she's engaged."
" Engaged! 'Don't say? What worlds of bliss
  Are in the announcement caged !

" I must her see, I mount, I fly,
  I must congratulate,
I must behold her dewy eye,
  And pat her pretty pate!"

WHAT DID THEY SAY?

FATIGUED by numerous calls of late,
  "Say I'm not in," the lady said.
"What did they ?" the lady prayed,
  As from the door returned the maid.
"Each in a breath the same thing said,"
  Replied the maid, 'How fortunate!'".

MISS HOOPLA.

TWO ladies meet, all in a glow,
  And one, demure and sage,
Midst other talk, asks "Do you know
  How old Miss Hoopla is?"

The other lady, blandly gay,
  A white, unprinted page,
Responds: "She sick! You me dismay!
  When heard you of it, Liz?

"I know she talks of heart-disease
  But still she's all the rage!"
"O," said her querying friend, "do, please,
  Forget the doctor, Jane.

"I heard that fifty was her age,
　And this my question meant,
But here she comes; the court, the stage.
　No beauty holds more vain."

THE DUKE AMUSED.

THE Duke of Lancaster, benign and calm,
　Sat in his chair, a judge 'twixt true and sham,
Midst things expressly to his lordship given,
Things not alone of time—the hour was eleven—
But, in this glorious autumn, things of heaven.

Just at this moment lugged a porter in
A pine box labeled, nor concealed a grin;
The Duke perused the marks, and with a hush
Upon his voice, which made it soft as plush,
Read: "Mrs. Sly," and "Fragile," and "Don't
　　crush!"

Now, this same Mrs. Sly an orator was,
As keen as is a saw that's called a buzz;
Gibraltar was not firmer, sure, than she.
The law had her pronounced as pure; and he,
How could he here a spur to levity see?

LE DIAMANT DÉSIRÉ.

[The reader will more readily appreciate the absurdity involved in the idea of giving to a provincial merchant an order for a hundred-carat diamond in recalling that very few diamonds of such size are known to exist. The Kohinoor, the Regent, the Austrian, the Orloff, are not greatly larger. The largest diamond, probably, in the United States is the President, of the weight of fifty-two carats. In diamond-producing countries a custom prevailed to manumit the slave who had the good fortune to find a diamond of the weight of seventeen and a half carats.]

I SAID, with solemn tone, and sober face,
    In chatting with a friend, a jeweler, " Try,
Go into all the world, search every place,
Cross sapphire seas where coral islands grow,
And me a hundred-carat diamond buy,
With not one less than seventy facets; cheap
You must not think to get it.   Let me know
Whene'er ·you find the jewel; do not sleep
Until you me report the price and stone,
And what land yields its high prismatic glow,
For much I wish to claim it as mine own."
With gravity mock the jeweler gave consent;
And, as I turned, and left his cozy store,
A rustic to the jeweler said, " He's bent
On having something stylish; isn't it more
Than he can, even in a town, afford?"
" No, that man buys regardless of expense,
He scatters money like a very lord,
He rolls in coupons, consols, bonds and rentes."

SWEET WAYS OF A LADYKILLER.

THERE is a ladykiller in this town
   Concerning whom the women are all mad.
  His pew at church is packed with ladies glad
  To do him homage; maidens cap and gown
Fix for his capture; he, silly, has no frown
   For anything in petticoats, and each has had
   From his sweet leer warmth like a liver-pad
Encouraging and gentle; but goes down
All hope again in each enchanted heart
   When things occur which show that this sweet
      man
   No fondness has for beauty, only when
'Tis gilded with a fortune; Cupid's mart
   Him only pleases when he bonds can scan,
   Lands, houses, and percentage, eight, nine, ten.

PUNISHMENT OF AN ILL-MANNERED
DANDY.

I MET a fop of sixty years and o'er;
  'Twas near his polished, aristocratic door.
I said, "Good morning, G * * ," and he
Responded with a tittering "Te, te, te."

" What ails you, friend?" was next my cautious
          quest.
" Well, John," he answered, "well, if I aint blest!
You've got you a new pair of pantaloons!
And, don't you know, such breeches many moons
Ago went to the dogs? They are a mile too wide!"
At my old dandy's want of courtesy to have cried,
Would have been joy to him, but I espied
Just down the street a tailor named Relief.
Well named, he held the cast of joy or grief.
" Rattle your dice, old man," I thought, " we'll
          know
Whether in style I am or is this beau.
For, know you, my own measure gave the size
Whereby my legs were fitted with that guise,
And knew I nothing of the fashions, nor
Cared one sole straw; not so my dandy bore.
" 'Lief," said I, as we came to where he stood,
" Here's a debate of fashions ? Be so good
As to disclose from all your stores of art,
Whose legs with fashion's ruling laws take part,
The legs of G * * here, like a pipe-stem small,
And pinched by trowsers almost make him bawl,
Or mine, in graceful ease reposing, in fair folds,
Which free the wind seeks, as it rolls and rolls
Their amplitudinousness ? You are made judge."
Responded 'Lief: " Against you, John, no grudge

I have; you're in the fashion, whereas G * *
Is 'way behind the times, and he must hus-
Tle to catch up. His legs, now look, betray
Neglect of sense, neglect of fashion gay."
I exultation felt, but not confessed,
It was an easy victory; I was dressed
In fashion's style, while manners dreadfully bad
In G * * received deserved revulsion sad.

A PROTEST AGAINST THE INCORRI-
GIBLE LIAR.

HE that will pry will tattle,
    And he that will tattle will lie;
She that will pry will tattle,
And she that will tattle will lie;
Pry and tattle and lie,
Lie and tattle and pry,
Pry and lie and tattle.
Why should the tongue so rattle?
Why against truth so battle?
Why should its still defy
All who its lies decry,
And incessantly lie and lie?

.

GRATITUDE.

FARMER BUCKWHEAT had met with a
  terrible loss,
  He had missed from his pocket a roll of bank
  bills,
Three hundred good dollars, the price of a horse,
  And it made him decidedly down in the gills.

But here comes a boy with an honest, bright face,
  Who the much-mourned-for treasure had found
  on the road,
And relieved his sad friend, with a very good
  grace,
  Of that grief which upon him weighed as a load.

"Ah, Tommy," the farmer said, "come to my
  heart,
  Such integrity fine should have a reward,"
For, relieved, by this salve, of a festering dart,
  The man, for an instant, the good boy adored.

And but for an instant; his worship returned
  To gold, and his caution again found its feet;
So he said, as he all sense of decency spurned,
  "Come, Tommy, we'll—draw cuts who shall stand
  treat!"

FRAGMENT OF A CRITIQUE.

.   .   .   .   .   .   society,

.   .   .   .   .   .   piety.

STELLWAG AND COCKRELL.

October, 1890.

I.

TWO cronies met, and stood upon the walk,
   There halted they to have a friendly talk,
They opposite were in politics, and quite near
Approached the fall election of the year,
For county offices, held, and those of State,
Judges, and clerks, and men to legislate.
Of Round Grove one was, Billy Stellwag named,
The other, Tommy Cockrell; Tommy claimed
His residence on that proud, ambrosial height
Called Oakland Hill, a hill where, in delight,
Live goodly men, and queens on social thrones,
Midst railroads, ravines, cliffs and telephones.
The electric lights were blazing keenly round,
The heavens above with twinkling stars were
    crowned,

The Scorpion held almost the south exact,
The east Andromeda graced, nor Pleiads lacked.
At hand stood Justice on her classic dome,
With sword and lifted scales, and quite at home,
So much so that the usual bandage worn
By Goddesses of Justice, in her scorn
Of things conventional, she had thrown aside,
And this caused some her rulings to deride;
And, sure, decisions there have been called law
Which men have heard, and devils, with wonder-
        ing awe.
Not far the Artesian Well was, with its spikes
Condemned by all philanthropists, where likes
The visitor never his first taste, but builds
A gradual liking up for its clear rills.
Thence sees the Frenchman, hero of two worlds,
The imbibing people happy, men, boys, girls,
Who, 'neath his feet can read the histories true,
Of men renowned as e'er fame's bugle blew,
La Fayette, Harrison, Digby, and Purdue.
Bankers around their offices have, and there
Admirers are of every widowed fair
Whose bank-account affords sufficient charms,
And bonds, and corner-lots, and shares, and farms.

II.

But let me now describe the walk whereon
This meeting was, a walk from nature won;
Furnished and set, no doubt, at usual rates,
It had come down from geologic dates,

Had been fog, fluid, jelly; was now stone,
Brought from the Greensburgh quarries; always
　　　prone
To wear too smooth, and walked upon with care,
Lest, as has sometimes happened, it the calm
Might mar of one who, as a battering ram
Is called upon to use his spinal column, fate
Which spoils the sufferer's temper, and his gait;
(For no one, as a catapult that's human
Likes to see fail high heaven's protecting numen;)
Not quite as costly as the best Berea,
But, when the bill comes in, sufficiently dear;
Blue limestone, in large flags, five wide, twelve
　　　long,
Put there to last forever, broad and strong.
A sidewalk 't was before the Temple Hall,
A mart for merchandize, of stories tall.

III.

But, truce to this.　There, on the Temple's sill,
Quite near the chatting gossips, with good will
To give them prices and to sell a bill,
A merchant stood; he heard their busy chat
Of tariff, temperance, candidates, this and that,
And stood there waiting till the climax came,
Or, rather, anti-climax, rout and shame.
The stone a secret flaw had, not yet known;
Beneath it was an area void and lone,
An utterly uninteresting hole,
Which had a place been to deposit coal,

Used before Natural Gas was introduced,
Whose Kempton geysers, drilled, and cased, and
　　　　noosed,
For enterprising capital formed a roost,
Piped thirty miles through roadways, and then
　　　　turned
By keys convenient in, where'er 't was burned;
And 't was supported only, was this flag,
At either end; but who'd suppose would sag,
And snap off in the middle, like the stem
A clay-pipe has, a stone should have the phlegm
To hold an army up, supposing e'er
The host could stand on feet just three score
　　　　square?
Eight inches was its thickness; it would seem
No weight could break it, accident, or scheme,
And yet it broke in one brief instant; snapped
As quickly as your eye could wink, and wrapped
In blank amazement these two men, whose
　　　　weight,
Scarce sixteen score of pounds, was adequate.

IV.

Cockrell had given his crony some huge point
In politics, or news, or (laying his finger's joint
Upon his nose) uttered some deep, wise saw,
Or, from his counsel fresh, a point of law:
That wages would go down, pearl buttons up,
Or prohibition dash the flowing cup,

Or that one party sought by fraud to win,
Or secretly disbursed, the other, tin,
Or that the murder case, just then in vogue,
Would end in the acquittal of the rogue;
When Stellwag brought his hand down on his
     thigh,
And said, impressively, " I don't believe it, I—"
A sentence he ne'er finished: there and then
The stone broke in the middle, and the men
Went with it to the vacant place below.
The incident stopped the breath, stopped logic's
     flow,
They danced, for a moment, just as gay Terpsi-
     chore
Might in a waltz, or, in a fight, old Hickory.
But, in another moment, " Where in the hell
Are we going to," said the astonished Stell—
Wag, as he clumsily floundered round, caressed
By his co-tenant in the darksome nest;
And, at the same time, the astonished Cock—
Rell as he saw the hitherto-solid block
Disintegrate, and its two fragments slid
So as to form an inverted pyramid,
Oblique in two divisions, in the pit,
And stunned and bruised: " Why, what sort of a
     cit—
Y is this?"   The merchant had quick aid, and care
Soon roped the men out of their casual lair,
Whence they arose a panting, famous pair;
And, sure, ne'er friends were, in so rough a muss,
Fished from an improvised sarcophagus.

FANNY KISSED ME.

IMITATION OF LEIGH HUNT.

FANNY kissed me when we met,
    Running to me 'cross the avenue;
Fame, good woman, never set
    This aside whate'er you have new!
Say I'm prosy, say I'm old,
    Say no Muse would e'er assist me,
Say aught else, all faults unfold,
    Press with firmer lips than yet
Pressed have on your clarionet,
    Blow, but, Dame, this ne'er withhold,
        Fanny kissed me!

THE BAPTISM DISTURBED.

"DIP *him* again, Boyd, *he's* a *dirty* dog!"
    The Elder heard, all heard, the blas-
        phemous rogue,
The river seemed to tremble with the wrong,
Already blessed with prayer and sacred song;
The police seized, the broken statutes fined,
Him whom no rules of decency could bind;

And high the Elder's indignation rose
'Gainst one he counted 'mongst religion's foes.
But said the Elder, later, " Friends, I must
Admit Reub Taylor's punishment was unjust,
The words were true which us so much annoyed."
And so agreed hot Reub and Elder Boyd.

EARLIER POEMS.

BEAUTY SEEN BY GLANCE.

'TIS in the great world's visions warm
    As in the moonbeam's trance,
There is a halo round the form
    Of beauty seen by glance.

Loveliest when rough clouds map the skies
    The peerless queen of night
Marks out to quick adoring eyes
    Her mimic seas of light.

There are some forms, that seem to glide
    Around our earth-wrought bowers,
We would detain, but is denied
    Their stay to bless the hours.

Such, though enshrined like stars that set
    But when our being ends,
Our outward vision scarce have met
    Ere space our rapture rends.

Have you not dreams you would not break,
    Linked thoughts you can't unchain,
Fair dreams of those thought can't forsake,
    Links binding heart and brain?

MUSINGS.

I'VE looked upon her ivory brow, I've looked
    upon her eye,
I've felt in homage to her charms I'd never cease
    to sigh.
The rude and boisterous storms of fate, or fortune's
    'wildering maze,
May mar me or may make me great: there would
    I ever gaze.

A thousand dazzling forms and fair may glitter
    in the light
Of fashion and of folly, where dark tempters try
    their might,
And beauty's ray, as bright, as pure, for others,
    round me shine,
But let me call, as its fond wooer, her peerless
    beauty mine.

The meekness of an angel's grace, the pride that
    loves the poor,
The winning terrors of a frown that make me
    love the more.
No wonder that ye all she slights; to love is to
    adore;
Ethereal splendor seldom lights our dark and
    heartless shore.

INDIAN PICTURES.

I HAIL each beauteous Indian scene,
  The American warrior's noble mien,
The graceful form of the prairie's queen.

In what halls doth this princess dance?
The prairie's skies her charms enhance,
Skies that gild fair this prince's lance.

Light is her step on her own sward,
And bright her smile by all adored,
Can greater charms the East afford?

All stern is thy keen eye, young chief,
There glory, power, vengeance, grief,
Mix they with love's emotions brief?

JOY AND GRIEF.

BALLAD.

I.

OFT, while the lover's knot is tied,
  And the happiest hearts united,
There comes to others a terror wide,
  And the hopes of earth are blighted.

Well on it was to midnight's hour,
　　The wedding-guests departing.
They passed a house where death his power
　　Had shown with vengeance darting.

O 'twas to them a contrast drear,
　　Their trusting bride's devotion,
The smile of love, of joy the tear,
　　The bridegroom's pleased emotion.

But in this room a drink-racked form
　　The widow's tears fell o'er him,
With liquid fire that pulse once warm,
　　The "devil's clutch" hence tore him,

Him seized on that same afternoon,
　　While bride and bridegroom waited
To hail the hour which now was soon
　　To see the lovers mated.

Then, while the bride her bonny hair
　　Was braiding for her bridal,
While glass and maids bespoke how fair
　　Was Mr. J'aimetu's idol,

While the blest bridegroom thanks his stars
　　For the gift that heaven has given,
His sober peace no terror mars,
　　His honest name by crime ne'er riven,

Then were there others plunged in woe
  Dark as his joy was grateful:
A drunkard sought his deadliest foe,
  Than human foe more hateful.

Grasping the liquor with a vow
  To drink and then renounce it,
That he would take his "last grog" now,
  And then the pledge, pronounce it,

He swallows like the leech that cries
  "Give, give, I cannot leave thee,"
Then backward falls, and groans, and dies:
  Ah! Woman, does it grieve thee?

· II.

The bridal throng had passed along,
  And light their hearts and merry,
They listened to the soft-tuned song
  Of the music-loving Marie.

The bridal pair stood in that hall,
  Glad friends their nuptials greeting,
The bride a queen whose graces fall,
  Like sun-light moon-beams meeting.

The goodly man who tied the knot
  Was there among his people.
His was a halo blessed the spot
  As crowns the church the steeple.

The church-aisle they had left in haste,
　The streets were passed sans leisure,
There was no thought of wrong and waste
　Where all was smiles and pleasure.

III.

Where, where, was then that hollow eye,
　That breast with anguish broken,
Where was that woman's carking sigh,
　Of ruined hopes the token?

That *was* thy last drink, suicide,
　Rushed o'er thy soul a torrent,
And swept it where the billows ride
　Eternal and abhorrent.

Scarce placing down that bucket vile,
　The "devil's clutch" still o'er thee,
Those curses broad, that bitter smile,
　To death's dark regions bore thee.

O 'twas a scene of horrid shame,
　That maniac-gulp was maddening:
The blight and ruin we should blame
　Red Bacchus for are saddening.

And I was one that passed in fear,
　And saw the candles burning
Round drink's pale victim's gloomy bier
　And comrades t'wards him turning.

Behind me was the dazzling glare
Of beauteous forms and faces;
Before me, with their demon stare,
Death's ignominious traces.

Ah, while the lovers' knot is tied,
And the happiest hearts united,
There comes to others a terror wide,
And the hopes of earth are blighted.

The foregoing ballad is founded on facts. A man had one afternoon committed suicide in the following remarkable manner: Yielding to the anxious pleadings of his wife, he vowed reformation, and promised to take a "last grog" and quit the practice. Then, taking up a bucket full of whiskey, which he had in the room, he swallowed an enormous potion, and immediately fell backwards, and shortly after, in great misery, died. Some persons returning from a wedding which had been solemnized that evening, were informed, as they passed near the house, of this melancholy occurrence. "The poor widow," said one of the party, "would receive no consolation, for she said that her husband had died 'in the devil's clutch.'"

Mr. J'aimetu was Mr. S. S. T.; the bride, Miss L. M.; and the officiating clergyman, the Rev. Samuel R. Johnson, a gentleman distinguished alike for his learning and his piety. The date was June 26, 1845.

DIRGE.

TIME is fleeting, breath is passing,
  Sieze each moment as it flies:
Sickness will, our frames harassing,
  Send our spirits to the skies!

Time is fleeting, breath is passing,
  Lose the first not, and the last
We shall yet, in love surpassing,
  Yield when life to us is past!

Time is fleeting, breath is passing,
   Towards eternity both hastening,
Time so long our sins amassing,
   Breath whose accents needed chastening!

Time is fleeting, breath is passing,
   Hasten then we on our path,
Patient through fatigues harassing,
   Watchful, such the Father hath!

LA FONTAINE.

A LAMENT.

[In compliance with the terms of the treaty of 1840, the Indian tribe, the Miamis, had removed to lands beyond the Mississippi. Accompanied by some sixty of his people, their principal chief, La Fontaine, was returning to Indiana in the month of April, 1847, with the design of spending the remainder of his days at his former place of residence near Huntington, as stipulated by the terms of the treaty. On his way up the Wabash he experienced severe symptoms of pneumonia, which at length terminated fatally at Lafayette, April 13, 1847. His age was thirty-nine. He was of mingled French and Indian descent, and by religious persuasion, a Catholic; a man of prodigious frame; remarkable for extraordinary courtesy; and possessing the entire confidence of his tribe.]

THE Chief had bade his exiled tribe farewell,
   And, weary, journeyed to his old domain,
But o'er his path the gloomy angel's veil
   Hung in dark folds, and shrouded him from
      pain.

Behold!—their thrones fast crumbling into dust—
   Earth cold clod closes o'er her forest kings,
Yet dims no eye keen sorrow's rising gust,
   No heart of ours its tearful homage brings.

Oh, Chieftain, resting with the royal dead,
   Why Pity, lonely, mourneth o'er thy grave?
Whence our indifference to thy kingly dread?
   Ah, why the oblivion of those ancient brave?

Last of the rulers of their native vale,
   Pride of thy people, in their distant home,
How will they proudly check fond nature's wail,
   How sink still deeper in their gathering gloom!

A race, the lords by right of all our soil,
   Theirs the wild forest and the prairie-sea,
Why among strangers rest they from their toil
   On Wabash banks and Oui-a-ta-non' lea?

Their deathless names even on our mountains
       graven,
   Their slumbering kingdoms all our valleys
       swell,
From Alleghany's pinnacles the raven
   Shrieks o'er no space where red men do not
       dwell;

Dwell 'neath the trophied honorable tomb!
　　Dwell 'neath the soil the Manitou had given!
Why roamed their children crushed down to their
　　　　doom?
　　Why hath not vengeance swayed the sword of
　　　　heaven?

Behold, the eagle of their native skies
　　Screams o'er the white man's heraldry of war——
Hark! Even now those notes of triumph rise
　　O'er fields empurpled by the Indian's gore!

Came bigot cruelty's and robbery's hour,
　　Dark "tyranny that hunted and reviled,"
False greatness that hath no remorse in power,
　　False, boasted right above the forest's child.

These tell the reasons of their fallen state,
　　And these the sources of their wounded fame;
Long on their hearts its grievousness hath sat,
　　The red man's sorrow and the white man's
　　　　shame.

O, who shall say what savage glories bright
　　Might robe in splendor now deserted thrones
Had not the terrors of the unequal fight
　　Broken the proud spirit of those glorious ones?

Had not the Christian desolating band
    Brought drink and vices stronger than their
        swords,
The echoes of this far-off western land
    Had rung them back La Fontaine's battle-
        words!

O'er yonder point where war's hot carnage rose
    (The hallowed field where Owen and Daviess
        sleep)
Now, Chieftain, might thy power appall thy foes,
    Like the red storm that blazes o'er the deep!

For thou hadst, Chief, what nobleness of form !
    A stature like the early kings of earth!
A mould invulnerable to the pigmy swarm,
    Like the old heroes of immortal birth!

If reared in days of vengeance and alarm,
    When warriors crowded to dark scenes of
        blood,
Swift deaths had hurtled from thy sinewy arm,
    And blood gushed freest where "The Foun-
        tain" stood!

What Pontiac wisdom might thy fame have sealed!
    Thine great Tecumseh's fearlessness of fate!
Pet-aw-lesh-aw-roo's chivalry in the field!
    And Ong-pa-tong-a's thunder in debate!

But all thy force was bent 'gainst fate to plead
  That honor might not yet be merged in peace,
Content that none but memory's wounds now
        bleed,
  And sorrowing that e'er long these, too, may
        cease.

For human destiny flow our sorrows forth,
  And hope, immortal, hath its earthward trace;
Lean thou on God; He knows, besides thy worth,
  The moral, passive courage of thy race.

Thus, then, thy simple virtues we enroll:
  (Compared herewith the wealth of fame were
        dross—)
He lived in peaceful dignity of soul,
  He died an humble follower of the Cross.

PERSONAL POEMS.

ANCESTRY.

YES, I go back a thousand years, and half
    Another thousand, to the date remote
When Gaul, at Soissons, changed its name to
       France.
There clashed the Salian host with legions trained
In Rome's high discipline, and there his sword
Syagrius unto Clovis gave, superb,
Clovis the King who led the Salian Franks.
There Bruno, chieftain, lustrous with renown,
Renown upon renown acquired brave,
And, more than Wellington he, reward
Proportioned to his merits: this he had
In that estate, far-spread, vine-clad, Deer Park
On the Rhine, lands, castles, mansions, over which
The sun the shadow throws of Strasburgh's spire.
There he his seat built, there his family grew,
And grandsons to the fiftieth degree have dwelt,
Some chieftains, prelates some, some bards, and
       some
Like to my humble self, who claim no fame
Nor merit, all content to know that days
Have been when honors hung around my race.

THREE CENTURIES.

LIVED of my ancestors one in centuries three,
    The sixteenth placed him on the family tree,
Wherein five years he passed in infancy.

The seventeenth throughout his progress saw,
And of decay he seemed to escape the law,
Midst health and wealth that never felt a flaw.

Years of the eighteenth passed he happily seven,
Mind, soul and heart of his were of good leaven,
Ye can his age tell when he entered heaven.

WELSTED.

WELSTED—1689–1747; POPE—1688–1744.

WELSTED of England flourished in Pope's
    time,
And with blank verse was skillful, and with rhyme.
Some said he Pope surpassed: they rivals were,
And mutual satires mild employed their care.
But mutual admiration, too, flowed forth
From hearts intent to recognize true worth.

Such promptings gave me freely history's Muse,
And gave me leave in my own way to use,
Free with her laureled praise and Sibyl-chants,
And that romance which England's annals haunts,
And sure that Welsted to my race belongs:
Thence claim I kinship with his name and songs.

TO MY MOTHER.

MARCH 4, 1889.

A ROUNDED space of ninety years to-day
    Marks of a life yet vigorous decades nine;
  Nine are the Muses, of the jubilant line
   They crown the birth, that, wander where it may,
It may the echoes rule of every lay.
   Come, Muses, then, inspire this line of mine,
   This wreath around her brows help me entwine,
  An honored life ancestral claims the bay!
Born when our land its great career began,
   Each year has seen my mother's graces grow,
   While she has seen these millions multiply:
May God ordain a hundred years her span
   Of life, midst children's children's smiles, while
      flow
   Blessings from Him who hails to seats on high!

TO THE SAME.

MARCH, 4, 1890.

NOW ninety-one! Yes, ninety-one is won!
　　Lived in three centuries past an aged bough
　Of our ancestral tree, and o'er his brow
　Graces of years a hundred and twelve were spun
By weaving webs of time; and what was done
　When felt Welsh mines his pick, Welsh soil his
　　　　plow,
　May once again be experienced, even now,
　When centuries three again are on the run.
For ne'er ancestral, ne'er historic line
　Gave than my mother better proof of health
　Corporeal, intellectual, than does she;
She may adorn the coming century; wine
　Of human tone and merit ne'er more wealth
　Of praise gave worthies famed beyond the sea.

TO THE SAME.

ON HER NINETY-SECOND BIRTHDAY, MARCH
4, 1891.

THOU of the jubilant voice, historic Muse,
　　Arise, and sing another natal day!
　Sound, sound, the cymbal, thou who givest the bay,
　Nor classic phrase, nor words of choice, refuse!

Not yet doth earth the pleasing presence lose
  Of her who lingers on her lengthening way,
  Content to go, content alike to stay,
  Behind her earth and all its mingled hues;
Before her heaven replete with lustrous stars.
  Sing, sing, O Muse, her many merits great,
  The elastic spirit, and the judgment clear,
The eye-sight, e'en, which not yet weakness
      mars,
And us, attending, prompt to show, elate,
  Continued praise with each revolving year!

TO THE SAME.

ON HER NINETY-THIRD BIRTHDAY, MARCH 4, 1892.

SAW Dante holiness in the number nine,
  Being, as 'twere, a triple trinity,
  The three developed by the number three.
  Thine anniversary, mother, seems divine,
Because it doth, for me, the twain combine;
  I see the twain united, dear, in thee,
  The reverent age of thirty threes and three,
  Symbol on symbol, sacred sign on sign.
So lofty is thine age, the retrospect
  Reminds me too of Dante's, for his sight,
  While Beatrice with him stood, a spiritual flame

Swept down throughout the stars the infinite
    flecked,
  And scanned the past, dim, dark, or dazzling
    bright,
  And memories fair of every lofty aim.

TO ALEXANDER POPE.

MARCH 4, 1892.

THE age thy mother reached, immortal Pope,
  Mine has attained, and that my constant love,
  Before she joins the radiant thrones above,
  May long attend her here, is my fond hope:
Thou who with wits of every age coulds't cope,
  And caustic mirth and blistering satire move,
  I who, in gentler times, am called to prove
  My gifts of melody, and my fancy's scope.
O teach me, favorite of the tuneful nine,
  Like thee to cherish memories filled with joy,
  While town, or fields, or forum, or far lands,
(Friends, duties, books, in copious measure mine)
  Work, study, musings, fortunate me employ,
  Grateful for myriad boons from her sweet hands.

IDAHO SPRINGS, COLORADO.

JULY, 1890.

BURST waves from out the caves of Santa Fé,
  Blest mount from which the fount ebullient
      springs,
  My praise employ with joy Isaiah* sings!
  Ye made me feel how much may heal your
      spray,
Which, like En-Rogel's Gihon's, Ophel's, play,
  Of health gives type and heavenly wealth, and
      wings
  Suggests whose fluttering to Bethesda clings,
  Sweet pool whose waters cool warmed in the ray
An angel's presence strange gave, deeply stirred!
  Long hail ye those who fail in bodily force,
  Long well your welcomes forth to distant lands
May pilgrims learn of ills the healing word,
  May your hot steam long gleam along its course,
  And pour to every door your golden sands!

---

*Therefore with joy shall ye draw water out of the wells of salvation.
Isaiah XII, 3.

A PRISONER OF WAR IN SPAIN.

[The flight of Queen Isabella of Spain to France in 1868 threw the government of Spain into the hands of the Republican party. Don Carlos proclaimed himself King under the title of Charles VII., and, with armies operating for the most part in the north of Spain, besieged several Republican cities with varying success. The Republic, in 1875, gave place to a Monarchy under Alphonso, and the Carlist cause was lost. On the 25th of November, 1874, I was taken prisoner of war by a Carlist force encamped in the Pyrenean mountains, under the circumstances detailed in the following lines.]

IN Spain, a prisoner fallen at Moloch's shrine,
   I little saw of war or of its woes;
'T was but an episode, and a surprise,
   That in the course of an excursion rose.

Thus was it: I was lodged full well at Lourdes,
   And, charmed with all the Pyrenean heights,
I could not rest till I had seen and tried
   Gavarni's snows and its sublime delights.

Ah, how the heart leaps in the Lavedan!
   What music in the Gave that sings to Pau!
I hear its murmuring voice come down the years
   As though around me pressed its beauty now.

Or stand I on the bridge that Paradise
   Commands and all the supernatural place,
And breathe the fragrance southern breezes send,
   And muse, midst proofs of rare celestial grace,

On thee, war's jewel of the ancient days,
   Nor wonder England claimed thee prize so
      long,
Nor that around thy walls foes camped in vain,
   And omens cheered thee worthy Roman song,

Or follow I the stream to Cauterets,
   Made famous by the laureate Tennyson,
Or, branching, seek Barèges les Bains, Vigne-
      male,
   Trounouse's Peak or prattling Gave d'Azun.

Ah, how the mountains cling around the soul!
   How they unite the lofty and the deep!
How like to joy the sunlight on their crowns!
   How sympathize their feet with those that
      weep!

Sighing midst rocks to reach ethereal planes,
   Ah, how the lofty temples of the pines
Soothe the tossed mind, while nature's infinite
      scope
   Is seen in all her flowers and ferns and vines!

The first third of my journey was by rail
   To Pierrefitte in Nestalas; a home
Me furnished there an inn, which seemed a toy
   Compared with its huge neighbor, Mount
      Soulom.

Why was I thus alone? My lazy friends,
  Of School Street one, one of the Golden Gate,
Had missed the time of the departing train,
  And on them I, enthused, refused to wait.

My Pierrefitte host would me have held an age;
  I saw, with him as guide, fair view on view,
But I at last said, "I must on my quest,
  We must give up the Pic de Balétous."

So, on the morrow, I the genial man
  Left while he urged me to look up his friend;
Saint Sauveur's sought I in a carriage; thence
  Must I on foot upon the journey wend.

But no, a horse could me convey as far
  As to the village at the mountain's base;
Therein I could to Manitou's snug site
  Beneath Pike's Peak resemblance somewhat
      trace.

Gavarni is the village at the base,
  Named from the mount. There I arrived, and
      sent
The steed back by a messenger, and again
  A garrulous host found to my service bent.

At Saint Sauveur's the Bergon's lofty peak
  In isolation sought the distance blue,
While round it towered its neighbor peaks, less
      high,
  But which no end of stirring romance knew.

On to the South, t'wards Spain, a ribbon shone,
  As shine the glimmering Pleiads in the night:
Against dark mountain barriers twinkled fair
  A cascade sparkling down Gavarni's height.

And, on my horse-back ride, full oft mine eyes
  On beauties of the stream were fed, or fields,
Or from the mystic summits came effects
  Kind nature to her fond observer yields.

Alighted I, near Chèze, an obelisk
  To see, which could not ask a lovelier site, ·
In memory of the lustre Queen Hortense
  Shed through this valley by her presence bright

At Pragnères I reined in my grey, aghast
  At seeing an humble rustic dwelling crushed
Beneath a giant rock that, sometime poised,
  Like Damocles' sword, from its steep height
    had rushed.

At Trimbareille, the halting grey I found
  Had cast a shoe somewhere upon the road:
Dismounted I, and sought a chestnut tree,
  'Neath which arose a shop and snug abode.

The shop, protected by its spreading bole,
  The smithy of a blacksmith was, and came
Into my mind our Longfellow's graphic lines
  Consigned, with more he wrote, to endless fame.

At Trimbareille I caught a glimpse of Spain,
　For t'wards the left of that fair ribbon's sheen,
Mont Marboré, concealing Perdu's heights
　And Cylinder's, could be distinctly seen.

Through Pyrenean mountain-gates came hosts,
　'Neath Hannibal's lead to bend the power of
　　Rome,
A power he bent not, but which broke 'neath tribes
　The north sent forth, and who here made their
　　home.

These northern tribes the Moorish armies' dash
　Here afterwards met, here smote Martel in
　　fight,
Here Christian hosts for Christ the victory won,
　And swept the infidel through these gates of
　　flight.

How could Illuro speak and Portalet!
　How might that murmur deepen of the Aspe's
Which rivals found, within her defile, shrill
　With triumph's cheers, and sad with terror's
　　gasps!

Yet still I never dreamed that Spain was near;
　Alone my thoughts were of the land of France,
Perhaps my talk, wherein all names were French:
　Held all my mind as in a lingual trance.

Past Cronmelie's heights and frowning Pic Méné
   I was by rocks met, mighty, savage, black,
Rocks thrown in such disorder that their name
   Of Chaos seemed in force somewhat to lack.

Or had some giants of the earlier days,
   Whose heads held converse with the clouds,
       there fought,
Or shook volanic thunders some steep height,
   And to the plain its mighty ramparts brought.

Romance on one a hoof-print plain descries,
   By Roland's horse Bayard 't was made, they say,
When Roland urged him at a single bound
   To reach this spot from heights four leagues
       away.

Joseph Victor de Mirabeau Dumont,
   So called himself the guide to me assigned;
I doubt if anywhere in all the world
   A better-mannered man you e'er will find.

On foot we toiled to towering esplanades
   In number many, often making pause
To view the ravishing delights around
   And ponder of such grandeur vast the cause.

The ribbon had a muslin veil become,
   With all the beauty of the sunlight white,
With all the charms which give to Undine's realms
   The rainbow and prismatic tintage bright.

Aloft the inaccessible summit shone,
　Crowned with pure snows that at no season fail,
And, as from nymphs aërial, floated down,
　In graceful undulations, that fair veil.

It floated down or into diamonds dashed,
　Or opals, or smaragdine gems, and round
Attendant cascades plunged towards the plain,
　And miracles made of vision and of sound.

Long feasted we upon the wondrous view,
　Long watched the foamy crests the mountain
　　　　tore,
As, down beneath, they sought the lower heights,
　And cascades formed which sought the valley's
　　　　floor.

Descended we towards the Porte Méné,
　A pass that outward leads towards the south;
I hurried on, and faster than my guide,
　And soon was gone far on beyond its mouth.

I knew not then what made the boy retreat.
　It was because he knew that flagrant war
Held Spain convulsed with armies, and that I
　Had passed of France the very farthest door.

This knew he and not I, romance held me.
　Before me rose a ruined castle's towers;
I climbed with weary footsteps it to seek
　Far up the steep sides of a hill all flowers.

Ruins I found, but also picket guards.
　'They speedily haled me to an inner gate,
And I, a student-tourist in the land,
　A prisoner stood within a donjon's grate.

And so one waking dream was made concrete,
　Nor could I at Fate's irony complain,
For I had found, with guns replete and men,
　A castle safe, a castle fair, in Spain.

Me interviewed the officer in command,
　And fully searched I was from top to toe,
And questioned was acutely, but at last
　The officer's faith in me began to grow.

"Tell me, my friend," were Caballero's words,
　"Unquestioned, all your story, hiding nought."
I did so, and he said: "You are no spy,
　And so to Saragossa I'll report."

He Spanish, I American, what plan
　Of mutual converse had we? Spoke French
　　　each,
And found a pleasant mode of interchange
　The accepted vehicle of courteous speech.

What did we talk about? Of everything,
　But chiefly of the lands beyond the sea,
And proud he was to hear me own that Spain
　Had given a hemisphere to history.

Him I recalled the lines that Claudian wrote,*
    The last great poet he of Rome's bright reign,
Who said no words of man can worthily reach
    To picture forth the wondrous world of Spain.

We talked of that Princess Antonia,
    Whom I within my native land had seen,
A dream of beauty and surpassing grace
    And sought by Spain from Germany as a queen,

And Leopold, her prince, the German chief,
    Of Hohenzollern's long and lofty line,
And all the turmoil of the war which cost
    Fair France her lordly states upon the Rhine,

And gave the Third Napoleon to disgrace,
    A ruler who in wisdom ruled his realm,
And whom his nation strangely then disowned
    When most his hand they needed at the helm.

And as, one evening, watched we star on star,
    He seemed by their magnificence quite pos-
            sessed,
And said: "The orbs of heaven observe the rule
    That sends all glories onward to the West;"

Nor heed would give my scientific plea
    When I observed: "Our globe's revolving east,
And 'tis this motion gives us the idea
    That moves, and westward, all this starry feast."

---

*Quid dignum memorare, tuis, Hispania, terris,
Vox humana valet!

"There sends the Bull," he said, "his horns abroad;
　He, as a God, Europa through the brine
From orient lands far westward bore, and gave
　To paths of nations an appropriate sign;

"The mythic hunter fronts him in the skies
　With club upraised and shield of lion's hide,
But shine the golden horns as brightly now
　As when at first they met the Giant's pride."

The guest of Caballero I remained
　A dozen days; arrived a courier then,
Who from headquarters orders brought in form,
　Which gave me back Gavarni's inn again.

MISCELLANEOUS POEMS.

PURE LIGHT.

RED, blue, green, yellow, violet, indigo, and
    orange:
Such is the Alexandrine line that shows
The true prismatic colors of pure light,
Light natural, intellectual, the same.   [blood,
There is dread war which clothes the earth with
There is reviving nature makes it green,
The violet which the labored furrows. charms, ˙
The auroral dawn divine, the yellow noon,
The indigo of storms, the blue serene,
The march of mind, the march of nature too.
From all the varied learning of man's life
The simple poem comes; from all the hues
·Surround life's changing battle comes the glow
Of light supernal, such as prophets saw
At times appointed, but which is reserved,
In copious everlasting floods undimmed,
For all who, in supernal realms, may claim
By merits earned, or charity given, a share.

THE DAWN.

I.

SAFFRON, and gray, and white, and then the
                    sun-burst!
Such is the progress of each glorious dawn:
The light comes not abruptly forth in one burst,
But, through marked changes, slowly, on and on.

II.

The tintage first that's seen is richly golden,
But, following it, the promise sinks to stone,
And blank the heavens become as calendars olden
Till shines at last of stars the central throne.

III.

So fare, through various zones, our longings
                    human;
Delayed the hopes of man are in the earth;
At last in heaven is seen the Almighty's numen,
Our saffron hopes attain celestial birth.

THE HEAVENLY TIDINGS.

GLORY to God, and peace to men,
      But not to all men, sung the choir,
The Angelic choir which chanted when
Of ages came the great Desire,

And why to all men is't not given
   To enjoy the peace which comes from God?
Why bound the charity free of heaven,
   And wield o'er men a tyrant's rod?

'Tis not of heaven to bless the base,
   No tyranny 'tis to praise the good;
What David sung with royal grace
   Has always as established stood.

The royal minstrel sung that peace
   Unto the wicked there is none;
This prophecy holds, and ne'er shall cease
   While mortal man his race shall run.

God made the will as free as strong.
   The angels recognize his ways,
And sing through echoing ages long
   To men of good will peace and praise.

HEAVENLY TRUST.

FORTY days the deluge poured
   Round the prisoners in the ark,
   Through the sunlight, through the dark;
   Then the olive-branch the dove
   Brought as sign that God is love,
And with grateful songs adored
Noah and his sons the Lord.

Forty years the struggling band
   Led by Moses every woe
   Suffered that the deserts know,
   Want and sickness, dread and pain,
   And their trust was not in vain.
God. at last, with His own hand,
Brought them to the promised land.

Forty days Christ passed, divine
   On the mountain, bowed in prayer,
   In the star-light, in the glare,
   Heeded not the tempter's taunts,
   Dared the treason, dared the lance:
Shall we mortals poor repine
And distrust heaven's high design?

Heavenly trust these lessons teach:
   Sorrow's waters flood the soul,
   But to Ararat they roll;
   Satan spares none in his guile,
   Let's distrust his guilty smile;
And the wilderness bids us reach
Forth to homes God gives to each.

MENTIBUS NOSTRIS INFUNDE..

INTO our minds infuse, O Lord, thy grace,
   Thy heavenly grace, that so we men, to whom
Was sent an angel in the earlier days,
To make us know that God Incarnate dwell
Soon would 'mongst us, may, through his suffer-
         ings, borne
On Calvary's heights, to realize be brought
The glories of the resurrection morn;
And this we ask through that same Christ our
     Lord,
To whom be praise and worship evermore.

MANIFESTATIONS.

NOT frequent have the manifestations been
   Whereby the Almighty has appeared to men;
Whereby the spiritual has become concrete,
   Describable by wondering voice or pen.

Only when rang throughout the adoring skies
   The jubilant words the heralding angels sung,
Was seen on earth, that all men might him know,
   The Incarnate God, the praise of eye and
     tongue.

Elsewhere men knew him only by report;
　　Moses on Sinai heard his voice in awe,
And Margaret at Paray-le-Monial;
　　And visitors to Louise his sufferings saw.

The Maid of Lourdes, the sacred form aloft
　　Saw, in the niche, of her who gave him birth;
To Bernadette the audience high was given,
　　And secret held from all souls else on earth.

Job his rebuke heard in the whirlwind's roar,
　　Job the impatient, wrongly patient called,
Made humble by the amazing, strange event,
　　And from his haughtiness by God's voice
　　　　appalled.

The fortunes of our lives not us allow
　　His footprints e'en in Palestine to tread,
But seen throughout the universe are His works,
　　Through them are we to know the Infinite led.

MOSES.

EXODUS, CH. XXXIV.

WHEN Sacred Writ speaks of the Mount and
　　　　Moses,
It thrice repeats the sacred name of Moses,
Thus making triple mention strong of Moses.

This doeth it twice: and first when from God
      Moses,
It says, came down with shining face; then Moses
Knew not that shone the honored face of Moses.

And then that o'er his face a veil placed Moses,
Before the trembling people, but that Moses
No veil wore when with God was speaking Moses.

BISHOP PAOLINO.

TO Bishop Paolino once there came
    A mother sad who said, "My son is ill,
A prisoner, in a dungeon, without blame.

"Help me, Lord Bishop, him to rescue thence,
   Else soon will me this carking sorrow kill,
This misery torturing heart, and soul, and sense."

"Your son is sentenced by the law," he said,
   "Upon some sufferer must it fix its hold,
And I will suffer in the poor boy's stead."

Forthwith he sought the dungeon, and the chains
   Would on his own limbs place, in grime and
      cold,
And bear, content, the gloom, and weight, and
      stains.

LIFE AND DEATH.

TO die is but to live again
  Diviner life in nobler spheres;
To live is but a moment vain
  Compared with never-ending years.

Hope steers a troubled voyage here,
  It watches stars that change and set;
Hope in the heaven's loses fear
  And wears a starry coronet.

How blest the memory of the just!
  How sweet their rest on Eden's shore!
They know where we can only trust;
  They praise where we can but implore.

If music here of singing birds
  And garish sunshine thrill the heart,
What joy must heavenly seraphs' words,
  Attuned to golden chords, impart!

Why, when our pure and good in peace
  Resign this earth for happier skies,
Should sorrow still refuse to cease,
  And grief's hot tear-drops sadly rise?

But no! Our tear-drops are the soul
  That bursts in pearls upon the cheek;
Good angels watch them as they roll;
  The eyes of God were mild and meek.

ISAIAH LXII, 10.

GO through, go through, the gates,
    Cast up, cast up, the highway;
Prepare ye, prepare ye, the ground,
That pass may, that pass may, the chariot.

Cast out, cast out, the stones,
    Make smooth, make smooth, the highway;
Speed onward, speed onward, and bear
To far fields, to far fields, the tidings.

World o'er, world o'er, make ye
    Men's hearts, men's hearts, a highway;
Let roll there, let roll there, the wheels,
And glow there, and glow there, the triumph.

THE RIVER.

TO S. H.

THROUGH yonder vale a river flows,
    Rippling o'er pebbly reaches wide,
Serene except when melting snows
    Or weeping clouds obscure its tide.

It dimples onward to the sea,
    Through hills of beauty, wealth of grain,
A land of braves where all are free,
    Whose glittering sword hews slavery's chain.

So flows the river of our lives:
    The same eternal hills are seen
And waving fields, and darkly strives
    Or brightly plays its silvery sheen.

TEACH US CONTENT.

O NORTHERN Pole
    Whereon all summer glows the attendant
        sun,
Whereon all winter glooms continuous night,
How doth thy lesson teach us hardihood won
    From fortune's moods of favor or of slight,
        In cheer or dole!

    O Northern Star,
Whereon our latitude looks throughout the year,
    Which, seen from sea or land, a Pharos shines,
How like the Light Supreme, unchanged and
      . clear,
    Is thine, which all of all the heavens combines,
        Or near or far!

    O rolling Earth,
Which, light or dark, in grooves appointed glides,
    And gives, in changing measure, joy or pain,
Teach us content, in all the ebbs and tides
    Of God's allotment, and the loss or gain
        Death gives or birth!

IN WHAT MOOD?

"ALLZEIT FRÖHLICH IST GEFÄHRLICH."

I.

HE who is always gay is oft in danger,
    He who is always sad a burden bears,
He on whom Fortune smiles is not a stranger
To strifes, illusions, envyings, dreams and cares.

II.

What then?   Combine them all, be cheerful
When mirth the moment rules; and then, with
            grace
Receive each serious word, each thought that's
            tearful;
And greet fair Fortune with her own sweet face.

GREGORY IN THE FORUM.

"WHOM have we here?" said Gregory the
            Great,
    As once in Rome he walked with little state,
    Just as, when judge, in friendly, kind debate
That forum he had trod, while from the court
    Would pour the crowd 'mongst children gay
            with sport
    And earnest men who haled from forge or fort.

'Whom have we here?"   He looked on English
          boys,
  Their large blue eyes he saw, and artless joys,
  And flowing curls the wind's caress employs,
Pearl-rose their faces, golden-hued their hair,
  Slaves, by the time's sad usage, in a fair
  Barbarians called, whereat all Rome might stare.

Response came from the boys: "We're Angeli."
  "Yes, angels are ye, that I well can see,
  And from what province may your origin be?"
"The province of Deira."   'T was the same
  That has Northumberland for its modern name.
  "De ira," said the pope, "conveys the blame

'At once and mercy free of heaven, and surely
          means
  De ira Dei, whence at once one gleans
  Angels of right may scan celestial things.
And by what name call ye your reigning king?"
  "Ælla," they said, and he: "Herein ye bring
  A promise ye shall Alleluias sing."

THE SPANISH AMBASSADOR.

CHARLES OF ANJOU Sicily lost,
      He was a Frenchman, they Italians,
Lost the French too in that island,
      Lives and weapons, steeds and galleons.

After vesper service closed
    Happened this one feast of Easter,
Easter Tuesday evening 'twas,
    And a slayer was each feaster.

For the hostile bands of soldiers
    Charles had placed within the city
Stung with insolence the Palermans,
    Who them slaughtered without pity.

Often cited, oft excused too,
    Cruel deed and ne'er forgotten,
It a warning stands that people
    Will resent a government rotten.

In France afterwards Henry ruled,
    Had passed over years three hundred,
Henry whose white plume in battle
    Order brought while nations wondered.

Said the King one day to Italy,
    In the person of her minister:
"I like not, sir, what your King says,
    Sweet words covering purposes sinister.

"If in this way he annoys me,
    Will soon cease the *entente cordial*,
I will try, sir, what may come from
    War's dread plans and blood's red ordeal.

" You may look to see me breakfast
  In your plaza grand at Milan,
And to dine where glare at Naples
  Sulphurous flames o'er saint and villain."

Although by this fling provoked much,
  Courtesy kept the minister silent,
He, a diplomat, made, wisely,
  No response to this speech violent.

All were awed, except one wag there,
  For there Spain had her ambassador:
" In doing this, your majesty, surely,
  Speed than usual you'd make faster.

" I suggest that when, at evening,
  Glows the ray serene called Hesper's,
You may reach Palermo's gateways
  In good season, sire, for vespers."

FREDERICK THE GREAT.

1740.

KING FREDERICK had a secret treaty
            made
With England, which pledged subsidies in aid
Of Prussia, as of jealous states are laid
The mighty plans, when foes, before they invade,
                        Embarrass.

The King then, prompt sly cutting quips to
weave,
And fixed the French ambassador to grieve,
Sent for him, and with nothing to relieve
The suddenness of it, asked him: "When d'you
leave

For Paris?"

THE MARK OF OSWALD.

THE blind have an interior inward light,
And other senses; these exert their might,
And Homers see without exterior sight.

Duke Oswald had been taken prisoner; long
His son him sought, until, expert in song,
He, as a singer, hunted out this wrong.

Duke Saneck's moated castle strong he sought,
And sung therein such minstrelsy as brought
Gold first, and then the father's rescue wrought.

The fine poetic fire delighted much
The lawless baron, and with pleasure such
He neighbors called to judge of voice and touch.

The wassail-bowl, the beakers, freely passed,
Duke Saneck's self in drink was ne'er the last,
And loud roared revelry free and gay and fast.

"Duke Saneck, goes report that Oswald's here,
The chief of Fürsteneck, and mightily fear
His friends has happened him some mischief
　　　　drear."

"H'm," said the drunken Duke, "not all reports
Are lies."　Another said, long bred in courts,
But drunken, "For his many slippery torts,

"Men say that you have made your prisoner blind."
He answered: "Gossips surely are quite kind.
What use for eyes can dungeon-dwellers find?"

"It seems a pity," said one standing by,
"Such harm to do the art of shooting.　Why
Of shooters sharp he was the leader high."

"I'll wager you," another said, "he yet
Can hit the mark, if he can only set
His mind thereon."　"Done! I will take your bet."

This was the rash engagement of Saneck,
This led him soon to suffer mortal wreck,
Upon a sea where rivals trod the deck.

All this passed while the son sat wondering there,
And pain and anger felt and heavy care,
But knew he cooped was in a tiger's lair.

"Bring forth the prisoner!" Oswald guarded came,
And heard the bet, and took the gun, and aim
Had well in mind, but not the very same

That Saneck meant. But, "Tell me," said he
    now,
"Just where the beaker is. Duke, place it thou,
And this charged bullet shall its centre plow."

"I place it on this table," Saneck said,
And instantly his breast was filled with lead,
And on the fortress-floor he tumbled dead.

The son drew sword, and said "He hath done
    right.
I as his son will answer this in fight,
Saneck both died and lived a caitiff knight."

The guests a moment thought, then said "'T is
    well,
Duke Saneck here hath wrought a deed of hell,
And goes the train of cursed fiends to swell."

THE IMPERTURBABLE.

IN the times Italian past,
   And in the domain of Florence,
One rough Duro, who a vast
Feudal dukedom had amassed,
   Had a vassal, honest Lawrence.

Duro, through his lands, one day,
　　Made a journey in his carriage,
That he might fair work survey,
Or his vassals find at play,
　　Sick, or meditating marriage.

Came he finally to where,
　　Cap in hand, the honest vassal
Met his lord with greeting fair,
Not, like others, with some prayer
　　Given that therewith he might wrestle.

" Ah," said Duro, " in yon row
　　There's a fig-tree that's a beauty.
Some of its figs please bestow
On your lord when further flow
　　Of the juice shall make them fruity."

Lawrence kept in mind his word;
　　In due time the best selected,
And in a new basket stored,
Ready for his feudal lord,
　　And ne'er thought they'd be rejected.

But caprice and sport and mood
　　Often ruled the tyrant feudal.
" What is here?" he said, " Here's food
Fit alone for hogs, that spewed
　　Would be by my lady's poodle.

" Tie him, men, to yonder tree;
    Let him thoroughly be pelted
With his worthless figs.   We'll see
How men fare who jest with me."
    Seized he was, and strapped and belted.

But, as oft as near an eye
    Came a well-directed plumper,
He was heard with warmth to cry
"God be praised!" and all asked why?
    And herein was found a stumper.

Of the man the pious phrase
    Was unto his lord reported.
Thought he, shall I blame or praise
Such demeanor, such strange ways?
    "Let him hither be escorted."

Thither brought, the fellow's face
    So besmeared was, of his vision
Seemed no longer any trace,
Even of where his eyes had place
    Seemed there to have been elision.

" Tell me," said his lordship, won
    By the man's forlorn condition,
"Why you show resentment none,
But, as answer to our fun,
    Piety rather, and contrition."

" It was, sir, because in mind
   I, when pelted most, revolved
Lucky 't was my present kind
Had me saved from being blind."
   Yet was not the question solved.

" But," he added, midst surprise
   Evident made by curious glances,
" Had of fishes of good size
Been my present, I no eyes
   Had borne hence for work or dances."

" Noble fellow, soldier, wit,"
   Then the suzerain lord exclaimed,
" Bathe him, bring him clothing fit,
And a purse, and be it writ
   Duro of his sport's ashamed!"

GRUNHILDA.

"CHILD, we had not missed thee, why
    Should'st thou wring those hands
      and cry?"
Thus the Lady Abbess spoke,
Anwered thus the moan of pain,
Answered thus the pouring rain
From the nun's sad lids that broke,

While the Abbess led the way
To the nun's sweet cell, where heard
Had been praying night and day,
Where the music of each word
Was of one who ne'er had erred.
Nor had she, Grunhilda, lost
Grace divine, of priceless cost,
Though of hope almost bereft.
She had with a trifler left,
Had the trifler's arts defied,
And had feared to be denied
Access to her convent cell;
In temptation's furnace tried
By a recreant, faithless guide,
She had come her tale to tell,
Come to risk contempt and scorn,
Thence perhaps to go forlorn,
Turned by holy hands from home,
Sent through misery's lanes to roam,
Sent, a leprous thing, to meet
All the scoffings of the street.

What was then her stunned surprise
To be met with favoring eyes:
Deemed she it but irony,
Feared she that the Abbess would
Plainly make it understood
That no tainted thing like she
Should be suffered by the good
Sisters of the convent,—wharf

Of a river where should land
Nought to harm the pious band,
Gerresheim-by-Düsseldorf.

O the heart! How oft it beats
With a clamor for the seats
Of the heavenly, the divine!
But how often it retreats
Only to lament, repine,
And to taste the bitter wine
Of distrust, and on the earth
Grope with thoughts of little worth,
Grope with dangers, grope with snares,
Seek for wheat and gather tares,
Seek for bread and find a stone,
Friendship, readiness to disown,
Mercy, and a cruel jeer,
Charity, a bitter sneer.

Consciousness of right may aid
The interior sense, but made
Is of more than self our life.
We are what the world us paints:
Uses it a color fair
It assists us in the strife:
Paints us dark, the hostile stare
Social leaders start us taints
With repute that's base, and God
Is alone our witness: Thence
Comes regard for that great world

Which can round us throw its fence,
Which can o'er us hold its rod,
Which can fiend or angel be,
Slavery give or liberty.
Tints none delicate are as those
Maidenly fame has, and no flower,
Lily, violet, tulip, rose,
Has of beauty such a dower.

Guardian angels sometimes gleam
Through the mazes of a dream,
Guide the life, instruct the heart,
Bid the tempter to depart;
But not often is it seen
Comes the angel in between
Fate and her endangered ward,
In such guise as came the Lord
Unto Peter when, in dread
Of the yielding waves, he said:
" Save me, Lord," on Galilee,
" Me betrays the treacherous sea."

Said the Abbess: "Thou hast thirst,
Eight days hath thy fast endured,
Eight days in thy cell immured,
Thirst and hunger must be thine!
Come, partake of bread and wine!"
She! Grunhilda! she accurst!
She into a frenzy burst
Of wild grief, and thought "I know

Comes at last the cruel blow;
I shall leave my home, my friends,
This on earth my happiness ends,
O the folly of my flight,
O that hideous, hateful night,
Night I shall forever rue!
O the vows of fealty true
Broken by the wretch whom fiends
Sent to tear me from my heaven,
Sent to sink my soul in dole,
Parched in sulphur, torn by levin,
Sent to dash me from the skies
Whereto all my longings rise,
O'er me horror's clouds to roll,
Driven from these delightful scenes!"

But the maiden had not deemed
Overruling destinies worked
For her aid the while she dreamed
Only that her feeble will
Aid afforded, and that lurked
'Neath the darkness only ill;
Strength was given her in the moil,
Prayer had saved her soil from soil,
Power given power ill's power to foil.

They approached, at last, the door;
Blind with tears she saw no more,
But the Lady Abbess voice
Gave to her surprise: "Are two

'Hildas in the convent?" Rose,
Softly as the zephyr flows,
In response, a tone so choice
She was stunned, and meekly threw
Eyes to heaven, for well she knew
Melody such was not of earth.
Superhuman was its worth,
And a heavenly visitant had
Place held of the absent nun.
Awe her being filled, but done
Was the angel's mission, glad
That to happiness brought again,
Through whatever gate of pain,
Was the maid unto her given
To protect, to warn, to screen,
To adorn with grace and mien
Meet for lives devotional, her
Prone to wandering, apt to err,
But from ill kept safe.   The tone
Changed to distant music; clang
Seemed it had with notes which rang
From the heavens when Bethlehem gave
Him to earth who came to save.
Sought she thus the ethereal zone,
And the splendor softly rose,
Sweetly as a perfume goes,
Vanishing into fields of heaven.

HEROICS, ELEGIACS.

A SERIES feigned of finger-joints, some long,
 Some short, of ancient poets' honored song
The structure was, compared at times to sounds
The ocean gives when on the shore it bounds,
Or to a silvery column in the air,
Which springs a jet thrown from a fountain fair.
By genius managed thence came dignity:
The sounds sublime are that gives forth the sea,
And nought more simply pure and grandly bright
Is than the fountain's leap into the light.
This is admitted, but the truth remains
That modern poesy has the greater gains.
The seashore and the fountain are not lost;
In modern poesy throbs the heart and soul;
Here mountain-brooklets lisp, and tear-drops roll;
The wide domain of nature fills the verse,
Or soft or sounding, or diffuse or terse;
And sweetness oftener comes in modern lays
Than in hoarse lines accorded boundless praise.

SESTINA.

THE POET DEFENDETH THE CLAIMS OF MODERN BEAUTY AND WORTH.

IF Petrarch worshipped Laura on the earth,
 And Dante followed Beatrice to the skies,
What yet remains for later poets' lays?

Already Homer Helen had given fame,
And Maro to Lavinia long renown,
And shines our mother Eve in Milton's song.

But have we now no dames deserving song?
Has Eve no daughters to inspire our lays,
Daughters whose charms have ripened as the earth
Ripens since paradise first spread her skies?
Have not our girls a heritage of renown,
And lineage long, and toppling fame on fame?

And why should Helen have been given to fame?
Her only merit sole beneath the skies
Was beauty. Why should Beauty lord the earth?
Why should she meed demand of peerless lays?
Why should she be the queen of loftiest song,
Song consecrating her wide-spread renown?

And while Lavinia, sure, deserved renown,
And Maro could not better grace his lays,
Yet rule domestic was her sphere on earth,
Although her race was ancient, and in fame
It well deserved fore'er in exquisite song
To shed bright rays through fair Ausonia's skies.

And why went Beatrice to the loftiest skies,
Preferred before so many for renown?
Was it to please the bard and aid his fame?
Was it to spread his verses through the earth,
And make supreme his queenly lines of song,
Graces divine assuring deathless lays?

And Laura, why was'she, in later lays,
Crowned sovereign queen of Italy's sovereign
      song?
Have we no Lauras worthy of renown,
Whose merits should be lauded to the skies,
And bear a crown all Kohinoored with fame?
Is Petrarch's land the favored spot of earth?

Yes, fame for our own dames we claim, and song
Them yields our zone of earth to raptured skies,
And them with lays we load and all renown.

TO A. L. R.

RHYME ROYAL.

AH, friend divine!
    Ah, learned and skilled
In minstrelsy e'er had seven circuits run
Thy life in revolution round the sun,
And ere thy years of girlhood had begun,
    An infant thrilled, high-willed,
    And lisping line on line!

    Come, sacred Muse,
    And touch my tongue
With ardor such as gave the Angel him
Who stood within the holy precincts dim
Of prophecy, Isaiah. Let me hymn
    The future's tongue; be sung
    By me its roseate hues.

There see descend
The lyric crown!
See Laura greet its rays, and calmly wear
Its honors gained by genius void of care,
And heights assume which none of us may dare,
And, with the crown's renown,
May God his blessing send!

CLARA LAURA LANG.

ON classic shores the far-famed Lorelei
Sings strains harmonious full of mystery,
But all the notes her fair lips ever sang
Yield to thy name, sweet Clara Laura Lang.

And Italy's bard, a busy honey-bee,
Wove round his Laura wreaths of poesy:
His numbers find in me no answering pang,
Since I've known thee, fair Clara Laura Lang.

Come songsters blythe from lands beyond the sea,
And bind our souls in spells of ecstasy:
No note divine in court or hall e'er rang,
My ear so thrills as "Clara Laura Lang."

Voices angelic, from earth's grossness free,
Have, in the past, praised heaven's high majesty:
Such voices might, with fitting melody hang
Round thy loved name, dear Clara Laura Lang.

THE LILY MAID OF LAFAYETTE.

"COME, dainty little beauty, a picnic would
you have?
The violets smile in secret nooks, the red-buds'
blossoms bloom,
The hyacinths, convolvulus, the heliotrope, the
rose."
" Yes, I would dearly like to go," said the dainty
little beauty,
"And what is 't now you're laughing at?
Cool grottoes are, Belle talked about, at fair
Tecumseh's Trail,
There wonders are of land and wave, and founts
with jet on jet,"
Said the lily maid of Lafayette.

" But, dainty little beauty, the place is rather far,
We'll have them hitch the horses up, and give you
quite a feast,
With Laura, Carrie, Elbra, joined, in Happy
Hollow's shade."
"Yes, I would dearly like to go," said the dainty
little beauty,
" And what is 't now you're laughing at?
There pimpernel and daisies, and footsteps seen of
fairies,
And you to go along with us we'll gladly, gladly
let,"
Said the lily maid of Lafayette.

WRITTEN IN THE ALBUM OF MISS U. G.

SHE has my heart, she asks my hand,
   Sweet Ursie and her dimple:
An asking I cannot withstand,
   I give it in fee-simple.
My heart, my hand, are now the girl's
   Whose album's page I write on,
She with her wealth of chestnut curls,
   And I as gray as Triton.
But love will always rule us two,
   Whichever lives the longer,
For ne'er was truth itself more true
   Than this: That love is stronger
When heart and hand together go;
   There summer's choicest roses blow,
There pansies bud beneath the snow.

EMMA CONNER.

THANKS, renown, and honor
   Be to Emma Conner!
That she guarded Glory's flag,
Symbol of a mighty Nation,
Saved by her from desecration,
   Nor allowed profaned to drag
   As a base, ignoble rag!

Thanks, renown, and honor
Be to Emma Conner!
   That her moved our soldiers' fame,
Grace her with Fame's fadeless roses,
And where valor's self reposes,
    Breathe with praise her patriot name,
    Waking ardor into flame!

Thanks, renown, and honor
Be to Emma Conner!
   Comes from blood the fire she shows,
'Twas her fortune to inherit
From her father faith and merit,
    Thence her brave devotion flows,
    Thence assail her freedom's foes!

Thanks, renown, and honor
Be to Emma Conner!
   That might float that symbol grand,
Precious blood spilt he in battle,
Now his life, amidst the rattle
    Of salutes and drums, the land
    Hails with raptured heart and hand!

Thanks, renown, and honor
Be to Emma Conner!
   Of a rustic school the head,
O'er the building she the banner
Placed, that in such pleasing manner,
    Might be love of country fed,
    And young minds therein be led!

Thanks, renown, and honor
Be to Emma Conner!
  But words fail the indignant tongue
To denounce the skulking traitor,
Of his land and flag the hater.
    Be his crime no further sung,
    Lost his name the base among!

Thanks, renown, and honor
Be to Emma Conner!
  Not alone when rages strife
May a patriot win devotion,
War's as permanent as the ocean,
    War to save the Nation's life,
    War to foil the traitor's knife!

Thanks, renown, and honor
Be to Emma Conner!
  Valor women have and nerve,
Shines at times a glorious maiden
With a State's fair honors laden,
    These the heroic impulse serve,
    These the people's cheers deserve!

TWO INSCRIPTIONS.

TO G. W. C.

IN THE FIRST VOLUME:

October 15, A. D., 1884.

LET not the forum's calls, my friend,
　　Thy thoughts, thy time, too much employ,
Lay briefs aside, relax, unbend,
　　And be awhile, with me, a boy.

IN THE SECOND VOLUME:

October 15, B. C., 70.

'Tis Virgil's birthday which I write
　　Upon this gift of Virgil's page,
Here where the Wabash courts the sight,
　　The Mincius of our later age.

THE CHILD, THE MAN.

"*C'EST que l'enfant toujours est homme,
　　C'est que l'homme toujours est enfant.*"

Always we see in manhood childhood's ways,
Always the child's a man of fewer days.

THE LADY-BICYCLIST.

CLIFF-DWELLERS were there in the
    ancient days,
They may have numbered ladies, knights and
    seers;
Before their dwellings we inertly gaze,
Because no history comes which their careers
Gives toned with joy and grief and strifes and
    fears.
Mound-builders were there, but their mounds are
    mute,
And furnish little for or pen or lute.
What lordliness of character was theirs
We know not, nor their triumphs nor their cares.
But this we well observe, and 't is the last
Great scene upon the unrolling scroll of time,
Which cancels all the losses of the past,
And shows in clusters rich the ages' fruit,
It is the lady-bicyclist sublime.
Her know we well; her joys, her cares are ours,
No cliffs she needs ascend, nor donjon-towers.
May she long cycle, needing ne'er a mound,
And be with homage as with merit crowned!
May she long drive, adorning height and vale,
And roses share her cheeks with lilies pale,
While we her pleasing presence gladly hail,
And deem the navigation of the air
At last has been accomplished by the fair!

FACIAL EXPRESSION.

(A FRAGMENT.)

COMPARE it some might to a Quaker's face,
    Or Presbyterian's, deacon's, priest's, or grace
Some other settled form of habit gives:
I only say that in the man's face lives
That he believes; an earnest, settled life,
And strong conviction gives son, daughter, wife,
An air serene, a settled, pleasing pose;
This we all see, and every one of us knows.

A LEGEND OF ALSACE.

THEY say in Alsace once was wine
    More plentiful, even, than was water.
So plentiful was't that once a shrine,
A lofty church, was built with mortar
Made from the mingled wine and lime,
And that each wife and son and daughter
Who lives in Thann, or since that time
Lived there, or in that pleasant quarter,
Can smell the fragrance of the vine,
And birds and bees love, too, to loiter,
When summer blooms, in that sweet shrine.

TENNYSON.

A H, Tennyson! A little quaint and queer,
 And sometimes angular, but always touched
With sacred inspiration! How I love
Thy little flower in the crannied wall,
And how I often wonder genius stops
Never at trifling, school-boy methods, else
Thy verse severe would ne'er have err'd to say
"What God and man is," meant to rhyme with
        crannies,
But would have said, with due regard to grammar,
And rhyming still, that God *is* and man is!

TRACING THE STARS.

December 16, 1889.

W HEN glorious winter spreads his pictured
        skies
Behold Orion's giant form arise:
His golden girdle glitters on the sight,
And the broad falchion beams in splendor bright;

A lion's brindled hide protects his breast,
And seeks his club each world-invading pest.
The river's shining streams beneath him pour,
And angry Taurus rages close before;

Behind him Procyon snarls and Sirius whines,
While full in front the whale enormous shines.
Nor bright Capella nor Medusa miss,
With snakes that through their horrid tresses hiss.

See Cancer, too, and, near, the Hydra dire,
With roaring Leo, filled with furious fire.
The timid Hare, the Dove with olive green,
And Aries, fly in terror from the scene;

The warrior Perseus gazes from above,
And the twin offspring of the thunderer Jove.
Lo! in the distance, Cassiopeia fair,
By Perseus aided, seems a W there,

While near Andromeda, her daughter, stands,
And vainly strives to free her beauteous hands;
She calls, distressed, King Cepheus to her aid,
Her father, powerless to assist the maid.

And see, beyond, around the glowing pole,
With shining scales, the sinuous Dragon roll,
The Greater and the Smaller Bear betwixt,
And with their never-setting splendors mixed;

While to the left glides on Arcturus famed,
As in the oldest extant writing named,
Which names the Pleiads too, and names, divine,
Our Hero-Hunter, who shall ever shine

As one who woman's warm devotion gained,
And whose sad death the chaste Diana pained.
Roll on, O Winter's stars, in beauty dread,
The world by ye to your Creator led!

[The foregoing verses were suggested by those of the late Professor
Green on the same subject, and in one instance, his phraseology is used
without change.]

PATRIOTISME, RAMPANT, ENRAGÉ.

Tending to show that the spirit of patriotism overrules all other influences and all other considerations, there is found in the vicinity of the town of Montefiascone, midway between Florence and Rome, in the churchyard of the church of St. Flavian, the tomb of a former bishop of the diocese, unhappily a German, a German bishop of an Italian diocese. His epitaph, in Latin supplied by Italians, accuses him of excess in the use of a wine, produced in that region, known by the peculiar name of Est. The Latin epitaph, followed by an English translation, is given below:

EST   EST   EST

PROPTER   NIMIVM   EST

JO·DE FVGA D·MEVS HIC MORTVVS EST

IS   IS   IS

ON ACCOUNT OF TOO MUCH IS

MONSIGNOR JOHN DE FUGA HERE DEAD IS

The epitaph is of unknown date. Dante, in his Purgatorio, Canto 24, line 20, has given Pope Martin the Fourth a similar aspersion under an allegation that he died, in this same neighborhood, in Bolsena, from a surfeit of eels and wine.

And he
A space beyond, the leanest face we see,
The holy Church held in those arms of his;
Of Tours he was, and make him penitent pine
Bolsena's eels, and grieve the Vernage wine.

The pontiff's real offense, in the mind of Dante, probably was that he was a Frenchman. In the Commedia throughout Dante takes repeated occasion to emphasize his hatred of France and French influence. And both instances deserve to go with that other, recorded in church histories, that the Italians, A. D. 939–942, disfigured with knife-cuts the face of Pope Stephen the Ninth to show their hatred of his German origin and to prevent his appearance in public.

In our times Bishop De Fuga's memory might have been thus libeled:

BIER   BIER   BIER

THROUGH TOO MUCH Bier

MONSIGNOR JOHN DE FUGA WAS BROUGHT TO

HIS BIER.

How ignoble do such epitaphs seem in contrast with that of Cardinal Alciati in the Church of Saint Mary of Angels in Rome!

VIRTVTE VIXIT

MEMORIA VIVIT

GLORIA VIVET

BY VIRTUE HE PREVAILED

HIS MEMORY NE'ER HATH FAILED

HIS SOUL'S IN GLORY HAILED

POPE AND HIS TREE, AND HIS SIBY·LS.*

'TIS *early* training forms the growing mind,
Just as the *sapling's* bent the tree's inclined.

*   *   *

Our buskined sibyls, redolent of *perfumes*,
Bathe *oft*, and *sometimes* in Castalian flumes.

---

*Pope's words, as will be remembered, are:
   "'Tis education forms the common mind,
   Just as the twig," etc.
   " A slipshod sibyl, meditating dreams,
   And never washed but in Castalia's streams."

COMMENT ON EMERSON'S "PROBLEM."

EMERSON:

"*THE hand* that rounded Peter's dome,
And groined the aisles of ancient Rome,
Wrought in a sad sincerity;
Himself from God he could not free;
He builded better than *he* knew;—
The conscious stone to beauty grew."

COMMENT:

Ralph, it was not a single man,
For many worked upon the plan.
Bramante laid the programme down;
La Porta earned therein renown;
Carlo Maderno built the nave;
Buonarotti, artist brave,
With Raphael, worked upon the piers;
Bernini, he and all his peers,
Built on, in prayer and zeal and hope,
Two centuries long, from pope to pope.

THE GERMAN BAPTISTS.

WHY call men a Tunker a "Dunkard"
When Tunʃen, to dip, means Βαπτιζω?
Let cease now the name, almost drunkard;
Muse, correction thereof you I bid sow!

THREE CONUNDRUMS.

I.

WHY are the French most abstinent of all
men?

Because, with them, one egg's always un œuf.

II.

Which race is it no care in eating shows?

The German, for it dearly loves the wurst.

III.

What cultured city has foul cannibals' ways?

'Tis Boston, through its fondness for baked bein's.

JE T'ADORE.

SHE spoke no French. The crucial time had come,
    The supreme moment, and his knees collapsed
Upon the brussels of her parents' home:
" The weird and solemn hour of ten has lapsed,
And let me say it, Hattie, je t'adore."
" Go on and say it then," thus in she cut,
" What need to talk about the door? The door!
.Why all the doors, you see yourself, are shut!"

N'EST-CE-PAS ?

SHE talked with him *one* evening, that alone,
But while abroad, she had quite learned grown,
And loved with foreign phrases to adorn
Quite common-place affairs, health, weather, corn,
Trips, picnics, and a thousand other things,
The fashions, and the races, and the Springs.
On this particular occasion the young man,
Who as a linguist was not in the van,
Observed that often she said "*N'est-ce-pas ?*"
And deemed it an illusion which not far
Concerned her father, for he thought " Nice pa!"
Was dutiful, but somewhat oddly brought
As comment upon almost every turn
Of conversation: Why the swain would learn.
And so he finally said " Ask his consent!
Your nice pa will it give, and be content
With me, I warrant, for his son-in-law !"
Alas, she then talked Dutch: "*Du lieber Gott !* "
"*Ach! Donner!   Blitz !*" and " *Ausgezeichne-
ter Spott !* "
With this she mingled laughter that brought tears,
Not to his eyes, but hers, and wordless jeers,
Which him persuaded to look up his hat,
And to adjourn without or this or that.

NAPOLEON THIRD.

NAPOLEON placed his N on pier
    And temple, arch and pillar, and a sneer
This brought from foes (until Sedan but few):
"*Il a ses ennemis partout!*"

NEWPORT.

"SOON, George, I'll visit Newport with ma
    mère."
" O Julia, give yourself for her no care,
For I will have the best of horses there."

A LESSON IN FRENCH.

NOW tell me, pray, what is the word
    Which often I in Paris heard?
It certainly was not French that's pure,
It had the sound of Empahrewer.

And not alone by this perplexed,
The Louvre found me mightily vexed
Because each careless laugh-renewer
Used much a word like Amachewer.

One by his friends was said to know
Whate'er belonged to art, but, O,
A number of the American boys your
Crowd contained called him Connoyzher.

And there stood on the Louvre stairs
One burdened with religious cares,
And said Jones to his friend, "Now ought yer
To speak of him as a Colporcher?"

THETA.

A GREEK PASTORAL.

In the following lines are introduced, as components of English sentences, *all* the letters of the Greek alphabet. The author has the suggestion, and a share of the lines, from Prof. J. B. L. Soulé.

ALPHA, a shepherdess, led the swains
Where rivulets purl o'er roseate plains,
And murmur bees, and wing on wing
Of dove flash where the shepherds sing
And shepherdesses, or in grot,
Or bower, on cliff, or sunniest spot;
But she a rival saw in θ,
Her sister, than a primrose neater,
And she would often flout and β,
And punch and pinch, and pound and pelt her;
Full many an angry blow she δ,
So that the birds, in air or μ,
By sympathy θ's sufferings ν,
And sympathy siezed each lamb and ewe.

For Alpha was so rude to θ,
That every time she chanced to meet her,
She looked as though she longed to η;
And oft 'gainst myrtled slopes she jammed
      her,
And, with her crook, all rose-wreathed, λ;
And afterwards nothing would denote her
Remorseful in the least ι ;
But, with a sly, deξning eye,
She out would cry: "Oh, coquette, φ!"
And then towards the willows fly.

Oft Theta, sweet with blush and clamor,
Would run and tell her grief to γ,
And γ, with a pitying Ψ,
Would promise her a piece of π,
Of meat, and fruits, and salsify,
And say, " Now darling mustn't X,
Wait, dear, until I put a K
Top of my head, and don a wrapper."

Two swains Hibernian of good make
Had grottoes just across the lake,
The lake wherein at shores not deep,
Would bathe nymphs, swains and meek-eyed
      sheep,
Their names O and Ω;
Both work and pastime found them eager.

The sward (which was no ύ*)
They sought while lingered yet the dawn,
The one as stout as *Σ*ringen
E'er saw, or vine-clad hills of Bingen,
And neither in " dyspepsy " gone,
Nor like a poet making yawn
All comers to his ε†

For Alpha, brilliant though severe,
Ω owned a friendship dear;
And Mike in love with little *θ*
Fell deep when first he chanced to meet her,
And made a deep impression too
On *Ω* her eyes of blue,
Her golden hair, her manners simple,
And here and there a crazing dimple.
And oft at eve the swains would ġo,
And on the glassy mirror *ρ*,
And leave their sheep to nip, in view
Of shepherdesses, mint or rue,
Osier, or ox-eye, or oxalis,
Plants needing never prop nor trellis,
But dear, in nature's dewy palace,
To Amaryllis, Maud or Alice.

So when the pretty envied *θ*
N Alpha was about to *β*,
She down upon the bank would *ζ*,

And call her friend (by diva done
No sweeter notes have plaudits won)
"Run Mike! Run Mi-kee! *O**!

And though ⌐aste gave him breathing rough,
He would of breath find quite enough,
As he for land would leave the water,
To say to baffled Alpha " *Tτ*!"
And check thus easily her abuse;
And the next day, while held the truce,
And thinking always of his *θ*,
And in what courtly way to greet her,
Would, in a billet-doux, make use
Of that new diphthong seen in Zαus,
Done to impress the little goose
With learning found not in her Homer,
And give her for reflection broma.

Needless to say that marriages two
Those scenes of sylvan beauty *ν*.

* O Mike, run !

INTERROGATION.

"TWIST thou its tail, and turn it upside
down."
"What, man! Treat thus the British Lion or
John Bull?
Such language, surely, well befits a clown,
But not a bard of wit and learning full."

"Well said.   The Greek interrogation point
   Is what I meant, a ; 'tis.
The tail, being twisted almost out of joint,
   John Bull would hardly recognize as his."

"Let me accost thyself, thou mark antique,
     Thee whom perhaps the Argonauts sought
          sublime,
Thee whom have sought all lands all sailors seek,
     All coasts whereon art gilds the mists of time.

"Thus twisted, wilt thou for a moment stand
     Poised, a trained athlete, on thy classic head ¿
And then, upright, as seen through land on land,
     In books by these our later readers read ?"

Books claim us where each honoring fashion
         stays:
     The Spaniard could not to the Greek say nay:
"¿ Que pueda," runs his psalmody of praise,
   "Igualarse con el Señor?" to-day.

THE TEACHERS' INSTITUTE.

STOOD forth the pedagogue in the Institute:
   "My friends, pronunciation has to me,"
He said, to hearers at his learning mute,
   "No difficulties, as you soon shall see.

" I meet, for instance, with a puzzling word
   Which halts, as in hard oak will halt a dry nail.
I see at once that never was there heard
   A word pronounced that's easier than *finale.*

" But, let me see, I would be careful here;
   I would not say a thing to make you grin all;
It may be that some very learned seer
   Might be correct, and prompt me to say *finale.*

" Why, yes, to be sure, there seems to be a choice.
   It may be, friends, I'm wrong herein, for sin 'll
Find easily the sinner, and the voice
   Be managed so that we shall make it *finale.*

" Indeed, the word may take another turn:
   I cannot act the despot over *my* Raleigh,
And cannot really undertake to spurn
   The idea of calling this strange puzzle, *finale.*

" But, friends, at my own wanderings, I'm aghast;
   I must my straggling senses in this din rally:
The counsel I arrive at, as the last,
   Is that you call the curious thing a *finale.*"

The rogue the bull's eye had still nearer hit
   In trying again, for then we might have seen
        Al
Akbar praised, and saved his blundering wit,
   At reach, at last, of this his happier *finale.*

THE THERMOMETER ANALYZED.

ABOVE eighty, torrid;
  Above ninety, horrid;
About seventy, chilling;
Below zero, killing.

THE GARDEN OF THE GODS.

MANITOU SPRINGS, AUGUST 4, 1890.

HERE, in this Field Olympian, strange and
        weird,
Aloft among the glowing cliffs remains
The Eagle's Nest supreme: but eagle none,
Nor eaglet, seeks the rock so fitly niched
The bird to couch Jove's footstool grandly graced,
Bird still of glory's heights the favorite guard;
For civilized man's approach has made him seek
An eyrie lovelier 'mongst remoter heights:
True symbol of the high poetic soul, which paths
        seeks out
All unfrequented, where the thunder's crash
Falls on the rock primeval wet with spray
Which leaps in foam down purple mountains'
        sides,
And blooms the sweetbrier in the laurel's shade.

Yet rocks around in wondrous beauty glow,
Glow with a ruddy radiance which the rage
Of æons passed declares, when the fierce heats
Interior of our globe threw suddenly forth
Hot, sputtering, pinnacles huge of tinted clay,
Clay that deep down its convolutions rolled,
Clamoring the earth within in mighty throes,
Then sprang at one wild leap towards the skies,
A wonder to all times, and where crowd men,
In frequent caravans glad, God's works to see
And ponder on the glory of his ways.
Then, after flame–convulsions, torrents came,
Torrents celestial, wearing to shapes grotesque
The amazing pinnacles born of fire: at times
An added fairy grace contributing;
At times constructing tracery fair of spires;
At others making seal kiss seal aloft,
Or, on a lower plane, but yet divine,
Figuring a mimic world of plastic forms:
The crocodile fixed in stone immutable,
The noisome toad, the hedgehog bristling rough,
All petrified into colossal shapes
That met the gaze of wondering nations gone,
They who the mossy mounds mysterious built,
Or they who in sheer cliffs high-laddered watched,
Or in dim caves which bounteous nature gave
To shield, delight, and puzzle, ages long
Of many peoples.   Last there came a race
Of learning wide and potent, and they asked
Of that one of those shapes who seemed to keep
Guard o'er the place, now Major–Domo dubbed,

Though stone, or almost stone, was then his state,
Yet armed by grace Apollo gave with speech,
Best gift of power that comes from Gods to men,
What *name* this unexampled glen should have.
"The mountains ask where Gods resort," he said,
"The lofty Peak there witnessing their ways:
This tinted, glorious place their Garden is;
Adore ye them whose works here glow; 't is
   meet
This Garden, yonder Peak, this affluence grand
Of mighty nature should devotion claim
And honor high for *all* the radiant Gods,
And have the name the Olympian Jupiter bore;
And his whose glory glows in Holy Writ,
Jehovah's, who from Sinai sent the law
Written on nature's tablets, graven on stone;
And his, the Incarnate Lord's, who in the Mount
Strove forty days in solitude and prayer,
And thence descended to the praise of men."

THE TRUE ROME.

OF Rome, true Rome, was no decline and fall,
 And history's course, by famed historians all,
Has been perverted: vicious emperors ne'er
Could more than murder; and it is not fair
Heroic peoples carrying war far forth
To distant states to smirch as of no worth,
To name barbarians from their length of beard,
Or claim had visages unwashed and weird.

No, kings are not the people, and the power
That brings a nation to its supreme hour
Is not the vice and folly of a few.
All nations are conservative, the true
And honest, modest, earnest, kindly, form
The nations all; 't is not the idle swarm
Of mendicants around the city's streets,
'Tis not the army that careers, retreats,
Advances, sets up monarchs vain, or holds
Its better citizens in terror's folds,
It is the great majority: these men
And women are of wholesome lives, and when
Nations decline it is when conflict comes
Between the pride of sovereign peoples: war
Is but the vent wherein for glory more
The noble pride of nations moves, and change
Comes not from manners rude or costumes
        strange,
Comes not from feeble emperors or their slaves,
But comes from foreign rivals and the braves
That national pride fans into flaming fire:
Thence war, thence revolutions, thence the lyre
Of bards immortal sounds heroic strains.
One nation loses while another gains,
For national jealousy solves many things
And patriotism conquers even kings.
Rome falls and Germany rises; national force
On either side has been contrasted; course
Has had that rivalry God's decrees have given
To all the tribes of men beneath the heaven.

The life of nations, as of man, is clash,
Some meekly wise are, others bravely rash,
And conflict is a part of nature's gifts,
And human levin shines through human rifts.
Incessant struggle is man's chiefest law,
This rules the people, rules it not the awe
That lazy kings or vicious princes wield,
'Tis in the battle felt and in the field
Where labor plods, and in the family's love
Caressed ancestral, where the greatest store
Of honor goes to him who fought,
And somewhat less to him who worked or taught.

ODE

FOR THE OPENING OF THE COLUMBIAN EXPOSI-

TION, 1892.

AS when, in Rome, the fruitage of ripe lustres
  Was sung by Horace, following Sibylline
    maidens,
So now a hemisphere, ours, the glory radiant
    Sings of Progress.

Shone forth, in earlier dates, the Games Olympic,
And, later, came the Amphitheatre Flavian,
And then the palaces rose of Gaul and Britain,
    Brilliant, lofty.

Sung well th' athletic limb the graceful Grecians,
And Phœbus sung and Luna stately Romans,
Art, last, and commerce sung the rivaling
        moderns,
      Lords of Ocean.

Grace, skill, and art, forever be ye honored,
And ne'er forgotten be ye, ancient eras,
But yield here, praised Apollo and Diana,
      To Columbus.

Strike ye the sounding harp, ye mighty minstrels!
Pour hence, adown the stream of time, the chorus!
Turn ye, to flowing measures, notes of Empire,
      In Chicago!

God, do Thou give these scenes thy Benediction!
O Thou who art of Land and Sea the Ruler!
O Thou who claimest all, the Past, the Present,
      And the Future!

Come, ye vast nations of the distant Orient!
Come, ye whose isles renown gave Ariadne!
And ye whose waves saw landward borne Europa!
      Be ye all welcome!

And lag ye not, ye of the land of Ferdinand,
And of our Christopher's friend Queen Isabella,
And of those shores Italian where young Colon
      Passed his boyhood!

Hither bring ye your prized, your marvellous
products,
Hither bring ye your speech ornate and various,
And here your pleasing ways and accents courteous
Teach Columbia!

Meet ye, pleased, here our miracles of invention,
The steam, the lightning, every pulse of science,
Meet ye, too, here our God-given ores prolific
And our harvests!

Pray ye that here long may the prosperous people
Fair mirrors be of all the saving virtues,
And here religion youth and age hold honoring
And contented!

Faith give ye, and give Law, for our example!
Return ye, friends, to harbor pleasing memories!
And come, midst clustering years, your children's
children
To renew them!

THE FALL OF ROBESPIERRE.

" GO flout him in his chosen seat, abase his
pride of power,
Select your men, let forty meet at such a place
and hour,

Break rudely in upon his speech, cry down his
    friends, declare
Him traitor, murderer; thus ye'll teach the timidest
    how to dare!

"Let, on a signal, daggers gleam, in forty hands
    upheld,
Then will his power pass as a dream by gallant
    courage quelled,
Else will he kill his fellows all, thee and the rest
    he hates,
And quickly act, his head must fall to save a
    thousand fates."

So Tallien's wife to Tallien spoke, and not too
    soon spoke she,
For vanishing in blood and smoke was France's
    liberty.
Then fronted they fell Robespierre, and on the
    signal given
Rose forty members, each his peer, by noble
    courage driven.

Collot, Fréron, Garnier were there, with godlike
    gifts adorned,
While Thuriot from his lofty chair the falling
    tyrant scorned.
"Down, despot, down!" each voice exclaimed,
    "this dagger seeks thy heart,
The demon discord shall be tamed, and checked
    the blood-clogged cart.

"Thy head the last shall feel the knife, and
France once more arise,
Yield then to France thy dastard life, claim it her
myriad cries!"
The woman's counsel saved the State, made strong
the timid peers,
And lifted from mankind a weight of crime and
dread and tears.

THE FOUR SOVEREIGNS.

A BALLAD OF PARIS TOWN.

One afternoon, in the summer of 1867, the author, while in attendance
on the Universal Exposition as one of the Commissioners from the United
States, met, in the *Place des Pyramides*, a public square separated only
by the width of the *Rue de Rivoli* from the main entrance to the Tuileries,
under the circumstances indicated in the following verses, the four
sovereigns named therein.

I.

'TWAS once a mighty autocrat walked through
the Paris streets,
Nor bodyguard had he at hand as one who danger
meets,
Nor trappings had he of his state, nor sceptre bore
nor crown,
O this dread sovereign on his walk in streets of
Paris town.

II.

Sickened at home with empty forms and crazed
with flattery,
In sooth he had his state laid by that he might
better see

How lived the people, how they talked, and what
　　were Paris sights,
This mighty emperor who of power had reached
　　the loftiest heights.

III.

Nor menials had he who might cringe, and watch
　　his slightest look,
His thumb he held where last he read within a
　　little book
Of places known for deeds of blood or other deeds
　　of grace,
A strawberry walking-stick supplied the lack of
　　sword and mace.

IV.

But three companions, garbed as he, and royal
　　sovereigns too,
Who each his fellow-sovereigns' names and great
　　dominion knew,
Each with his little stick and book, made up his
　　company,
And all were from the curious crowd and grim
　　assassin free.

V.

Albeit, while rode, a few days thence, the Czar in
　　landau gay,
With France's idol by his side, upon the Elysian
　　way,

Burst from the crowd a pistol-shot which Poland
    sent, but aim
Too rash and hasty sign alone gave of a slumber-
    ing flame.

VI.

And who were these three brethren great, who
    made the stately four,
O would you hear, then let me tell the occasion
    great which bore
These wondrous men to Paris streets and wind-
    ings of the Seine,
They who at home led armies forth to risk the
    embattled plain.

VII.

'Twas when the world came trooping up from
    every shore and sea,
And traders sought from far and near Louis and
    Eugénie,
That all the sights of Paris town and all the
    merchandize
Might, midst fair fêtes, for prizes strive, and
    dazzle wondering eyes.

VIII.

And every clime its products sent and every
    nation men,
And all went gaily to this Fair, and were assem-
    bled then

Those who at home were singled out for beauty
    or renown,
The fairest troop of knights and dames e'er
    thronged to Paris town.

IX.

But O who were the sovereigns three who, with
    the autocrat,
Bore walking-stick and guide-book there, black
    boot and silken hat,
That thus of citizens enjoyed the easy, plain attire
Which to these sovereigns was beyond all price
    or kingdom's hire?

X.

O one from Cleopatra's realm came through the
    tinted waves
That Africa's northern border-lands and Europe's
    southern laves,
But he had laid aside his arms and his insignias'
    store,
And but the customary dress of Paris men he
    wore.

XI.

The land wherein the lotus blooms and heard is
    Memnon's voice
Should always lofty thoughts inspire and inspira-
    tions choice,

But she, a ward of lands remote, bows to a foreign
yoke,
And Ismail for his throne in vain shall England's
aid invoke.

XII.

Another from the Orient came, he was the great
Soldan,
He who, at home, wore baggy suits by sovereign
worn and man,
The garments trim and high-crowned hat upon
his person drew,
And, like the Viceroy now disguised, none from
the crowd him knew.

XIII.

And who was he the last that came? Ah, here is
destiny shown,
King William, Prussia's king, was he, to be as
Emperor known:
The guest whom France received with joy her
made to bleed and sigh,
Ah, many a man he met that day his legions
doomed to die!

XIV.

Him none would deem a chief severe. Garbed as
the rest was he;
None would this gentleman, sure, have driven
from this his liberty;

If shrewd surmise the others had in their disguise
    found out,
None would have said 't is he shall hold of Paris
    each redoubt,

XV.

Shall hold each fort that circles there, shall hold
    their garrisons all,
Hold every gate and battery ranged on slope or
    height or mall,
Shall, while Napoleon's triumphs gay from tower
    and arch look down,
Hold in his strong hand all the hosts and gold of
    Paris town.

XVI.

And who is he that comes with bland and cheer-
    ful mein along
While something makes him single out from all
    the pulsing throng
These sovereigns four he dealers deems in sugar,
    wines, or wool?
It is a Paris citizen of wealth and leisure full.

XVII.

" Sir," then unto the Czar he said, " I see you're
    strangers here,
To show you up and down the town wherein for
    many a year

Of pleasant residence I have dined, read, thought,
and talked, and slept,
A town wherein myself was born, will you my
aid accept?"

XVIII.

"Kind sir," the Czar made due response, "our
meeting's opportune,
We take your kindly offer as an unexpected boon,
We strangers are, and started forth your beauteous town to view,
And we shall feel forever, sir, indebted unto
you."

XIX.

He showed them much, one walk is slight, however, to see all,
He showed them where Lutetia stood, upon that
island small
Where law-courts and Our Lady's shrine now
grace a varied scene,
Of these and other sights lacks time more than a
glance to glean.

XX.

He showed them where, a tilery once for making
bricks, now glowed
Imperial palaces wide whence art's and government's honors flowed,

That where, in Clovis' time, the wolf prowled
　　　with his stealthy mate,
The radiant Louvre now displays its Melian
　　　queen elate,

XXI.

The Palace of the lazy kings, the boulevard Saint
　　　Germain,
The Invalides, the Pantheon, the blood-besprinkled
　　　plain
Whose history Luxor's mystic shaft can ne'er
　　　from men conceal,
The Luxembourg, the place where stood the
　　　world-renowned Bastille,

XXII.

And Bosio's charioteer and steeds where once
　　　Lysippus' stood,
Mint, Printing House, and Library, and ('t was a
　　　satire good)
The cannon Russia lost in war now to her Czar
　　　brought home
In that proud shaft, for fates reserved, the Column
　　　of Vendôme,

XXIII.

Sweet charities in God's Hotel, saints in the Mad-
　　　eleine,
Sweet troops of children driving sports upon the
　　　well-trimmed green,

And there, on asphalt wide and long, the lordly
    equipage,
Where flowers and perfumes and delight charm
    matron, youth and sage.

XXIV.

Much were they pleased, as debtors to the courte-
    ous citizen,
The sovereigns four, who thus at hand, the bour-
    geoisie, its men
And women saw, and history lived, without the
    carking crown
Which would have thrown at distance far the
    sights of Paris town.

XXV.

Low sinks the sun, and they, fatigued, must
    lodgings seek perforce,
When just at hand upon them gleamed, all
    mounted on a horse,
In bronze colossal, a fair Maid, a work of sovereign
    art,
A dream to bless the five good friends just at
    their time to part.

XXVI.

And would you know what Maid was she that
    thus upon them smiled?
From fields where flowers of fair romance fame's
    gory path beguiled

Her name comes down, and latest fame with
　　　jubilant trump shall tell
'T was she who bore Saint Catherine's sword,
　　　the worshipped La Pucelle.

XXVII.

And spoke the Czar, " Sir, let me say, now that
　　　is closed our stroll,
We thank you for instruction given and comment
　　　sage or droll,
And since it may be that some day you may us
　　　meet again,
Let me tell you that when at home we royal state
　　　maintain.

XXVIII.

" This gentleman the Viceroy is of Egypt's realm
　　　antique;
The Soldan this, whom tribes diverse for rendered
　　　tribute seek;
And Prussia's crown this wears; and I of the
　　　Russias all am Czar,
We hope that we may see you where men know
　　　just who we are."

XXIX.

"The Soldan! Czar! The Viceroy! King!
　　　A brave and sly quartette!
But let me tell you, you, my friends, your suzerain
　　　lord have met,

I rivers own that run with gold, I've chests of
    diamonds full,
And, when at home, unnumbered slaves me call
    the Grand Mogul!

XXX.

" Good evening! But let me one word of honest
    counsel add,
That is, if ye the police 'scape, thereof ye may be
    glad,
This Fair of ours brings rogues about, but seldom
    in such crowd,
Or with slick tongue so oily quite, and impudence
    so loud."

XXXI.

Then left in haste, and greatly miffed, the man of
    Paris town,
While stood I near the peerless Maid who looked
    upon us down,
Us five, the sovereigns four and me, and I a
    sovereign too,
Then mirthful looks the four exchanged, and
    t'wards the Tuileries drew.

XXXII.

There gave they to their merriment vent, and
    joined in that same glee
The cordial roar of Louis' voice, the laugh of
    Eugénie,

And soon it burst the palace.walls, and flew o'er
      Paris town,
And joined therein maid, matron, knight, and
      blouse, and cap, and gown.

LOCAL LYRICS.

In explanation of the three local lyrics here given, it should be said that the city authorities of Lafayette, Indiana, had determined that the people should not be allowed to rest themselves at the public drinking-place, the Artesian Well; and to prevent their using the convenient low stone fence, near the fountain, as a seat, the authorities fixed heavy and sharp iron spikes in the fence. The lyrcis failed to make any impression upon the brilliant authorities. It is said that against such people even the Gods meet with no success.

I.

WHAT THE OLD MAN SAID.

APRIL 17, 1887.

"DOWN with the spikes!" the old man said,
   Who came along and saw them there;
"The place is public, but instead,
   Some narrow mind would steal our air.

" Down with the spikes!   No Bastille's here!
   The fount of God here freely flows!
Why should the pampered townsman sneer
   Because fatigue he never knows?

" Down with the spikes! Draw near we will,
   And sit where we care not to stand?
Our farm's remote, or up the hill   .
   The homestead by our fathers planned.

"Down with the spikes ! No˙eyelids raised
   By ambling fops who loafers' scorn,
Can make us yield our rights, while praised
   Is public right of freedom born.

"Down with the spikes ! For 'public use'
   The words read on yon corner stone;   .
Where our own Wilson spoke. excuse
   Is none, which would his words disown.

"Down with the spikes! My dusty feet
  Have found repose in other towns;
And elsewhere ne'er did iron greet
  The dusty foot with friendless frown."

II.

WHAT THE PEOPLE SAID.

APRIL 25, 1887.

"MAMA, I heard a man say 'damn!'"
   "It must have been a loafer, son."
"No, 't was a farmer, so said Sam;
  He had his boy, and team, and gun.

And other people said 'he's right!'
  A lawyer slapped him on the back,
A preacher said, ' My friend, polite
  Your phrase is not, but has the smack

Of things that men of old have said;
  If there's a hell it is for men
Who have for fellow-men a dread,
  And would them in hard limits pen.'"

"And where did you hear preachers such?
  Of course 't was not our pastor, dear;
It sounds just like the *nosty* Dutch
  Who smell of cheese and Wagner's beer."

"I know not who the man was, ma,
 But he a cane had, and the staff
He raised against each iron bar,
 And said, ' The man who would here quaff.

From this Artesian Fountain wealth,
 Had better leave his manhood home,
Had better seek God's Fount by stealth,
 And bate his breath 'fore yon cheap Dome.'"

" And somewhat else he said, I think,
 Of 'Pharisees' and 'taxes'—sure
The man forgot to take his drink,
 And wended homeward quite demure."

III.

WHAT THE BOY SAID.

APRIL 29, 1887.

"MAMA, I see a picture here,
 A park in Europe, where are seats!
Can it be that the loafer's leer
 Their ignorant way of living greets?

Why, here no man can sit him down,
 Nor woman either, in our Square;
' Drink and pass on,' the police frown,
 Nor at our Hoosier beauties stare.'

And when I closer scan this scene,
  I see here idle people sit,
The young, the old, the proud, the mean,
  The beggar, and the man of wit.

The nurse here brings her knitting forth;
  The idler, turned from tasks that pay;
And baby limbs, and aged worth,
  Have seats which to them 'linger' say.

Why is it that in Lafayette,
  A foot-worn idler cannot stay
Around the spot where friends have met,
  Perhaps to see the fountain play?

Don't you remember Roswell Smith
  Met us one day in Union Park,
And seats were there; a man of pith
  Is he, The Century bears his mark!"

The boy had said, and waited till
  His mother pursed her pretty mouth.
" These foreign pictures always fill
  The mind with notions of the South

Of Austrian, or Parisian, ways,
  Of idle people born for nought,
Who know not of King David's lays,
  And have no spark of godliness caught.

A man who stops upon the street,
  Or woman either, near a well,
A loafer is, and such should meet
  A seat which should such laziness quell.

And such a seat of spikes should be,
  Of various heights, arranged to catch
The Pharisaical eye, and free
  To all, a couch to catch the wretch."

"Why, ma, I heard that Lafayette
  Was born in Europe, and in France;
I think that he would feel regret
  To find, instead of rest, a lance.

And once I heard, in Sunday-school
  That good men lived 'neath Southern skies,
And at Samaria's Fountain cool
  Heard words from One divinely wise."

TRANSLATIONS.

DIES IRÆ.

PREFACE.

The task of translation is a difficult one. Its chief difficulty arises from the almost impossibility of substituting the
idiom of one language for that of another, or of suggesting
paraphrases to take the place of idiomatic expressions.
Translations, therefore, must to some extent be always failures. They must mar, or neglect, or fail to reveal in all their
fullness and truth, the words of the original, and the translator cannot achieve even a comparative success without a
ready knowledge and an easy use of both languages. He
must have studied them both *con amore* in spite of their mutual jealousy. Such felicity is rarely vouchsafed to the most
fortunate student. For one Cowper deserving immortal
honor for his translation of Homer, we have fifty Derbys deserving, as Diedrich Knickerbocker might say, to be utterly
famous for their deliberate want of success in the same work.
The difficulty increases when it is proposed to treat a religious subject, and becomes more formidable still if the composition be metrical. The success of an original composition of
this character entitles it to claim a position among the works
of genius, and the achievement of a creditable translation of
such a work entitles its author to a cordial recognition in the
ranks of scholarship. Such a work is the classic hymn, the
"DIES IRÆ," a description of the Day of Judgment—a subject of dread sublimity, and yet, in the original, at least,
treated admirably in rhyme, and that rhyme double, and not
in lines double only, but triple.

The authorship of the poem is a question for archæologists.
For them it is to decide between the claims of Gregory the

Great, of Thomas of Celano and others—perhaps to fix the merit upon some shrinking scholar modest as Virgil condemning his Æneid to the flames.

English translations of the poem in the trochaic measure are rare, and still rarer are those in triple rhyme, or what might be called the triple double rhyme, the "*terza rima*" of the Divine Comedy. The trochaic measure, short and strong, has the ringing vigor of a descending sledge-hammer. It has those forceful notes which in the nether world the Trojan hero heard, ages before the modern troubadour brought the anvil without metaphor upon the stage to emphasize the chorus of romance—

"Illi inter sese multa vi brachia tollunt!"

In all the translations of this great poem which have fallen under my notice, I have observed certain palpable wrongs done to the original. Let me note one in the very outset of the poem—the determination of all translators to render "IRA" into "*wrath*" or "*vengeance*." Now the literal word is not wrath or vengeance, but "ÀNGER." DIES IRÆ means Day of Anger—of Divine Anger. On that day the Redeemer will appear as a Judge. Rage and vindictiveness are not the attributes of the judicial office—they are characteristics rather of demons. Anger, on the contrary, is a characteristic of good men and of the good God. When, at the sight of the golden calf, Moses broke the tables of the law, his anger waxed hot. And when, too self-sufficient, the same law-giver smote the rock in the desert, the anger of the Lord came up against him, and against all Israel. In the new dispensation the sense is the same, for it is an apostle who says "Be ye angry and sin not." Shakespeare uses the right word when he makes the good Duke of Vienna counsel Isabella about redeeming her brother from "*the angry law.*" In this instance the excuse so obvious in other instances, cannot avail the translator—for here there is no necessity, actual or supposed, of neglecting the sense for the benefit of the rhyme.

Another wrong which is usually, if not always, done to the original is that the translators treat the poem as if it were not upon the Day of Judgment but upon the Day of Despair. Judgment does not necessarily imply condemnation. Sinners will in quantity surround the judgment seat, but there will be multitudes, too, of saints. The seven-sealed book will contain not only the lives of the wicked, but also of the good. It will have in it pages red with crime, pages black with fraud, but also pages white with purity and effulgent with sanctity. The opening of the sixth seal will reveal a great multitude, which no man can number, of all nations and kindreds and people and tongues, clothed in the white robes of innocence and bearing in their hands the palm-branches of victory.

Some translators fail to reach

"——to the height of this great argument."

They affect to circumscribe even the extent of the Resurrection. Hampered by the rhythmical difficulties of the situation they fail to give to an event embracing all the nations of the earth its universal scope. To read their lines one would suppose this event might be restricted to some patrimonial graveyard, or at most to a parish cemetery. They even fail to find room in their lines for words prominent in the original, and which to the unsophisticated might seem of prime importance, like the word "resurrection" itself, or that upon which rest the hopes of a fallen world, the "crucifixion."

Another wrong consists in this, that whereas the verses of this poem are remarkable for natural and unaffected diction, for ease and flexibility, the verses of some of the translations are remarkable only for stiffness and quaintness. As comparatively free from these faults, however, I am glad to note the efforts in this direction of Dr. Abraham Coles and General John A. Dix. Of this poem Dr. Coles published, in 1868, in an elegant volume, with other gems of Latin verse, no less than thirteen original translations all by himself. The first in the series is as a whole by far the best, and aided by a stanza from the sixth and a word from the eleventh, has been so highly appreciated as to be adopted by the Catholic Publication Society of New York in their favorite manual of prayer, "The Mission Book." The translation by General Dix is published in Judge Nott's "Hymns óf the Middle Ages," and has been recently reproduced in " Scribner's Monthly."

As to General Dix's translation, I regret that I must qualify my commendation by observing that, as it seems to me, he has rejected his best stanza, the first, urged to it in part, it would seem, through sensitiveness at a quip of Thackeray's —a poor authority, I fear, for the acceptance or rejection of anything whatever, and especially for the rejection of anything savoring of good taste and sound learning. I regret, too, in his translation to observe, in the eighth stanza, the use of the word "tremendous" as applied to the Deity. It can scarcely be said to be justified by the word in the original, where it is tremendæ (in the genitive, agreeing with "majestatis") fear-inspiring, causing to tremble, again not through demoniac horror but through divine power. I submit that the word is one which is seldom or never used in English in a good sense. Gibbon uses the word to give voice to the appalling summons of the barbarians at the gates of Rome: "The tremendous sound of the Gothic trumpet." Motley, appreciating, too, the English sense of the word, speaks of a "tremendous mischief." Doubtless it would be proper to say of a king—mayhap of a judge in an exceptional moment—that his temper had betrayed him into a tremendous explosion of rage, but to any characteristic of a king clothed with awe-inspiring majesty and seated in solemn state to exercise the office of a judge, the English use of the word "tremendous" seems inapplicable ; besides, the use of the word by this translator has other disadvantages. It imparts an exceptional turgidity to that part of his translation, and betrays him into the use of the plural "us," in the style of the litanies, where the context and the style of the poem require the use of the singular "me." Beyond all this it is perhaps no idle comment to say that the translator, carried away by a ponderous word, like a prisoner of war in irons, has missed the "free salvation" accorded to all who seek it in the middle of the same stanza.

It should be remarked that the poem divides itself into three parts:

I. The first six stanzas are occupied with a description of the *Day of Judgment.*

II. In the next eleven stanzas are comprised the *address of the suppliant* at the bar of God.

III. The last stanza of the poem is a *prayer of the poet* that God will spare his guilty creatures.

DIES IRÆ.

PARS PRIMA.

DESCRIPTIO.

I.

DIES iræ, dies illa!
Solvet sæclum in favilla,
Teste David cum Sibylla.

II.

Quantus tremor est futurus,
Quando Judex est venturus,
Cuncta strictè discussurus!

III.

Tuba, mirum spargens sonum
Per sepulchra regionum,
Cognet omnes ante thronum.

IV.

Mors stupebit, et natura,
Quum resurget creatura
Judicanti responsura.

V.

Liber scriptus proferetur,
In quo totum continetur,
Unde mundus judicetur.

VI.

Judex ergo quum sedebit,
Quidquid latet apparebit,
Nil inultum remanebit.

DAY OF ANGER.

FIRST PART.

DESCRIPTION.

I.

DAY of anger, day of burning!
   All the world to ashes turning!
David's and the Sibyl's learning!

II.

On this day of grievous trembling
Judge and people are assembling—
Now's an end to all dissembling.

III.

Through the graves of every nation
Sends the trumpet animation—
'Fore God's throne each takes his station.

IV.

At the creature's resurrection
Nature greans in every section—
Death is stunned at the defection.

V.

Then the books of records hoary,
Full of guilt and full of glory,
Of the world shall tell its story.

VI.

Then the Judge, His seat assuming,
All things hid His Light illuming,
Good exalts, while evil dooming.

PARS SECUNDA.

SUPPLICATIO.

VII.

Quid sum miser tunc dicturus,
Quem patronum rogaturus,
Quum vix justus sit securus?

VIII.

Rex tremendæ majestatis,
Qui salvandos salvis gratis,
Salve me, fons pietatis!

IX.

Recordare, Jesu pie,
Quod sum causa Tuæ viæ;
Ne me perdas illâ die!

X.

Quærens me sedisti lassus,
Redemisti, crucem passus;
Tantus labor non sit cassus!

XI.

Juste Judex ultionis,
Donam fac remissionis
Ante diem rationis!

XII.

Ingemisco tanquam reus,
Culpa rubet vultus meus:
Supplicanti parce, Deus!

XIII.

Qui Mariam absolvisti,
Et latronem exaudisti,
Mihi quoque spem dedisti,

XIV.

Preces meæ non sunt dignæ,
Sed Tu bonus fac benignè,
Ne perenni cremer igne!

XV.

Inter oves locum præesta,
Et ab hædis me sequestra,
Statuens in prate dextra!

XVI.

Confutatis maledictis,
Flammis acribus addictis
Voca me cum benedictis!

XVII.

Oro supplex et acclinis,
Cor contritum quasi cinis:
Gere curam mei finis!

SECOND PART.

SUPPLICATION.

VII.

Wretched me, what shall I say then?
Through what patron shall I pray then?
Shall I see of hope a ray then?

VIII.

King of power and grace unending,
Free salvation's blessings sending,
Save me, on Thy word depending.

IX.

Jesus, Savior, O remember
Pains for me felt in each member,
Save me from each dreaded ember.

X.

Weary, Thou my load hast lightened,
Crucified, my dark sins whitened,
O let my sad hopes be brightened.

XI.

Righteous Judge of retribution,
Grant me gift of absolution
On this day of execution.

XII.

Like a wretch from justice rushing,
Groans my heart, my face is blushing,
Spare one whom his guilt is crushing.

XIII.

Mary, contrite, was forgiven,
On his cross the thief earned heaven,
And I too with hope have striven.

XIV.

Worthy of reproach, scorn, ire,
And perennial pangs of fire,
Yet I to Thy love aspire.

XV.

With Thy faithful sheep divided,
When the impious goats are chided
Let me to Thy right be guided.

XVI.

When the wicked sink with curses
Into fiery hell's reverses,
Let me share with saints Thy mercies.

XVII.

Low I supplicate Thy power,
Care for me when tempests lower,
In this dread supernal hour.

PARS TERTIA.

PRECATIO.

XVIII.

Lacrymosa dies illa
Qua resurget ex favilla
Judicandus homo reus;
Huic ergo parce, Deus!

THIRD PART.

PRAYER.

XVIII.

In that grevious day and fearful,
Man will make the ashes tearful;
May his sins so heaven-daring,
Find his Judge benign and sparing.

ISTE CONFESSOR.

THIS day, seats sacred to the saints in Heaven,
    He whom the people praise in every clime,
God's con'fessor, ascended, glad to reach
        Eternal Rest.

Sweet, gentle, learnéd, humble, modest, blameless,
His life on earth he trod with soberest footsteps,
    His mortal frame awaiting from its Maker
        The Life Divine.

Such were his merits, full beyònd all measure,
    That grievous ills, that sickness verging death-
        ward,
Fled at his word, his touch bore instant healing
        As of Our Lord.

Therefore the chorus follow him; the grateful
    Pæan and the waving palm speak forth his
        praise,
And with unceasing love the world salutes him—
        "Pray, pray for us!"

There where he sits the Triune and the Only
    Sheds through the skies transcendent splendors
        worthy,
As guiding all our worldly ways in wisdom,
        Homage profound.

CRUX FIDELIS.

ONE noble tree there is alone
　　Among all forests found;
In germ, in leaf, in flower supreme,
　　It sanctifies the ground.

Its wood is sweet, and nails therein
　　A perfumed odor give;
It is a tree whereon who looks
　　In Paradise may live.

Such is the tree whose transverse arms
　　Sustained our suffering Lord,
Such is the tree yields fruit divine
　　By earth and Heaven adored.

VEXILLA REGIS.

"VEXILLA regis prodeunt:
　　Fulget crucis mysterium,
Qua vita mortem pertulit,
Et morte vitam protulit."

Forth comes the standard of the King:
The effulgent mystery of the Cross,
Where life bore death, and, wondrous thing,
Death brought back life, gain following loss.

O GLORIOSA.

"O GLORIOSA Virginum,
  Sublima inter sidera,
Qui te creavit parvulum,
Lactante nutris ubere!

"Quod Heva tristis abstulit
Tu reddis almo germine;
Intrent ut astra flebiles,
Cœli recludis cardines!"

O Glory of the Virgin Choir,
Sublime amidst the starry skies,
Thy milk thine own Creating Sire
Sustained, a Babe whom angels prize.

What hapless Eve had taken, thou,
Through thy blest womb restorest, glad
To help the grieved whom burdens bow,
And ope Heaven's doors to pleadings sad.

PETRARCH'S VISION OF THE MILK-WHITE FAWN.

IN sleep I saw, with wondering awe
  (Ye ken well what it warns)
While glowed the dawn, a milk-white fawn
  Come near with golden horns,

Erect its head, where laurels spread,
　　And 'twixt two silvery streams.
And came the sun his course to run,
　　Within that land of dreams.

The pictured hind, in grace outlined,
　　Seemed formed of love and hope;
Lightly it stepped, and distance kept,
　　Like the timid antelope;

And kind yet coy; with secret joy
　　.Its image filled my soul;
And o'er the sense soft influence
　　Of sweet reflection stole.

Great diamonds gleamed and rubies beamed
　　On the collar that it wore;
Words too, and theirs were characters
　　Of old imperial lore:

"This beauteous land an Emperor's hand
　　Hath to me freely given;
For me here gleam fount, flower and stream,
　　Beneath a favoring heaven."

The day's lord now, with radiant brow,
　　Climbed t'ward his mid-day height,
Yet still mine eyes, as at his rise,
　　Drank in that glorious sight.

A voice was heard—the spell was stirred—
The beauteous vision passed;
Yet in my heart it dwelt apart,
And shall while life shall last.

For the suggestion of the metre of, and for one of the phrases used in the foregoing composition, I cheerfully own my obligation to Francis Mahoney.

AU FORT DES ALARMES.

A U fort des alarmes
Ni camp ni gendarmes
Ne sauvant le roi;
Le per, le courage,
Sont de nul usage,
Éternel, sans toi.

The chief, in alarm,
Shouts, " Rouse, men, and arm,
I die by their swords!"
O chief, 't is thine hour,
Thy hosts have no power,
All strength is the Lord's!

In the heat of the fight
It is no earthly might
That saveth the king:
When the battle ends
The victory descends
On an angel's wing!

EARTH-SHADOWS.

FROM THE GERMAN.

CLOUDS, on threatening skies, we see
  Fix their tints and colors dread:
On the earth this may well be,
  Not on heavens above them spread.

Undisturbed those heavens are bright,
  Reck they nought of black or grey,
And their ether beams with light,
  Beams with blue empyreal day.

And must be thy heavens the same;
  Days of doubt and hours of qualm
On thy sight may strike, but claim
  Freedom for thy heart's deep calm.

Child of God, will come the hour
  Will its nobleness impart,
And earth's shadows lose their power
  O'er the heaven of thy heart.

HEART-EXAMINATION.

FROM THE ITALIAN.

IF one hath spoken against thee in despite,
   Do thou within thy conscience refuge take,
   And of thy heart examination make.
If thou be culpable, the infliction's right;
If innocent, an excellent lesson's light
     Hath reached thee, this: That always to
       forsake
     Those frivolous words and ways which idly
       break
     Life's earnest course and calm in this world's
       fight
Is better for thee; profit thus shall spring
   From either source; the poison foully mixed
   Shall turn to honey; and the embittered foe,
That sought from thee hot sighs or schemes to
     wring,
   Thy secret friend shall be, intent and fixed
   To thy wronged soul his due amends to bring.

THE ODE TO ARISTIUS.

This Ode, otherwise known as the TWENTY-SECOND OF HORACE'S FIRST BOOK, was sung, in the original Latin, as part of the obsequies of President Garfield at Cleveland. The singing was by the German societies of that city, and, it is said, added much to the impressiveness of those solemn and affecting rites.

The ARGUMENT of the Ode, if it needs one, is, that, on one occasion, when the poet was chanting, in the depths of the forest on his Sabine farm, the praises of Lalage, a person the subject of his unbounded admiration, he was confronted by an immense and powerful wolf. The animal and the man exchanged, in mutual astonishment, intent and earnest looks, an interchange which resulted in the precipitate retreat of the ferocious beast. It may be remembered that Dr. Hayes, the Arctic explorer, had a similar experience in encountering, without a weapon, and at a point remote from aid, a huge polar bear.

The person to whom the Ode is addressed, Aristius Fuscus, the poet speaks of, in one of his Epodes, in terms of affectionate endearment, as a cherished friend. He was a brother-poet, and, in his time, of some celebrity. It is he, too, who is described, in the Ninth Satire of the First Book of Satires, as maliciously leaving Horace in the hands of the bore. Horace says, hopefully and suggestively, to Aristius: "You have some private business with me?" Aristius runs away, saying, as he goes, with mock gravity: "No, this is the Sabbath-day" (the Jewish dispensation, of course, being referred to) "and I can have no business with any one on the Sabbath-day." And so the empty and impudent tormentor of Horace had his own way with the helpless poet.

As appropriate to a funereal occasion, the Ode would seem to partake rather of the character of a love-song than of a psalm of requiem, but, certainly, its opening words were of rare appropriateness, and the words which follow are fairly allowable as explanatory of the incident in relation to which the poet uses so elevated a sentiment. Besides, it is known that President Garfield was an ardent student of Horace.

I.

MY friend, he who a life can claim
　　　Without a flaw, and free from blame,
　　The Moorish pike
Needs not nor bow, nor quiver's birth
Of poisoned arrows which to earth
　　　Their victims strike,

II.

Or wends through sultry Syrtes' sands
His path, or through Caucasian lands
　　　Which know no guest,
Or where the dark Hydaspes licks
Its fabled banks, and horrors mix
　　　In nest on nest.

III.

For, once, as in my Sabine woods,
Unarmed, in one of my gay moods,

My Lalage's praise
I sung, met me a wolf, and glared
On me surprised and calm, then fared
 On his wild ways.

IV.

No such a portent crouches grim
In warlike Daunia's forests dim,
 Nor nurses, dire,
King Juba's realm, where lions roam,
Parched, in their arid desert home,
 With frenzying fire.

V.

And yet I live my Lalage's face
And voice to sing, her artless grace,
 Her laugh, her form,
And all her charms; and thus my song
Would soar aloft on reaches long
 Of peace or storm,

VI.

Although I might, on sterile coasts
Where summer ne'er its glories boasts,
 An exile, sigh,
Or, where the effulgent Sun his steeds,
Drives hot above the suffering meads,
 A wanderer, die.

HANNIBAL'S SOLILOQUY ON THE ROMANS.

(Horace, Odes IV. 4.)

". . . THAT race, inflexible as brave,
　　Which, from the flaming walls of
　　　Troy,
Across the untried Tuscan wave,
Bore parent, wife, and prattling boy,
And household Gods, and daughters coy,
To far Ausonian towns, to destined grief or joy.

"Like as the ilex axes lop
Of all its boughs, where richly rise
The woods which Algidus o'ertop,
All shorn its loss it can despise: ·
Where every slaughtered army lies,
It draws from hostile swords a strength that
　　　never dies."

CONTENTMENT.

HORACE'S ODE TO GROSPHUS.

REPOSE desires the Ægean sailor, thrown
　On raging waves, what time, with dark-
　　ness sown,
The heavens nor moon nor glimpse of star-light
　　own,
　　　Malignant.

Repose desires the Thracian battle-stained,
The Mede to bear the beauteous quiver trained,
Repose, my friend, which wealth has ne'er at-
      tained,
         Benignant.

For vanish not the tumults of the mind
Where fretted ceilings shine o'er menials kind
And treasures vast, and rods the axes bind
         Of lictors.

Wisely they live content with moderate state,
Proud of some heir-loom of an ancient date,
And meeting sleep, with slight or no debate,
         As victors.

Why strive we for so much in life so short?
Why need we alien suns and tempests court?
Should not our native land as shield and fort
         Be cherished?

The bronze-beaked ships ascends devouring care,
Nor from armed ranks drives it the trumpet's
      blare,
Beneath it fleets and camps in grim despair
         Have perished.

He whom the present satisfies is wise;
The future will not yield for all our cries;
Some things in life e'en seen with smiling eyes
         Are bitter.

O'ercame the great Achilles sudden death,
Wears down Tithonus e'en immortal breath,
Than lessons these nor song nor legend saith
.   Aught fitter.

For thee, my friend, sleek herds a thousand low,
Mares four-abreast before thy chariots glow,
The Tyrian purple robe is thine: Art thou
                    Contented ?

While I am wise, love for my little farm,
And courtship of the Grecian Muses' charm
Shall never find that I ambition's harm
                    Repented.

COMMON NATURES.

"QUANDO mulceter
            Villanus
    Pejor habetur;
    Ungentem pungit,
    Pungentem
            Rusticus
                Ungit."

Treat gently a boor,
The return will be poor;
A rustic you grease,
And he will you teaze;
A rustic you punch,
And he will you lunch.

THE ORIGIN OF "E PLURIBUS UNUM."

FROM THE MORETUM, OR SALAD, OF VIRGIL.

IT manus in gyrum; paullatim singula vires
Deperdunt proprias; color est *E pluribus unus.*

Spins round the stirring hand; lose by degrees
Their separate powers the parts, and comes at last
From many several colors one that rules.

SIC VOS NON VOBIS.

VIRGIL.

SIC vos non vobis nidificatis aves;
Sic vos non vobis vellera fertis oves;
Sic vos non vobis mellificatis apes;
Sic vos non vobis fertis aratra boves.

Thus for yourselves not ye, birds, build your
nests;
Thus for yourselves not ye, sheep, wear your
wool;
Thus for yourselves not ye, bees, make your
quests;
Thus for yourselves not ye, bulls, ploughshares
pull.

MÆNALIAN VERSES.

FROM VIRGIL'S ENCHANTRESS.

NOW know I what is Love: His guileful ways,
　　His treacherous methods, well have I found
　　　　out.
Produced that boy no race of mine, no blood;
From Tmaros' doth he come or Rhodope's rocks,
Or hath his lineage from those rugged realms,
The last of earth, where Garymantians dwell.
Begin with me, my luckless pipe, begin
Mænalian verses low and sweet though sad.

ORPHEUS AND EURYDICE.

FROM THE FOURTH GEORGIC.

AND now, his steps retracing, he had passed
　　In safety every form of ill and chance
Adverse, and with Eurydice restored,
Was pressing onward to the upper air,
She following on behind (such was the law
That fair Proserpina gave), when seized, alas!
The incautious lover's mind a madness strange
And sudden, which, indeed, might well expect
Forgiveness, if forgiveness were a thing
The phantoms knew: He stopped and turned, and
　　　　looked
At his Eurydice, now with the light
Of day itself almost upon her face,

Unmindful of his word, and overwhelmed
In mind.   And, in that very moment, all
Was gone, his labor lost like water poured
In sands, his covenant snapped in twain; the King
To whom must be his prayer for mercy made
An iron King; and thrice was heard across
Avernus' pools the thunder peal.   And she:
" What, Orpheus, wretched me hath so betrayed
And thee?   What fearful frenzy great?   For lo!
The cruel Fates again have my return
Required, and sleep e'en now my swimming sight
Seals up.   And now farewell!   The mighty night
Surrounds and bears me on, while hold I forth
Weak hands to thee, alas! thine hands no more!"
She said, and suddenly from his eyes, as smoke
In thin air lost, she fled apart, nor him
Saw e'er again, as he in vain his hands
Reached unavailing forth her shade to stay,
And many things his eager lips would speak;
Nor him would Orcus' ferryman again
To pass the dread opposing stream allow.
What should he do?   Where go, when now his
                   bride
Had twice from out his arms been snatched away?
By what excess of mourning could he move
The Powers below, or with what voice of prayer
The heavenly Thrones?   And she, cold, cold, her
                   way
Was making in the Stygian boat, lost, lost.

THE GENIUS OF ROME.

FROM THE SIXTH BOOK OF THE ÆNEID.

"WHO thee shall leave unmentioned Cato
      great?
Or Cossus? Who the Gracchi's race? Or who
The Scipios grim, twin thunderbolts of war
And Libya's scourge? Fabricius strong, though
      poor?
Or thee, Serranus, from thy furrows called?
Or where drive ye, great Fabii, wearied me,—
Ye, of whom thou the greatest, art the one
Who by delay to us the state restored?
More softly others may bright bronzes mold,
Until they seem to breathe, and better bring,
As freely I concede, from marble carved,
The living features forth, and better plead
The cause, and with apt lines the measures trace
Of heaven, and tell where rise and set the stars;
But thou, O Roman, mind thee the great arts
Of government to learn.   These shall be thine.
Thou shalt thine empire on the peoples lay.
Thou shalt the ways of peace unto them teach.
Thou shalt the conquered spare, but shalt fight
      down
The proud contemners of thy state and laws."
Father Anchises thus had said; and then,
To those who heard and marveled at his speech,
These further words he added thereunto: . . .

CAMILLA.

FROM THE SEVENTH ÆNEID.

HER all the youth from field and threshold
    poured
To gaze upon; and stood amazed the crowds
The mothers made, who came her progress proud
To see, the while for wonderment dumb their
    breaths
They held: What royal honors roll in bars
Of purple, thought they, o'er her rounded limbs!
How with a golden clasp she loops her hair!
How like a Queen her quiver sets her off!
How conscious seems her war-steed of his charge!
And how her shepherd's staff of myrtle wood
Ends in a spear-point polished for the fight!

VULCAN AND THE SHIELD OF
ÆNEAS.

FROM THE EIGHTH ÆNEID.

"LAY all aside," he said, "postpone your work
    Begun, Ætnean Cyclops, and hereto
Your minds apply. Arms for a man of might
Now must ye make. Now need of strength there is,
And rapid hands, and all art's mastery shrewd.
Throw headlong all delays." No more he said,

But quickly all fell to, and equally nerved,
The labor shared.   Flows bronze in streams, and
      flows
The golden ore, and in a furnace vast
Melts the vulnific steel.   And plan they out
A huge shield's scope, one which shall match all
      spears
That Latin men may hurl, and orb on orb
They fold it seven times o'er.   Some air draw in
To windy bellows' depths, and drive it thence.
Some to the lake the shrinking bronzes touch,
And groans the cavern vast with anvil-strokes.
Sounds roar, arms raise, blows clang, clang in
      chorus;
And quick clip, turn, beat they the flat masses.

TRIUMPHS OF AUGUSTUS.

FROM THE EIGHTH ÆNEID.

AND there the Nile lay opposite sunk in grief
And spreading wide his breast and garments
      all
And to his branching streams and bosom sad
The conquered calling swift their course to bend
But Cæsar, borne the Roman walls within,
'Midst all the glories which three triumphs gave,
Was unto Gods Italian rendering thanks,
And vows performing on three hundred shrines.

These through the city testified its joy.
But joy shone everywhere, in games, in cheers,
In raging storms of cheers, which boiled where'er
The conqueror's chariot bore his form caressed.
In every temple Roman mothers sung;
At every altar Roman mothers stood;
At every shrine slain bullocks strewed the earth.
Himself on Phœbus' snowy threshold sat,
And there received of conquered peoples' wealth
The costly gifts, and them in order placed
Against the pillared temple's gates superb.
Pass on, in order long, the conquered tribes,
In dress and arms as various as in tongues.
Here had the skillful fashioner's art set forth
The Nomad tribes and Africa's nude sons;
And here the Cari fierce, and Lelegi grim;
And here Gelonian clans who arrows bear.
Here flowed Euphrates with a milder stream.
Here were Morini, most remote of men;
And here the Rhine which boasts its double horns;
The Dahæ unsubdued; and the Araxes' waves,
Whose rage its Macedonian bridge destroyed.
  Such things, so spread on Vulcan's shield the
                  gift
Of her his parent, much his wonder move;
And, ignorant he of all their histories hid,
Fill him with deep delight their images traced;
While lifts he high as reach his shoulders broad
The fame and fortunes of the future Rome.

EURYALUS AND NISUS.

FROM THE NINTH ÆNEID.

AMAZED, and struck with mighty love of praise,
Was now Euryalus' mind, and to his friend,
So wrapt in patriot zeal, he answers thus:
" And dost thou, Nisus, therefore seek to escape
Uniting me to thy supreme attempts?
And shall I thee alone send forth to meet
The danger dire? Not so me taught, to war
And blood accustomed, he, my father brave
Opheltes, me in face of Greek alarms
And Trojan suffering placing. And not so
With thee have I yet fared, since followed I
High-souled Æneas and his direct Fates.
There is, there is, in me, a soul which scorns
The light of life, and deems it well one's life
To throw away in purchase of such fame
As thou dost seek to compass by thy deeds."
　　And Nisus then: " Indeed, of thee I feared
No such a thing. Thee so I would not wrong.
No, no. So may great Jove thy friend bring back
'Midst glad ovations, Jove or whosoe'er
With favorable eyes my deeds may see.
But if, but if, I say, some adverse chance,

And, in such risks, thou seest how such may come,
. Or if some God my life should snatch away,
Then I should wish that thee I had not taken.
Thine age is worthier life.   Let there be one
Who me from combat borne, or bought with gold,
May unto earth commit; or if, as seems
Our usual fate to be, this be denied,
Who may oblations make and pile the tomb
With garlands fresh for him the absent dead!
Nor would I be of so much grief the cause
Unto thy mother sad, she who alone
Of many mothers, boy, hath followed here
Her son, naught caring for Acesta's walls,
Wherein remained such numbers of her sex."

But he: "In vain these empty arguments fond
Thou weavest.   Fail they all my mind to budge
From its fixed purpose.   Therefore let us haste."

He says, and stirs the guard for their relief.

ÆNEAS, PALLAS, TURNUS.

FROM THE TWELFTH ÆNEID.

STOOD keen in his bright arms
   Æneas, and as moved his thought so moved
His eyes, and held he back his hand and sword,
And more and more were softening him the words
That Turnus spoke, when he perceived, alas!
On Turnus' shoulder that unhappy badge

That Pallas wore and all the bravery gay
That in the boy's familiar sword-band shone,
Whom, by a wound o'ercome, Turnus had slain,
And stripped from him, and in defiance wore.
He, when of harrowing grief this monument loved
The sight his eyes had drained, by Furies fired
And terrible now with rage: "And shalt thou me
Escape, decked out in those dear spoils that wore
My boy? No! Pallas thee destroys. The wound
I give thee Pallas gives. His hand his foe
Doth immolate and righteous vengeance takes
On his accursed blood!" And with his words
In glowing wrath his sword within his breast
He buried deep. Came chilly death. Fell loose
The warrior's limbs, and, groaning, fled
His scornful spirit forth unto the Shades.

THE GATEWAY OF HELL.

FROM THE INFERNO, CANTO III.

"THROUGH me are found the grieving city's
walls,
Through me the way is to eternal pain,
Through me those lost are never found again.
Justice the founder urged of my grim halls
And Power Divine which reared the courts
above
And Wisdom Infinite and Primal Love.

Save things eternal, was created naught
  Before myself, eternal I and drear.
  All hope surrender, ye who enter here."

Mine eye the legend's sombre colors sought
  Above a gateway's lofty arch of gloom;
  "The meaning's hard ; it speaks an awful
    doom."
I to my master said; but he, as one
  Prepared, made answer: "All distrust lay by;
  Within thine heart let slavish terror die.
For we the place whereof I spoke have won,
  Where we the souls shall see in misery tost
  Who God, the mind's best dower and prop,
    have lost."

His looks were looks of joy, his welcome hand
  Reached forth for mine, its clasp brought sweet
    relief,
  And into secret things led me my chief.
Here wailings deep and screams and sighs
  Stirred all the starless air of that black deep,
  Whereat at first I could not choose but weep.
Tongues diverse, deafening yells, and horror's cries,
  Accents of grief and voices deep and hoarse
  And hands together struck with frenzied force,

A tumult made which its incessant whirl
  Strewed through the eternal tint of that grim air
  As sand when whirlwinds breathe on deserts bare.

DANTE AND LATINI.

FROM THE INFERNO, CANTO XV.

SO I; and he: "If follow thou thy star,
    Thou canst not of a glorious haven fail,
If in that world I rightly scanned thy sail;
And if so early had not been the bar
    That closed my life since heaven so favored
        thee,
    Cheers would thy work have always had from
        me.
But that neglectful, that malignant race
    Which came from ancient Fesole's gnarled
        stock
    And of the mountain smacks yet and the rock,

"Will, for thy well-doing, thee forever chase;
    And cause there is for this, for ill its fruit
    The sweet fig bears where sour sorbs have their
        root.
Report on earth of old proclaims them blind;
    Envy and greed and pride are in their smile;
    Look that their manners do not thee defile.
Reserves for thee such fame thy fortune kind
    That, for thee, hunger will both sides harass,
    But from the goat far off shall be the grass.

"And let the Fesolan beasts their reeking stye
   Of their own stock make up, nor touch the
         plant,
   If growth to such their rank enclosures grant,
In which revives the sacred seed whereby
   She Romans counted then when stood confessed
   That stye of malice foul the favorite nest."
"Were my complete desire fulfilled, you yet,"
   I answer made, "would not have banished been
   From all on earth that men's affections win,

"For in my memory's fixed, my heart's regret,
   Your image dear, paternal, kind, when taught,
   From hour to hour, your words, with wisdom
         fraught,
How man himself eternal makes; and long
   As life is mine, my deeds should all reveal,
   And my tongue tell the gratitude great I feel.
What of my course predicts thy friendship strong
   I write, and keep it, and a text beside,
   For one, a Lady, able to decide

"Their meaning, if I reach her sphere. Believe
   That conscience only is the goad I fear.
   Let Fortune, as she pleases, then appear.
Not new divinings such do I receive.
   So, Fortune, turn thy wheel as suits thee still,
   And, boor, thy mattock as it suits thy will."
And thereupon my Master his right cheek
   Towards me turned, and, looking at me, said,
"He listens well who notes, and so is led."

LAST VOYAGE OF ULYSSES.

FROM THE INFERNO, CANTO XXVI.

"WHEN me from Circe forth the land-
 breeze drove
 (At Gaëta me more than a year she claimed,
 Port through Æneas' grateful memory named),
Nor fondness for my son, nor filial love
 For mine old father, nor affection due
 To my Penelope left, of wives most true,
Could quell the burning zeal I felt in me
 To know more of the world, to sally forth
 And study men, their weaknesses, their worth.

"With but one ship I ventured on the sea,
 The deep, wide waste, and with those followers
 few
 Who yet desired my fortunes to pursue.
Both shores as far as Spain beheld us guests,
 Far as Morocco's and Sardinia's coasts,
 And isles besides that inland ocean boasts.
Tardy and old, at last, 'neath various tests,
 The narrow pass we gained where Hercules
 placed
 His warning landmarks which the adventurous
 faced,

" That outward further might no pennon wave.
   Seville upon the right was passed; the left
   Already us of Ceuta had bereft.
' Ye, through a hundred thousand dangers brave,
   Brethren ' I said, ' have safely reached the West,
   And now apply that vigil brief the rest
Of your prolonged existence is, to learn
   The unpeopled world which lies behind the Sun!
   Consider whence your origin great is won!

" ' The noble blood that in your veins doth burn!
   Ye were not born to live like brutish beasts!
   Virtue and knowledge hail you to their feasts!'
This brief speech ended, all demur was gone.
   Indeed, so eager for the voyage wide
   My men became, they could not be denied.
And then our stern we turned towards the dawn,
   And to the foolish flight gave wing each oar;
   Towards the left we always somewhat bore.

" The other pole, with all its stars, rose soon;
   Fell ours so low that never came its light
   Upon the glow that ocean spreads at night.
Five times its light had changed the rolling moon,
   Quenched, kindled, turn by turn, since on the
         path
   We drove where dangers lurk and ruthless
         wrath,
When brought to us a view remote relief:
   A mountain with the distance dim; its height
   All others I had seen exceeded quite.

"Alas! gave way our transient joy to grief!
    From out the new land rose a tempest dark
    And struck in its forepart our quivering bark.
Three times round all the waves it made her
        whirl;
    The fourth time rose the stern, the prow went
        down,
    And it Another pleased, with potent frown,
Us into ocean's ravenous jaws to hurl."

TRAJAN AND THE WIDOW.

FROM THE PURGATORIO, CANTO X.

WAS heralded there the immaculate glory
        high
That Roman Ruler gained, whose deed benign
To his great victory Gregory led divine.
The Emperor Trajan 't was, and there, near by,
    A weeping widow at his bridle stood,
    Grief-clad and frenzied, with her tale of blood.
Around about them knights in full troops thronged,
    And eagles, struggling with the wind, in gold
    Above them gleamed where War's dread
        banners rolled.

And 'midst them all, the unhappy woman wronged
    Seemed to be saying: "Give me vengeance,
        Sire,
    For my dead son, me, in my trouble dire!"
And he to answer seemed: "Now, wait until

I have returned." And she, like one whom grief
    Impatient makes: "Shouldst thou not come, O
        chief?"
And he: "Who shall be in my place will still
    Avenge thee." Then: "The good that others do,"
    She urged, "slight help will be, my Prince, to
        you!"

"Take comfort, dame," at length he answers,
      "right
    It is I hear this cause ere hence I move;
    Justice this wills; pity doth this approve."

WHAT DANTE SAW ON THE TER-RACE FLOOR.

FROM THE PURGATORIO, CANTO XII.

I SAW, on one side, him, to whom b'yond all
   God's other creatures nobleness was given,
Fall like a thunderbolt driven down from
    Heaven.

I saw, on th' other, Briareus' limbs in thrall
    To darts celestial, prone, their vigor lost,
    And round their fiery sinews mortal frost.
I saw the Thymbræan, Pallas saw, and Mars,
    Still, in their armor, rallying round their Sire,
    While giants mangled were by his swift fire.
I saw shrink Nimrod, he who sought the stars,
    At foot of his huge work, whence he, dismayed,
    His Sennaarite helpers ruefully surveyed.

O Niobe! with what o'errunning eyes
  Thee I beheld upon that pictured plain
  Betwixt thy seven and seven loved children
        slain!
O Saul! how sad was there thy guise,
  On thine own sword then fallen in Gilboa's
        Mount,
  That since nor rain nor dew-drop e'er could
        count!
O fond Arachne! thee I there beheld,
  Half-spider now, climbing the web's thin lines
  Wherefor in vain thy punished spirit pines!

O Rehoboam! fears thy front have quelled,
  While hurls thy chariot thee with terror stung,
  Thee on whose flank no foe pursuing hung!
Showed forth, moreo'er, the adamantine floor
  What Alcmæon made a luckless bauble cost
  His mother, who thereby her rash life lost;
Showed how his sons with bloody frenzy tore
  Sennacherib vain, within the temple dread,
  And how they left him, prostrate, bleeding,
        dead;

Showed the destruction and the carnage red
  That Tomyris wrought when Cyrus' head she
        dipped:
  "Bloodthirsty tyrant, be it by thee sipped!"
Showed how, dismayed, the proud Assyrians fled
  After that Holofernes' life was lost,
  And how on seas of slaughter all was tossed.

I saw there Troy, ashes and caves her towers;
  O Ilion! thee how humbled, how debased,
  Showed forth the saddening lines that there
      were traced!

BEATRICE DESCENDING FROM HEAVEN.

FROM THE PURGATORIO, CANTO XXX.

I HAVE beheld ere now, when dawn would pale,
  The eastern hemisphere's tint of roseate sheen,
  And all the opposite heaven one gem serene,
And the uprising sun, beneath such powers
  Of vapory influence tempered, that the eye
  For a long space its fiery shield could try:

E'en so, embosomed in a cloud of flowers,
  Which from those hands angelical upward
      played,
  And roseate all the car triumphal made,
And showered a snow-white veil with olive
      bound,
  Appeared a Lady, green her mantle, name,
  Could not describe her robe unless t' were flame.
And mine own spirit, which the past had found
  Often, within her presence, free from awe,
  And which could never from me trembling
      draw,

And sight no knowledge giving me at this time,
  Through hidden virtue which from her came
        forth,   .
  Of ancient love felt now the potent worth.
As soon as on my vision smote sublime
  The heavenly influence that, ere boyhood's
        days
  Had fled, had thrilled me and awoke my praise,
Unto the leftward turned I, with that trust
  Wherewith a little child his mother seeks,
  When fear his steps controls and tear-stained
        cheeks,

To say to Virgil: " All my blood such gust
  Of feeling moves as doth man's bravery tame;
  I feel the traces of the ancient flame."

THE EAGLE OF THE PARADISO.

FROM THE PARADISO, CANTO XIX.

AND now the Eagle's wings before me gleamed,
    That bird of beauty which those jubilant souls
Held interwoven in its feathery folds.
A little ruby each of those souls seemed,
  And upon each the burning sun's clear ray,
  Refracted, did in my glad vision play;
And that which now to shape in words I seek,
  Ne'er voice hath said, it ink hath written not,
  Nor fancy's shell e'er muttered in its grot;

For speak I saw, and heard discourse, the beak;
  And *I* and *My*, not *We* and *Our*, of choice,
  Came all divinely from his glorious voice.
"Being just and merciful," it said, "I here
  Exalted am to summits such that higher
  Cannot attain conception nor desire;
And all the earth my memory doth revere,
  For precepts mine the wicked e'en commend,
  Although their lives they do not to them bend."

THE EXQUISITE BEAUTY OF BEATRICE.

FROM THE PARADISO, CANTO XXX.

WHEREFORE my love, and loss of other
            view,
  Me back to Beatrice and her homage drew.
If what of her hath been already said
  Were in one single eulogy grouped, 't would ill
  Her meed of merit at this moment fill.

The beauty which in her I now beheld
  B'yond mortals goes; her Maker, I believe,
  Hath power alone its fulness to receive.
Myself I own by obstacles stronger spelled
  Than in his labored theme was ever bard
  Whose verses, light or grave, brought problems
            hard;

For, as of eyes quelled by the sun's bright burst,
　E'en so the exquisite memory of that smile
　Doth me of words and forming mind beguile.

Not from that day when on this earth I first
　Her face beheld, up to this moment, song
　Have I e'er failed to strew her path along,
But now I own my limping numbers lame;
　An artist sometimes finds his powers surpassed,
　And mine succumb to beauty's lance at last.
And I must leave her to a greater fame
　Than any that my trumpet gives, which sounds,
　Now, hastening notes, which mark this labor's
　　bounds.

THE BEATIFIC VISION.

FROM THE PARADISO, CANTO XXXIII.

THE mind becomes, in that light's presence,
　　filled
　With adoration, such that its intent
　Can ne'er from contemplation such be bent;
For all the good which will for object claims
　Is here combined, and, out of its demesne,
　The thing imperfect doth here perfect reign.
And feebler falls my failing speech, which aims
　To tell of what I yet recall, than would
　Soft babyhood's talk through milk not under-
　　stood.

Not because more than one sole semblance rayed
   In that keen, living light whereon I gazed,
   For it, as ever, with one radiance blazed;
But through my sight, which strengthened was,
      and stayed,
   By constant gazing, one appearance sole
   Changed as I changed, as though 'neath my
      control.
In that subsistence clear and lofty came
   Three circles, diverse each in hue, but planned
   With one dimension; beautiful they, and grand.

The second showed the first's reflected flame,
   As rainbow might ray rainbow, and the third
   Seemed fire, by breath from both the others
      stirred.
O how doth this conception all speech quell
   Beneath its mighty import! And e'en thought
   How less than little, near such wonders brought!
O Light Eternal, thou that dost sole dwell
   Within thyself, and, unto thyself known,
   Dost love and smiles to thyself give and own,

That circle which, in my conception, drew
   Within thee light reflected, when mine eyes
   Had somewhat rested on its heavenly guise,
Within itself, of its own proper hue,
   To me seemed painted with our effigy; thence
   I on it pored with interest most intense!

As one who, versed in geometric lore,
  Would square the circle, but whose mind finds
        nought,
  Long pondering, of the principle vainly sought,

E'en so did I survey this splendor o'er;
  I would divine how found the image place
  The round within, and their relations trace;
And had my wings assailed unyielding bars
  Were it not then that came my mind upon
  A flash of levin wherein my wish was won.
Came failure, then, which towering fancy mars;
  But yet the will rolled onward, like a wheel
  In even motion which that love doth feel

Which moves the sun in heaven and all the stars.

INDEX.

[The titles in small capital letters are those of the principal divisions of the work; those in lower case are single poems, or the subdivisions of long poems.]

www.ingramcontent.com/pod-product-compliance
Lightning Source LLC
Chambersburg PA
CBHW031051110726
47900CB00003B/890